Slaughter Park

Lauren Biel

Library of Congress Cataloging-in-Publication Data

Slaughter Park/Lauren Biel 1st ed.

Cover Design: Qamber Designs

Editing: Sugar Free Editing

Interior Design: Sugar Free Editing

For more information on this book and the author, visit: www. LaurenBiel.com

Please visit LaurenBiel.com for a full list of content warnings.

This book is dedicated to everyone who just lost The Game.
Sorry, not sorry.

Chapter One

Quinn

I pull the shawl tighter around my shoulders and try to shake the feeling of being watched. Of course I'm being watched. I'm a fucking cam girl. The ticker on the bottom of my screen shows that exactly seventy-six pairs of eyes are currently open and staring at none other than me as I prepare to put on a show. But this icky feeling isn't coming from my computer.

It's coming from the bedroom window.

I school my face and smile. This fear is silly, and it's going to fuck with my bottom line if I'm not careful. These people are paying good money to see me at my best, and that's what they're going to get.

Another group of people is also paying me good money, though their machinations are less about devious perversions and more about the cause of my constant fear.

"Just a few more minutes before we get started today," I say with a glance at the clock.

My public show runs for thirty minutes, followed by a

call for private chats afterward. That's where the real money is. All I have to do is show a little skin, fake a few orgasms, and watch the bank account climb. Best of all, I make enough to pay the bills and squirrel a little extra away for my bank account.

This wasn't my dream, but I want my luxury lifestyle. I already have the beach house, thanks to a lucky find on Zillow during a late-night scroll session a few months ago. Now I just need the flashy car, a few pairs of sexy shoes, and enough cash in the bank to support my lobster-tail obsession.

The money will come a lot quicker if I can help my new "friends" find Desmond.

The chat grows restless as I play with my loose golden curls. I let the pale-blue shawl fall open a bit more, revealing a hint of cleavage. Men furiously type with one hand as they start beating their dicks with the other, resulting in comical messages like MMM B B OPAN BOBS and YOI ARE SO HIT BB. Their desperation is kind of cute, not gonna lie.

The shawl dips lower, and I let it.

A few tips start filtering in. Little flowers pop onto the screen each time someone sends a dollar. Daisies, to be exact—my online namesake.

It's an homage to my mother. It was her favorite flower. I can remember the field that grew behind a duplex we were lucky enough to stay in one winter. That following spring, daisies filled the field with pops of yellow, pink, and white. We'd go out and pick a basket of them, then dry them over the stove. We may not have had much, but I had a very happy childhood with my mother. I was loved.

When she abandoned me at an amusement park, it came as a shock. Despite our dire circumstances, she never lacked as a mother. It's just unfortunate that addicts aren't often given second chances in our society. Not even when they want help. As a result, she couldn't find a job. What she ended up doing for what little money she earned wasn't so different from what I do now. The main difference is that I don't think she was very proud of her job.

Wherever she is, if she can see me now, I hope she knows that I don't feel any shame about what I do. And that I forgive her.

The clock dings on the hour, and I stretch my arms to let the shawl fall away. With an arch of my back, I nibble my lip and peek at the camera. "Are you boys ready to get warmed up?"

Strings of words fill the screen faster than I can read them. A few regulars catch my eye, like HornyandHung24 and FingerBlaster3000. They tip very well and usually request a private about once per week. It's mostly vanilla stuff with those two. Bend over and show me where the sun doesn't shine type shit. At nearly twenty-seven, I'm still pretty flexible, so they get their money's worth.

"Do you guys want a dance today? Or maybe we could do a little light reading?" I pull my librarian glasses from the desk and slide them onto my face. They make my green eyes look too catlike, but the men seem to like it. I grab a dark romance book from beneath the monitor and flip to the marked page. "Let's see where we were. Ah . . . it looks like the masked man was just about to chase his sexual conquest through the forest. God, just thinking about it is already getting me so hot."

I fan my face before pulling off my low-cut cami. This is the most they'll get in the public room—a little cleavage and maybe a nip slip. I'll eventually rub myself through my panties once I've read a few paragraphs, but if they want to watch me shove stuff in my ass, I need more than a few Daisy Dollars.

Before I can even get through the first paragraph, another familiar name pops onto the screen. Instead of feeling excited, a warm wave of dread pushes through me.

Fucking Desmond.

A private message opens in the corner of my screen. He's found a way behind my security attempts. Again.

```
Desmond: Two weeks is too long
without seeing you. I won't let you
shut me out again, Daisy.
```

Two weeks is the longest I've kept him out of my computer—and my life—so at least we're making some fucking progress. Then again, the goal was for him to break through eventually.

I lean forward and close the private chat window. I'm not terribly worried about pissing him off. He knows where I live, but I know where he is too, and I'm not concerned about a man who's currently threatening me from a hovel in Cameroon. He isn't the only one who knows his way around a computer.

Granted, I don't know malware from marshmallows, but I met someone who does. He magically popped up right around the time Desmond appeared. It sounded like the start of one of my books at first, all romance and fate, but it was no coincidence. He offered a large chunk of change if I would allow them to hunt my stalker in the background. It sounded too dangerous at first, but when he assured me I'd be safer baiting him with their help than dealing with him without them, I agreed. The promise of money certainly helped.

I pull out my phone and consider texting him, but there's no need. He's already spotted the problem. Another private message pops onto my computer screen.

ScotlandYard842: The team is having trouble tracing him. Are your doors locked?

I smile sweetly at the monitor despite the fear roiling to life in my guts. Maybe if I shit myself on camera, Desmond will lose interest. But my handsome new friend is watching too, and I don't want to run *him* off.

Though he isn't exactly running *toward* me, either. He's been in my orbit for nearly three months, but he's very hard to read, what with his brooding, quiet demeanor and dedicated focus to his job . . . whatever it is. He hasn't really told me what government entity he's from, and I haven't wanted to ask. His credentials were enough for me—a strong jaw, powerful muscles, and dark eyes that make my toes curl.

"Guys, we're having some technical issues on my end, so let's plan to meet back here in a bit."

I click out of the application and logout before the angry messages can fill my screen. Isn't it enough that I have to deal with one psychopath? I don't need an entire army of angry men with boners. God, could you fucking imagine the mob? Instead of wielding pitchforks and torches, they'll be brandishing bottles of Jergens and fisting their cocks as they beat down my door.

After typing a quick response to my savior, I hurry to check that I actually locked the doors. Not that the locks will do much fucking good. I bought this beach house on the Carolina shore six months ago. Even though I got this place for a bargain, I can barely afford the mortgage, let alone replacing the shitty doors with something more substantial than particle-board crap. A bargain in this housing market is still highway fucking robbery. I can't wait until I can afford to upgrade some shit around here.

The front door is latched and locked when I reach it. The house is quiet, aside from the intermittent *tick-tick-tick* from the ancient fridge. Nothing stirs on the beach. Not even the birds have ventured out to watch the sunset, though the clouds in the distance might indicate why. In spite of the ominous storm on the horizon, the sight begins to calm me. I'm alone.

I pad on silent feet to the side door and give the knob a jiggle. It's locked as well, so that just leaves the back door. I cut through the kitchen and down a narrow hallway that opens into a small mudroom. The lock is visibly engaged, but I give the handle a jiggle anyway. It's perfectly secure.

A sigh of relief eases out of me as I hurry back to my bedroom. The message window for ScotlandYard842 is still active, but it's hidden behind another of Desmond's messages. He just doesn't know when to quit.

```
Desmond: Don't run from me, Daisy. It
only makes me want to chase you that
much more.
```

With a shudder, I move the cursor over the X in the corner of his message window. While I would love to be chased and pinned down by a man, it requires a level of trust that I just don't have with this guy. Something tells me he'd never let me go if he caught me, and I'm not willing to test that theory. I press the button to get him off my screen.

Chaos ensues.

"No, no, no," I whisper as hundreds of message

windows cascade over my screen, all of them bearing his horrible name at the top. "Desmond, what the fuck do you want from me?" I scream.

The boxes stop reproducing, disappearing almost as quickly as they appeared until only the single box covering ScotlandYard842 remains. Two lines of text fills the box.

```
Desmond: You know what I want, silly.
Now come outside and give it to me.
```

A scream lodges in my chest as I hurry to close the message box. My fingers shake, and I shut my eyes so that I don't have to see my computer if it's going haywire again. Because he's lying. He's just trying to scare me, and I can't let him win. There is no way in hell he's outside my house.

But then I ease my eyes open and see the message that was hidden just behind Desmond's.

```
ScotlandYard842:  Get   out   of   the
house.
```

A shadow moves outside my window. It's little more than a flash of darkness before it disappears, but I saw it. Someone is out there.

I grab my shirt from the floor and pull it over my head. Desmond has taken enough from me over the past few weeks, and I'll be damned if he's getting anything more. My gaze darts around the room, looking for anything I can use as a weapon. I really should have taken my friend's advice and gotten something more substantial than a fucking golf club. Looking at it propped in the corner, I realize how inadequate it is. Skinny and useless, just like my ex's dick.

"Fuck it. This is what I have. I'll make the best of it, just like he did." I hurry to the corner and grip the golf club in my hands. What do I plan to do with it? I have no fucking clue. At least it gives me some distance.

I give it a few practice swings. My hands shake, and sweat slicks the grip as I readjust my fingers. The heavy driver weights the end pretty well, and if I aim carefully enough, I can probably do some damage. I'm concerned that the thought of killing this asshole excites me, but I'm sure plenty of women in my shoes have felt the same way. I'll tell myself it's normal for now and deal with the fallout in therapy.

With a deep breath, I leave my bedroom and head for the front door. My closest neighbor is nearly a half mile down the beach, but that's where my Scottish bodyguard friend suggested I run when we formulated a plan in case shit ever went south. I'd say we're heading toward the Equator at this point.

I'm accustomed to running in the sand, so if it comes down to a foot chase, I have home-field advantage. And I've seen Desmond. Well, his outline. He's always in shadow when he comes on cam, but he doesn't strike me as the type to do well in sand. He's bulky as fuck, and all that muscle will drive him down.

I reconsider the plan to run down the beach. My neighbors are elderly, and I'm not sure they'll even open the door for me, but I've glimpsed the little German man's weapon room through his bedroom window. Something tells me he'll come in clutch in a fight. That or he has a secret anime obsession, because who else buys that many swords?

But what if no one is home? What if I get to the door and end up looking like fucking Laurie on Halloween night? I'm not final-girl material. I'm just not.

"Fuck it, Quinn," I whisper to myself. "You won't be anything if you let that asshole get his hands on you."

I consider calling the police, but that's not really an option. When my friend agreed to help me, it was with the promise that he would handle all of my personal security needs. I promised never to involve cops, and he promised to keep me safe. So far, he's held up his end of the bargain, but things aren't looking so good right now.

Trust him. He won't let anything happen to you.

God, I read far too many romance novels. They've rewired my brain. As I stand here at my front door, gripping a golf club and fighting the urge to scream, that realization has never been clearer. A stalker is now at my house, and I haven't even started a paper trail on this asshole because I've been too enamored by the dark-haired stranger with a funny accent. I've put my faith in him, all because he makes me think dirty thoughts.

But this isn't a romance novel and he isn't coming to save me, so it's time to save myself.

I unlock the door and wrench it open with a scream. I'm the vision of a mental breakdown as I burst off the porch and tear down the shore with the golf club swinging like a death threat at my side. Fear blinders narrow my vision to a pinpoint, and I focus on the porch light in the distance.

The clouds have gobbled up the remnants of fading sunshine, casting the beach in darkness. Hot breath saws in and out of my chest as my legs pump beneath me. But then I realize it isn't my ragged breathing in my ears. Someone is behind me, and they're getting closer.

A scream tears from my throat as I dare to glance backward. A powerful, lumbering figure barrels toward me at a speed I can't hope to surpass. Each forward step is met with an explosion of sand and salt. His fists are large and clenched as he rushes headlong into the darkness, closing the space between us at an alarming rate. There's an animalistic growl with each gulp of air he sucks into his lungs. I can't even see his face through the shadows, but I imagine he's wearing a scowl as he grits his teeth and fantasizes about how he'll kill me.

I turn back to my neighbor's house. I'll never make it. The sand seems to stretch further with every forward lunge. I can almost feel his hands snaking around my throat, his hot breath against my cheek. With a guttural screech, I wheel around and swing the club. Pain sings through my palms as he catches the driver on the downward arc and wrenches it from my hands. I sprawl face-first in the sand, then scramble forward. But it's too late. He's on me.

Rolling onto my back, I open my mouth to scream for help, but his sandy palm smashes over my lips. I'm in a blind panic, unable to see his face just inches from mine as he says something over and over again. When the words and accent finally register, I go limp.

"I've got you, wee lass. It's your buddy, so no worries, aye?" He brushes the hair from my face and looks down at me before glancing around. "You aren't safe yet, though. Let's get you to Grim's."

With that, he bundles me into his arms and runs toward the house in the distance.

Chapter Two

Aven

I'm pacing the floor in front of the window when Jim arrives at the beach house. It's the first time I've seen a man trudge through sand in a hand-tailored business suit. Though, I guess it's not nearly as shocking as watching Grim doing downward dog in a Speedo each morning.

These people are so fucking strange. I've lived among them for a few months now, and it never gets any easier.

For starters, they're too fucking chummy for my liking. I get that they feel like a family—and some of them are literally related—but the entire dynamic just feels so unnatural. Killers shouldn't run in packs. Duos, maybe. Small groups, aye. But this mass of people who take joy in eating dinners together? I'd rather not, thanks. I only agreed to stay on and take this special assignment because it involved me working mostly on my own.

For the next phase of the plan, however, I'll be forced to work on the island. I cannae fucking wait. Cue the sarcasm.

The door flies open, and Jim barges in. Rain mats his

hair to his forehead, making him look younger, somehow. He shakes off his arms, sending a spattering of water to the hardwood floor. "Where is she? Was she injured?"

"She's in the guest bedroom. She's a little scratched up."

He reaches out and grips my shoulder with a firm squeeze. "Straight to the point. Good man." He glances around to ensure we're alone. "And you haven't let Grim in on the . . . ?" He raises his eyebrows.

I shake my head. "Secret is safe with me, pal."

His hand relaxes, and he pats me twice before pulling away. "Good man. Good man, indeed. Yes, well, it looks like we'll have to change plans a bit, hmm?"

A change of plans is an understatement. I was supposed to play friendly with the girl and keep her safe until Desmond shows up for the retreat. Then King and Jim were to swoop in and take charge during the retreat, leaving me free to carry my happy ass back to my homeland. This shifting timeline is bullshit. Not to mention the fact that I already know what Jim's about to push for, and I refuse to go to the island. I need to head him off before he forces me to join in. If the cruise experience taught me anything, it's that I don't play well with others.

"We should tell her everything so that she'll agree to stay here with me until you guys head to the retreat," I say. "She's more than willing tonight because she's scared, but when she has a clearer head, she'll want to go home. That lass has an independent streak a mile wide."

Jim fingers his bottom lip as he studies the floor. "Yes. Perhaps we should divulge some of the secrets to her. Maybe not all, though. If she learns she's a Carter sibling before she's mentally prepared, that could end badly. I don't want any of the others to know, either. Remember that your bonus—"

"Ach, I know. Enough already. I said I wouldn't tell a soul, and I haven't yet."

Jim learned of her sensational parentage when he went through Frankie's mother's computer. The woman had been cyber-stalking Quinn for years, likely jealous of the fact that the love of her life was also the love of someone else's. When the DNA test confirmed the suspicions, Jim offered to tell the group, but they chose to learn about Slaughter Park instead. Now he's holding them accountable for their decision, and it's in my contract that I'm not allowed to tell anyone. If I do, I lose my bonus, and the money is the only thing keeping me here.

Jim says something else, but I only catch the tail end of the sentence. I surely didn't hear what I thought I heard.

"Sorry, what was that?"

"I said that we'll need to convince her to join us on the island. We won't be able to protect her here, not like we can there."

My hopes and dreams of working alone sift through my fingers like sand. "I don't think that's necessary. This house is secure, and I'm perfectly capable of hunkering down and playing guard dog. No need to drag her out there and expose her to what we do."

And no need to force me to participate, either.

"If you aren't up to finishing the job, I'm sure I can find someone more eager to collect that money."

My jaw drops, because *what?*

His mouth forms a hard line—a look I haven't often seen on his face. "Speaking of money, that's another issue we'll have to tackle. She can't continue her cam show. Not until we have Desmond in hand. But when we tell her that, she'll likely dig in her heels."

"You could offer her more money. Tell her we're putting

her in witness protection for a few weeks, and this is part of it."

His mouth screws up, and he recoils as if I've just pissed on his leg. "Handouts? Absolutely not. Give her your cut if you'd like, but I'm not a bloody charity."

"Bloody?" I roll my eyes. "You've been hanging around King too much."

Jim sighs. "No, it's the island or nothing, I'm afraid. Are you in or out?"

Fuck. Fuck. Fuck.

I want the money. With it, I can finally return to Scotland. I haven't seen my native land in nearly twenty years, and I can't go back until I've paid a serious debt for a mistake made in my late teens. It's the only place I've ever felt at home. The green hills and solitude call to me daily, even from this distance.

But is it worth putting up with Jim's dysfunctional-family shenanigans?

"Do you think we could wrap this up before everyone gets to the island for the week-long retreat?" I ask. Because if I can avoid the games, I can avoid the socialization. "I mean, you don't want her around all the murder anyway."

Jim's lips pinch together as he fights a smile. "Say it again."

"Huh?"

"Better yet, say purple burglar alarm!"

"Oh, for fuck's sake. Are you going on about my accent again? You cannae focus on anything. Ach!" I throw my hands in the air and pace in a circle. It's better than socking him in the chin. "I'll fucking do it, but I'm not running interference if the games commence while she's still on the island. You can figure that out."

He raises his hands, palms out. "Fair enough. Now you just need to convince her that this is a good idea."

"Convince me that *what* is a good idea?"

Jim and I spin on our heels to face Quinn, who materializes in the hallway like a phantom. Despite the red rings around her puffy eyes, she's still uncommonly pretty. Her dark blonde hair reminds me of honey as it falls over her shoulders and kisses the tops of her breasts. A snug cami hugs her midsection before bowing out along the line of her full hips. She's thick in all the right places, especially that extra bit of softness around her stomach.

Stop sexualizing your primary.

It's bodyguard 101, for fuck's sake. I'm here to protect her and keep her safe, not violate her with my dirty thoughts.

Even if she forces me to think them each time she does a show.

"We were just discussing how best to protect you, dear girl," Jim says with all the sweetness and gentleness of a father. "But where are my manners? My name is Jim Madigan, and I'm—"

"You're the man who sold me the beach house," she says. "I've never met you, but I saw your name on the paperwork. Have you been stalking me?" Her gaze flicks to me. "Was this all a setup? Are *you* Desmond? Oh my god, it all makes sense now! You're fucking Desmond!"

With a squeal, she bolts for the front door. I step into her path, and she collides with my chest and bounces back as if she's struck a brick wall. She lands in a heap on the floor, eyes wild and mouth agape.

I offer her my hand, but she scoots backward like a terrified kitten, hissing and fluffing and swiping her claws.

"I'm not Desmond, lass. I'm Aven Slade, same as I was

yesterday and same as I'll be tomorrow." I nod at the most nonthreatening man to walk the planet, despite his disgustingly high body count. "That's Jim, my boss, and we want to keep you safe, I assure you."

She licks her lips and blinks much too quickly as her eyes jump between us. Outside, thunder rumbles overhead as sheets of rain patter against the tin roof. It's as if even God means to terrify her.

"I've been keeping an eye on you, that much is true," Jim says, "but my motives were not nefarious in nature. Convincing you to buy the beach house was a little devious on my part, but it was all to protect you. You've been on Desmond's radar far longer than you realize."

"You convinced me to buy that beach house?" Quinn looks between us, but her eyes land firmly on me. "And you? We didn't just meet by chance?"

"Afraid not, lass." I stuff my hands into my pockets and shrug. "Our meeting was more orchestrated than I led you to believe. But the rest of it is just as he says. You're in more danger than you realize."

"Desmond is . . ." Jim looks at me, searching for a way to put it that won't freak her the fuck out.

"He's a serial killer, and you're his current obsession," I say, putting it plainly, which is usually the easiest way, if not always the best. "If he gets his hands on you, that's it. You'll be dead within a day."

"We don't know much about him, but what we do know isn't good," Jim adds.

Quinn gulps and places her hand to her chest. "And what, you guys are with the FBI and just happened to take a vested interest in a sex worker because she's the target of the top guy on your most-wanted list? Is that what this boils down to?" She scoffs and shakes her head, a bit of her fire returning. "Listen, I appreciate the help, but maybe it's best if we involve the local police now. I'm feeling a bit like a worm on a hook here."

"We have connections to the FBI, but we are not a government entity," Jim says. "And your assumption is correct. We have used you as bait to lure him out, but your safety is more important than his eventual capture. I realize it's asking a lot, but you'll need to trust us." Jim looks at me. "Both of us. Your life very literally depends on it."

We hang on this moment, holding our breath as she determines whether we do this the easy way or the hard way. Personally, I wouldn't mind the hard way.

"No," she says with a gentle shake of her head. "I'm sorry, but I'm not comfortable taking off with two strange men to avoid being attacked by a third strange man. You can see how this makes no sense, right?"

"Told you," I mutter to Jim.

"Besides, I still have money to make. Does your island even have Wi-Fi?"

I pull up a chair and take a seat by the window. Lightning splits the sky in half as Jim and Quinn continue to argue. He begs her to reconsider, and she refuses to budge. After ten minutes of spirited debate, I've had enough.

"C'mon, lass. I'm taking you home." I rise from the chair and head for the front door.

Jim grabs my arm, stopping me before I can step onto the porch. "You can't be serious. Aven, you pinged his location. He's somewhere in town, and knowing him, he has been since we blacked out his system a few weeks ago. He's pissed."

I shrug him off and keep going. "Not my problem."

I shove my hands in my pockets and hurry down the steps. When my feet meet sand, I turn left and step into the rain. It's tapered to a trickle now, but more is on the way, judging by those dark clouds.

The door slams behind me as someone steps onto the porch, but I don't turn to see who it is. I already know it's Quinn, and I already know what she'll say as soon as she reaches me.

I hope Jim has the boat ready to go.

Chapter Three

Quinn

A lack of information is a debilitating thing. These men seem to have the answers to questions I haven't even thought to ask, and that's the only reason I'm now seated on a tiny boat as we bounce over waves. The rain forms needles that jab my skin, and I rub my arms to chase away the sting.

Ultimately, the money got me here. Jim offered to pay a hefty bonus for my cooperation. That—on top of the money I'll make once they catch the asshole—almost made this impossible to pass up.

Though, hearing that my stalker is actually at my doorstep certainly assisted my decision. A touch.

Jim notices the way I'm rubbing my arms, and he begins pulling off his suit jacket. He spares Aven a scolding glance before dropping the silk-lined garment over my shoulders. Aven looks out at the ocean and pulls his black leather jacket a little tighter against his chest.

"Isn't the abandoned amusement park out this way?" I yell over the buzz of the small boat's engine.

Jim nods and looks out at the ocean. "She isn't so abandoned anymore! I bought the whole lot and fixed her up! Wait till you see her!"

Despite my fucked-up circumstances, a thread of excitement winds through me. My mother brought me to Laughter Park several times when I was little. She saved for an entire year just to afford a birthday trip for her girl that final night. She disappeared during the fireworks show, almost as if she meant to leave me with one good memory before my world was ripped apart.

It worked. I can't think of that last day without smiling a little.

Almost as if it were orchestrated, the bright lights of the Ferris wheel twinkle to life in the distance. Like colorful diamonds, the bulbs glisten through the rain and never-ending darkness. More lights come into view as we draw closer, but instead of heading toward the bright twinkles and strobes, the boat's driver—a bald guy with a thick mustache and an equally thick Texas accent—turns the bow toward a darker area off to the right side of the island. We eventually pull up to a low-lit dock that must serve as the service entrance.

The bald man hurries to hop off the boat and tie it to the dock before the wake can rock us backward again. Unfortunately, he miscalculates pretty seriously and ends up slipping between the boat and the narrow pier. He lands in the waves with a shout.

"Well, that won't do," Jim says as he jumps to his feet. "Aven, can he swim?"

Aven spares the floundering man a glance. "Today is a good day to learn if not."

My eyes widen, and I dare to look into the water. I'm relieved when I see the man's mustache bobbing closer to the ladder. He isn't a very strong swimmer, but at least he isn't drowning. I'm not sure how I'd explain that trauma dump to my therapist.

Oh, some strange men showed up to save me from a stalker, and then their friend drowned because he missed the dock, so now I need to up my meds, thanks.

With a groan, Aven gets to his feet to tie down the boat before we drift away. He strolls to the ignition, sets it in gear, and eases the nose forward until it kisses the dock. When he goes to jump onto the dock, he does so with the grace of a gazelle, unlike his wet friend.

"You'll have to excuse Ice P—" Jim gestures to the soggy creature now pulling himself up the ladder and onto the dock, but a crashing wave muffles the end of the man's name. "He gets a bit overzealous around pretty ladies."

I don't have a chance to respond because Jim exits the boat, leaving me alone with my bags. Aven doesn't even offer a hand. Instead, he follows Jim up the dock and toward a set of iron gates at the end.

"I guess they don't need to be chivalrous so long as they keep me safe," I mutter to myself.

The wet man—Ice Pack?—approaches the side of the boat and offers to help me, but visions of my bags falling into the ocean have me shaking my head. I'd rather make three trips than be on the six o'clock news for causing mass sea turtle deaths when they choke to death on my monster dildos and various vibrators.

It was my one sticking point before agreeing to their plan. I have to continue working. When I was sitting in that little guest room, the massive loss of income was all I could think about. If I can't stream, I'll lose my subscribers. It took years to gain a foothold in a world where pretty girls are a dime a dozen. My gimmicks—reading from my favorite smutty novels or dancing to classic rock songs—draw them in. What I'm willing to do in private sessions keeps them coming back. It may not be what I always wanted to do, but it's what I'm good at. I've worked too hard to lose it all now.

"You'd best get a move on before the storm moves further in," Ice Pack says. "Just hand those bags to me, and I'll handle getting them to your room."

"I can manage," I say with a smile. And I can. I think.

I spend a few seconds figuring out how to Tetris all my things, but it's impossible. I have way too much shit. Finally, I relent and allow Ice Pack to take my suitcase filled with everyday clothes. Losing my work outfits, toys, and equipment isn't an option. I only breathe easy once he has it on the dock and at least five feet from the edge.

Once I haul my other bags onto the dock, we join Jim and Aven near the iron gate, which begins to open as we approach. A loud buzzer shrills as the towering bars ease away, and I note the barbed wire running along the fence that borders the property back here. Makes sense, I suppose. It's a long boat ride from shore, so it's not likely someone would come out this far to snoop, but they can't take the risk of someone sneaking into restricted areas. Still . . . it reminds me more of a prison than an amusement park.

But as we step further into the gates, my mood begins to change. A ukulele song glides through speakers hidden somewhere in the tropical foliage. The distant scent of funnel cake and roasting meat reaches my nose. My stomach grumbles and tries to touch my back. I haven't eaten anything since breakfast, and deep-fried dough is kind of my weakness.

"Are the food booths open?" I ask. My little legs struggle

to keep up with the men and their long strides, but I do my best. It doesn't help that I have to keep stopping to situate the luggage. "If not, does the hotel have room service at night?"

Jim glances over his shoulder with a smile and a nod. "The food booths had a practice run today, but they're closed for the evening. Our chef will take care of you when you reach your room."

He doesn't seem bothered by the fact that I'm fighting for my life with these bags. I guess his chivalrous streak ended with offering his coat. Now that garment feels like a burden more than a benefit. I'm sweating. Heavily.

I'm seeing Aven in a new light as well. That brooding masculinity looks more like the cold shoulder now. All those half-baked daydreams of falling in love and being swept off my feet splinter and disintegrate in front of me. He isn't protecting me because he has a thing for me. I'm a job.

It's no different from the men who think they're falling in love with me. What I do sort of lends to the fantasy, and what he does is similar. Men get off on ass and tits, but most women get off on the idea of being protected. There's something so hot about it.

Another set of iron gates looms ahead, situated between two massive gray buildings that look like airplane hangars. As we draw near, the alarm buzzes again as the gates separate. We pass through a security checkpoint, then step onto a garden path lit by small lights built into the curb. After a few twists and turns through more tropical foliage, the path opens up and we step onto a wide thoroughfare lined with shops on either side.

The group stops, and Jim points out some of the changes he made. We're in the section of the park that used to be themed to dinosaurs a la Temu *Jurassic Park*, but the gaudy statues have been ripped down and replaced with ornate, weathered fountains and elegant statuary. The area has a Polynesian vibe, and I kind of dig it. It beats the hell out of a T-Rex with splotchy paint and holes where its front arms should have been.

"It's very different," I say as I take it all in. "Did you make changes to most of the park?"

Jim clasps his hands behind his back, beaming as he rocks on his heels. "Oh, yes, yes. Many changes. Spared no expense! If you've been here before, I dare say you won't recognize most of it. A few of the rides are the same, like the carousel near Center Street and one of the coasters. I didn't alter the gondolas either, but . . . yes, it's a bit different."

Aven gives him a look and starts walking again. Without offering to help, I might add. At least Jim has the decency to let me stop for a breather. I'm all for being a strong woman, but if we have much further to walk, I'm not going to make it while lugging this shit around. Jim seems to realize this, and he must not want to bother with carrying any of it either, because he pulls a walkie from his belt and radios for help. Seconds later, a golf cart wheels around the corner.

Seated in the driver's seat is a squat little man with protruding eyes, thinning hair, and a dent in the side of his skull. He wears a bright yellow shirt and a jovial smile that raises his chipmunk cheeks. The cart comes to a stop beside us, and he hops out quick as a flash to grab my things.

"Gary, you'll take her to the resort by way of Dead Man's Cove," Jim says. He turns to say something to Aven, but he's already halfway down the strip of shops. He shouts for him, but Aven just keeps walking. Flustered, Jim turns back to Gary. "Take her to the resort. Aven will meet you to take her from there."

The little man nods, then motions for me to join him in the cart.

"I could ride back with her," Ice Pack offers. "I don't mind if I miss the dinner. I've already seen the rehearsal for the show."

"Oh, no, of course not." Jim wraps his arm around Ice Pack's broad shoulders and starts walking away. "She'll be just fine with . . ."

Their voices fade as they draw further down the street, the two of them headed toward a brightly lit circus tent in the distance.

"Guess that just leaves us," the little man says with a laugh.

I guess it does. So I hop into the golf cart and let yet another strange man lead me further into madness. I can only hope this growing feeling of dread can be cured with a good meal and some sleep. Something feels off about this place, and I don't think I want to find out why.

Chapter Four

Aven

She chooses to take her meal in the hotel's central courtyard. A large oval pond dominates the center lawn, and a statue of a topless lass stands in the pond's center. A jug rests on her marble shoulder, pouring water into the pool below. The gentle sound of rushing water is enough to cover my whistling nose as I hunker behind a large king fern and watch Quinn eat.

She glances over her shoulder, clearly feeling my eyes on her. Or maybe she's still keyed up from our earlier run down the beach. I certainly am.

It's one of the reasons I took off once the boat docked. I always think more clearly once I've cleared the pipes, so I hurried back to my room to rub one out. Imagine my surprise when she was already in the lobby by the time I arrived at the hotel. My selfish needs will have to wait a bit longer. No bother.

Quinn scrapes the last of the rigatoni pasta from the plate, then sits back with a sigh as she chews. I can't see her face, but I imagine her eyes are closed. She reaches into her pocket, then stops herself. I assume she's reaching for her phone, but Jim took that from her before the boat ride. He claimed it was to ensure her safety, but really, it's to ensure ours. We can't have her bringing hellfire down on the event before it's even begun.

Not that I'd fucking care. I don't even want to be here.

Quinn pushes the plate away and rises to stand. I step out from behind the plant and walk in her direction, timing it so that she practically bumps into me the moment she turns around.

Her hand flies to her chest, and she jerks with a start. "Shit, you scared me. How long have you been creeping around in the shadows?"

"I just popped down to have a check on you, lass. No creeping here. You ready to head back to your room?"

She blinks up at me and looks around. "Am I under house arrest or something? Am I not allowed to explore at all?"

"Aye, you can explore, but aren't you tired?"

She considers this, then rubs her arms. She must be cold. Winter still drags its icy asshole over this patch of sand in the evenings and early mornings. I consider offering my jacket, but I don't want to give the girl the wrong idea. It's hard enough to make sure I don't get the wrong idea myself, but I'm not one to mix business with pleasure, no matter how pleasurable the temptation might be.

"I'm not tired, but I guess I should try to get in a shift before bed." She looks down at her sandals and wiggles her toes. "Now that I know what's really going on, could we discuss a way to do physical jobs safely?"

"No, that's off the table."

She groans and stomps her foot. She'd been gearing up

to begin receiving physical clients before all of this Desmond shit started. The money from the clients, plus the residual pay from the videos, would have set her up for life, she said. I never talked to Jim about it, but I said no on principle.

My principle.

"Why?" she asks. "You have me on this prison island, and you clearly know who comes and goes. Can't your people vet my clients to be sure they aren't Desmond?"

"Head on to your room, lass. If you want to make money, you'd best do what you can. It's not up for debate."

Hurt flashes in her eyes. It's brief, almost imperceptible, but it's there. "All this time, you really weren't my friend, were you?"

"No, I wasn't."

Her head jerks back, and her eyes widen as her jaw falls open. "Jesus, you don't even try to soften the blow. You just fucking say it."

"Aye. I'm not in the habit of mincing my words. If you don't want the truth, don't ask the question." My shoulders rise in a shrug. "I've been tasked with making sure you don't end up looking like Swiss cheese. That's my only focus. Friendships only complicate things, so you should see this as a positive."

"Yeah, I guess." She nibbles her lip and wiggles her toes some more. I've hurt her pride a bit. That much is clear by the way she won't look me in the eye, instead choosing to micro-analyze the tiny beetle inching over the paved stones near the tips of her shoes.

I'm about to give her a nudge to start walking, but she doesn't need it. She grabs her plate and starts toward the stone trash can standing near the lobby entrance, and I stroll along behind her. She sidesteps the tiny beetle, so I do the same.

She glances at me over her shoulder as she dumps the plastic plate and utensils into the gaping hole. "You aren't planning to follow me all the way to my room, are you? I know the way."

"Aye, I do. Just want to make sure you make it there okay, pal."

"No need to call me that. We aren't friends, remember?" She gives me the cheekiest smile I've ever seen, and I have to give her credit where it's due. The blow lands.

Now she's the one giving me the cold shoulder as we make our way to the elevator. I can't say I much care for the tables being turned, but so long as we're both at the same table and aware of what's going on, I can't be bothered. She doesn't have to be friendly with me any more than I need to be friendly with her. And so long as I can keep enjoying the view, I have no reason to complain.

Her hips sway back and forth as she walks, each step driving her full ass into the perfect pendulous movement. It hypnotizes me as I wander behind her. She nearly catches me staring when she stops to press the elevator call button, but I avert my gaze and pay very close attention to the safety signage to the right of the doors.

"Making sure you're familiar with the evacuation route in case of a fire?" she asks with a playful lilt to her voice.

I nod. "I've memorized the building's layout already, but it never hurts to take a refresher course."

"And what refresher course were you taking when you were staring at my ass?"

The elevator doors ding open, and she steps inside with a flick of her hair over her shoulder. Guess I wasn't as sneaky as I believed.

I step onto the elevator and press the button for her floor. I'll need to be more cautious if I want to steal glances. Or maybe I should stop stealing glances at all. It's not like I haven't seen everything she has to offer. I've seen her pussy more often than her gynecologist at this point.

But it's different in person.

My internal voice argues with me, telling me what I don't want to hear. Because it's speaking a truth I don't want to admit. The woman affects me more with her clothes on than she does with them off. It was almost easier before, when I was playing at being friends. Now that the rose-colored glasses are off, now that we're both aware of what's going on, I almost find it more difficult to focus on the task at hand.

Then again, she doesn't know everything. She is still blissfully unaware of her heritage. Or of the fact that in a circus tent a few blocks from here, Jim and Ice are probably watching a child molester get his head lopped off.

And that's the biggest difference between me and these people. I don't want the kill brought to my doorstep. I want to work for it. I want to *hunt*. I feel like the dinosaur in *Jurassic Park* when they plopped down a fat cow for her. Yeah, it would quell the hunger to take the kill, but it wouldn't satisfy the urge to kill. It's not the same thing.

Maybe that's why Quinn intrigues me more now than before. As we step off the elevator and turn right down the hallway, that theory gains a foothold and begins to climb. Pretending to be her friend took away any effort on my part. It was too easy. Now that it's hard? It's going to be a problem. A man never wants something more than when he's told he can't have it, and a man who has to work for what he wants is more apt to appreciate it. Murder and relationships are not so different.

But I don't want a relationship. I don't want any stumbling blocks to prevent me from reaching my ultimate goal. Quinn is a means to an end, and that's all she'll ever be. Once Desmond is dispatched and she's reunited with her family, I'll collect my pay and be on my way to Scotland before they've even realized. No, I won't allow anything to stop me from getting back to my homeland. Not even her devilish green eyes will sway me otherwise.

"Enjoy the show," she says with a roll of her eyes as she opens the door to her room. "I know you'll be watching."

Aye, I will. But with my eyes a little more open this time.

Chapter Five

Quinn

I sit on a lounger by the pool and shimmy my shoulders to the upbeat island music drifting through speakers tucked away in the little bursts of greenery scattered about. Sweet flavors tickle my tongue as I suck down the best piña colada I've ever tasted. Lying back, I grab the digital camera Jim gave me so that I can continue to make content without my phone.

It's a high-tech device that creates beautiful images, but it's clunky and much harder to use than my point-and-click cell phone. In the week that I've been here, I've managed to drop this camera on my face no fewer than six times. Today is no different. As I frame the overhead shot and push my cleavage into God's face, my fingers lose their grip. The heavy camera slips from my hand and crashes into the bridge of my nose. I let out a yelp and clutch my poor face.

"Being so self-centered is dangerous," Aven says beside me.

Yeah, that's still going on. My watchdog never lets me

out of his sight. Even in my room, he's watching. I've found the cameras. The only place where I'm free from prying eyes is the bathroom.

I hope.

If anyone has been watching me in there, I'll be mortified. My diet doesn't usually consist of this much red meat, and my bowels haven't exactly adjusted well. At least the chef has been diligent about avoiding my allergen.

Another clue that he was watching me was the way he'd always pop out of his room the moment I planned to leave mine. That first night, I tried to sneak out, but he was right there waiting for me when I emerged in the hallway. How convenient that his room is directly across from mine.

And today, when I stepped out of my room in a swimsuit, there he was in blue board shorts, ready to join me. He even made me put on sunscreen. It's quite annoying, actually.

I hold the camera toward him. "Could you take the picture for me so that I don't end up with a concussion?"

He folds his arms over his muscular chest and shakes his head. "Not a chance, lass. My duties begin and end with keeping you safe."

"Wouldn't preventing self-imposed bodily harm be part of that?" I wiggle the camera and refuse to relent. "Please?"

With a rumbling grumble from deep in his chest, he stands and reaches for the camera. Pleased, I hand it to him and begin planning poses. This will be so much easier now that—

Click, click, click.

Aven tosses the camera at my bare feet on the lounger. "There. I took your damned pictures. Can we just sit quietly now?"

"No, we cannot just sit quietly. I've been sitting quietly

for days, and I'm bored. We can't visit the amusement park. My subscriptions are dropping off because I'm not posting as much content without my phone. And we haven't even heard a peep from Desmond since the day you hauled me to this vacation from hell! I'm beginning to wonder if this entire exercise is necessary at this point."

"Just because he isn't saying anything doesn't mean he isn't scheming in the background." He flops onto the lounger beside mine and places his hands behind his head without a care in the world. "Suit yourself, though. If you want to take a risk and go back to the mainland, be my guest."

"Do you mean it?"

"No."

I snatch up the camera and my wrap and get to my feet. "Fuck this. I'm going to do another show in my room."

"Didn't you do a show this morning?"

"Yes, which is why I said *another*. God, is it your first day using the English language?"

My handsome shadow stands and follows me into the lobby. It's a shame he's such a prick. It's also a shame that I'm so painfully attracted to him despite his piss-poor attitude, but isn't that always the way? We most want what we can't have. If he showed the slightest interest, my vagina would dry up.

Why are we like this?

We take the elevator to our floor and part ways at my door. He does his duty and waits until I'm safely inside before retreating to his room. I haven't been in there, but I imagine him surrounded by a wall of monitors, with all the screens tuned to me. It's three parts creepy and one part kind of hot. I like being watched. That's why I'm so good at my job.

Well, I like being watched when the people doing the watching aren't psychopaths. Desmond isn't the sort I enjoy performing for. But as I said to Aven, he doesn't seem to be a problem anymore.

I'll give this another week. If he hasn't shown his face by then, I'll have to find a way to break the news to Aven and Jim that I'm not willing to be used as bait any longer. Sure, they want to keep me safe, but only until they can get Desmond to rear his ugly head. Will they be so eager to save me once they have him in their sights? That's what I'm unsure about.

I grab my half-assed setup and pull it onto the bed. I miss my multiple cameras and expensive mics, but they're all back at my house. I'm forced to make do with the laptop and small webcam that I could fit in my bag. There wasn't much room among all the toys and outfits, and the men couldn't care less if I'm faking orgasms in 4K or ten frames per second. So long as I look good while I'm doing it, they'll pay.

I pull out a lacy red teddy and change into that. It doesn't bother me that Aven is probably watching me. He's seen it all anyway, and it's not like he's doing anything with it. It almost annoys me to know he doesn't beat his dick to me.

How do you know he doesn't . . . ?

That's a good point. For all I know, he's on his knees with his dick in his hands as we speak. There's one way to find out.

Other than the few workers I've seen roaming around the hotel grounds, there aren't any other people staying here. I haven't even seen Jim since he gifted the camera. With this information as my encouragement, I step half-naked into the hall. The red teddy barely covers the lacy panties, and the majority of my ass is out for the world to see. My nipples harden with the cool air, all their pointy glory visible behind the sheer fabric.

Thankfully, the hall is empty, just as I expected it to be.

I stand outside my closed door for a moment, waiting with bated breath to see if he steps into the hall to catch me. He doesn't. After several seconds, his door remains closed. Does this mean he needed a little time to put his dick away?

A smile slides onto my face. Maybe Aven isn't as unaffected as he'd have me believe.

The smile shifts into a smirk as I sway my hips extra hard on my way to his door. I raise my hand to knock . . . right as the elevator dings at the end of the hallway.

My eyes widen. My heart hammers. My asshole puckers. I hear the doors sliding open in slow motion, followed by female voices laughing and growing louder. Closer. In just a few seconds, they'll get an eyeful of a half-naked woman knocking on a hotel door, and I can't even blame them for what they'll think. The funniest part is, they'll be right. I'm definitely a sex worker. This just isn't a call on a client.

Turning back for my door, I remember that I failed to grab my lovely keycard on the way out. I must look like a squirrel on a back road as I dart back and forth before the car hits me. A very sexy, confused, and panicked squirrel. My brain finally kicks into gear, and I slam myself against Aven's door and bang on the metal with all the desperation I can muster. My palm stings with each slap, but I really need him to open this door.

I'm out of time. The three women have their backs to me as they exit the elevator and begin gathering their luggage, but they'll turn around and see me at any second. I grip the handle on Aven's door and give it a wiggle, but it's not opening. What the fuck is he doing?

His door flies open, and I nearly fall into his arms. His very bare, very wet arms. A towel drapes his waist, and a thick lather coats his dark hair in frothy bubbles. I guess he wasn't beating his dick to me after all. He was too busy taking a fucking shower.

But I'm too relieved to worry about any of that right now. I hurry inside and close the door behind me before the women can spot me. It looks like we're no longer alone at the resort.

Chapter Six

Aven

She's a breathless ball of nerves as she goes to the bed and snatches up the comforter to cover herself. I'm grateful. It means she hasn't had the time to notice I'm a bit breathless myself. When I realized she was leaving her room and headed toward mine, it was a mad sprint to put away the laptop and lube so that I could pretend I was doing anything other than what I was. The faux shower was a nice touch, but if she stands too close, she'll realize this is body wash in my hair, not shampoo.

I panicked.

"What happened to your plans for a show? I thought you'd be occupied for at least the next thirty minutes." I motion to my current state of undress. "Can't you give me a break, lass? A man needs some downtime."

She stutters and stumbles over her words before finally landing on a coherent sentence. "I saw people out there."

"Dead ones?"

"No, you moron! Women. I thought you said we were wrapping this up before Jim opened the resort?"

She skipped right over my question and fired back one of her own. But now it's my question too. We were supposed to have another week alone at the resort—Jim said he altered the timeline—so why are people showing up? And who are they? Jim promised no Normies to complicate things the way they did on the cruise. No fucking feds, either, aside from Frankie and King. I don't know why he lets those suits sniff around, and I don't know who would have arrived early, but I'd like to find the answer to the second question.

"You stay put, aye?"

She nods and pulls the comforter tighter against her chest. It's the first time I've seen real fear in her eyes since that night I ran her down on the beach, and it's doing something to me. The towel starts to rise as I imagine chasing her down while she's wearing that teddy. The fear in her eyes would be mine. All mine.

I turn for the bathroom before she can notice the way she's turning me on against my will. Once I'm tucked out of view, I swipe the suds from my hair and drag on some gray sweats and a blue t-shirt. Unlike the bonnie lass, I like to keep my bits and pieces a surprise.

Now that I'm fit to be seen, I step out of the bathroom and remind her to stay put again. She agrees with a grumble, and I exit the room.

A door clicks shut at the end of the hallway, just as I'm stepping out. Jim put all of his favorites up here in the suites, so it has to be one of his core group members. I stroll down the hall and knock on the door, which is opened seconds later by none other than Eve.

She's a sight in a silver gown and micro braids pulled

into a perfectly round bun on top of her head. She leans her chiseled cheekbone against the door and smiles at me.

"Aven Slade, I can't believe it's you. We didn't think you'd show up after the way you kept disappearing on the cruise. What changed your mind, honey?"

Cat pushes in beside her. "Damn, now I owe Kindra twenty bucks."

"I thought you lot weren't arriving for another week. I dinnae realize Jim pushed up the timeline."

Eve and Cat exchange a look before Eve says, "No, this has always been the timeline. Jim wanted us to have our fun before the college kids get out for their break. He plans to turn this place into a public space, only shutting it down for our event in the spring each year. The man loves his business prospects."

I turn and storm off, heading straight for Jim's room. The girls say something behind me, but I care fuck all about whatever it is. When I agreed to this job, it was under the assumption that I had all the facts. Without them, I can't do my job properly. I'd say this was a pretty serious fact to leave out.

Jim opens the door shortly after I start banging on it. He's wearing a royal-purple smoking jacket, and a thick, unlit cigar perches between his lips. But that isn't the only thing that's perching, because he also carries a large white bird on his outstretched arm.

I ignore the bird and go straight for the issue at hand. "You said you were giving me another week before everyone started to arrive. What changed? And why wasn't I included in the conversation?"

The bird squawks and flaps its wide wings, flaring the large white crest on its head as it knocks the cigar from Jim's mouth. Jim cowers and tries to escape the onslaught of wing wind, but the bird keeps its death grip on his scrawny appendage.

"Lower your voice! You're frightening Kenny!" He ducks and dodges his way toward the couch in the lounge area of his suite. As he flops onto it, the bird takes flight and lands atop its cage near the bed. "He doesn't like shouting. He came from a very sordid home, and he prefers calm voices."

"I wasn't the one shouting, you numpty," I grumble. "Why'd you lie to me, Jim? You said we had another week, and unless your science division stapled a fucking flux capacitor to my asshole while I was asleep last night, a week is what I should still have."

Jim leans forward and rubs his hands against his eyes. An exasperated sigh exits his lungs, though I'm not sure what he has to be exasperated about, exactly. He isn't the one trying to lure a serial killer into the open while keeping the bait intact.

"This complicates the fuck out of the mission. Or didn't you think of that?" I say.

The bird flaps its wings and starts squawking.

"And when the fuck did you get a bird?"

He holds a finger to his lips and closes his eyes. When the bird stops screaming, he motions for me to have a seat. I plop down in the tufted chair beside the couch, but only because it seems to calm the bird. I can't take another second of that sound.

Judging by the way Jim's currently rubbing a hole in his temples, neither can he.

"I might have . . . fudged the dates a little," he finally admits.

"A little? Okay, pal." I grit my teeth and shake my head. "You've just complicated matters by a lot, and I'm dangerously close to walking away from this entire shitshow. It's a right mess. Desmond hasn't made a move since that night, and we needed this week to really bait him out. How am I supposed to do that with everyone hanging around?"

There's a knock at the door, and Jim winces. "I might have fudged your mission a bit as well." He hurries for the door before I can ask what the fuck he means. When he returns to the lounge area, he has King in tow.

The tall, gray-haired man offers me his hand, so I stand and accept it with a firm shake. He's aware of what's going on with our hunt for Desmond, and his team has been integral in helping us track him. Even so, his presence now gives me an uneasy feeling. I thought our little trio didn't keep secrets, but it appears I've been the odd man out all along.

Jim and King take a seat on the couch, and I'm too pissed to let Jim know that he's just sat his luxury asshole on a massive glob of bird shit. I hope that bird ruins every expensive thing he owns, starting with that ridiculous smoking jacket. With a grunt, I flop back into the tufted chair.

"All right. Let's cut the shit and get right to it. What's really going on here?"

Jim sighs. King frowns.

Finally, King clears his throat and looks at Jim. "This is all my fault, I'm afraid. The hunt for Desmond is a personal one. I've been after him for twenty years, but I've never been this close to squeezing him in my fist. We needed a very specific set of circumstances to bait him into the open, and you and Quinn were part of that."

I shake my head. "Why me? I understand Quinn's part in all of this, being that she's Desmond's current obsession, but you could have used any of your goons for this job. Ice Pick, Grim. Hell, even Rosie could have done this."

"Not quite," Jim says. "I had our psychology department run scenarios, and the greatest probability for a successful outcome involved using you. Granted, in most of the scenarios, you end up sacrificing yourself to save the girl, but Desmond gives us what we need in every case. We thought it seemed a fair trade."

If that's what his experts deduced, he needs some new experts. I'll ignore the bit about my life being expendable, but they're off their heads if they think I'd sacrifice myself for anyone. "The girl is nice and all, and beautiful to boot, but I like breathing air. You would have been better off telling the boys they have a sister. Family ties and all that."

I go to stand, but King grabs my arm.

"Wait, let me explain fully before you make any decisions," he pleads.

But I'm not some weak-kneed woman. He can't sway me with his smooth accent and perfectly styled hair and a jawline that could cut steel. "No thanks, pal. I've done my part and held up my end of the bargain, which was to keep Quinn safe until the party started. Now it's your problem. I'll take my pay and be on my way."

"I'll throw in a bonus," Jim adds as he rises to stand. The bird screams from its perch and flaps its wings, so he sits down and drops his voice to a whisper. "Fifty grand to stay for the retreat."

"No can do. Just wire what you owe me, then lose my contact info." I head for the door without a single regret. Quinn was starting to grow on me, and I'll probably think about her the next time I beat my dick, but the sooner I can put this place behind me, the better.

"I'll double your base pay," Jim says. "Five hundred grand total."

My feet freeze. "Now you might be talking my language."

"Gaelic?" King says with a scoff.

I roll my eyes. As if the Queen's English is any easier to understand.

"There's just a small catch," Jim adds, and why don't I like the sound of this?

Then he explains the small catch, and I like it even less.

Chapter Seven

Quinn

Aven bursts into the room after leaving me in here for what feels like hours. I've already rummaged through his duffel bag and changed into one of his t-shirts. I was sick of sitting in sexy lingerie without anyone to look at it. That's the only reason I wear the shit. It certainly isn't comfortable, what with all the strings and tassels ramming into every crack and crevice.

He eyes my ensemble and rolls his eyes. "Get over to your room and put on something nice. Preferably something that belongs to you. I'm taking you to dinner."

"Oh, like a date?" I say with a flirty wiggle of my shoulders. My unrestrained breasts sway beneath the baggy shirt, but he doesn't even look. He's too busy digging through the closet.

"No, not like a date," he grumbles. He stands upright and snatches off his shirt, giving me a glorious view of his chiseled chest. He's built like a brick shithouse, with a barrel chest and a wide waist. Dark hairs paint a path toward his sweatpants, but my eyes are drawn to the tattoo running up his side.

I cock my head and point to it. "Is that a dragon?"

He raises his arm and looks at the tattoo as if he needs to see it to know what the fuck I'm talking about. "Aye. Ever heard of the Edinburgh Dragon?"

I haven't, so I shake my head.

"Well, when you get bored, do some research and learn about it."

"Or you could just tell me? Isn't that how conversations typically work?" I nibble my lip and patiently wait for him to pull off his pants.

"I suppose. If we were having a conversation. Which we aren't. Go get dressed." He grips the waistband of his sweats and waits. "Go on."

I grumble and slink toward the door. "You're no fun. But how do I get into my room? My keycard is in there."

He reaches into the pocket of his sweats and tosses a card to me. "A spare key to your room. Make sure you give it back at dinner."

I tuck the card into the panty string on my hip and leave the room. Maybe I'll give it back. Maybe I won't. We'll see how I feel later.

Aven shows up at my room an hour later. He's abandoned his jeans and leather jacket for khakis and a white button up. A black tie circles his thick neck, and he's rolled the sleeves, exposing his tattooed forearms. I've never seen him so dressed up, and it's a shock to the system. A good shock, though.

"You clean up well, Mister Slade," I say as I step closer and give him a twirl of my lavender cocktail dress. The hem flares wide, making me feel like a slutty princess.

He fusses with his tie, not even sparing me a glance. "Don't leave my side at this dinner."

I stop spinning. "Aren't you going to compliment my dress?"

"Why would I do that? You already know it looks nice. Isn't that why you were doing the dreidel impression just now?"

I set my jaw and snatch my purple clutch from the bed. "A girl still likes to hear a compliment."

"If you weren't so full of yourself, it might leave a little room for someone else to offer a compliment." He shrugs and stuffs his hands into his pockets. "But seriously, don't leave my side at dinner."

As he turns and leaves the room, I follow him into the hallway, but I don't miss a chance to make a face at him behind his back. He thinks he's so high and mighty, like he can shit on my confidence and then tell me what to do.

"What's wrong with having a little confidence?" I ask as we step onto the elevator. "Besides, confidence sells in my business. Oh shit, I forgot my camera!"

I go to step off the elevator, but Aven bars my path with his arm and presses the button for the doors to close.

"No photography in the parks, wee lass. Jim's rule, not mine."

My eyes light up. "We're finally going to the park? How exciting! But why can't I take any pictures?"

Aven checks his watch, then blinks at the ceiling. "Because right at this moment, a group of serial killers is currently preparing to join us, and they don't want their faces plastered all over your porn site."

I practically choke on my spit, because *what?* "Serial . . . killers? You aren't one to joke around, so what exactly do you mean?"

The elevator stops on the ground floor, and we move toward the lobby. I spot my German neighbor at the desk. His silent lady friend stands beside him, fiddling with something in her purse as he checks them into a room. Aven stops walking and points to them.

"That's Grim, but he's known as *Der Sensenmann* in Germany." His finger moves slightly, pointing to the woman. "That's Maudlin Rose, a killer from the Midwest. Her husband slashed her throat and rendered her incapable of typical speech. Now she goes around killing men who piss her off."

I roll my eyes because he can't be serious. My neighbor is odd, but he's not a serial killer. There is just no way. His little old lady doesn't look the type either.

"So you're telling me that you've brought me to a hotel that is now filled with serial killers when you're supposed to be protecting me from a serial killer?"

"Aye, that's exactly what I'm telling you. But we aren't a danger to you."

"*We?* You're saying you're one of them?" Okay, I can almost believe that, what with his cold affect and disinterested demeanor. But still . . . he's fucking with me. He has to be.

He starts walking again, and I hurry to keep up with him. If he's telling the truth, I don't want to find out the hard way. I don't believe him—this is just too ludicrous to be true—but there's a fire ant of doubt that won't stop biting my brain.

He pauses at the doors leading into the outdoor pool area. "I've killed, lass. I've killed plenty. And I've plenty more killing to do before I'm caught." He grips the handle, then releases it with a sigh and a shake of his head. "Jim asked me to keep some of it from you, but I don't feel right about it. You need to be given a choice, so I'm keen to offer that to you."

Oh, he's really playing into this, but I know what he's trying to do. He's trying to frighten me. Well, I won't be roped into his silly prank.

"I'm not afraid of you, Aven, and I don't believe that you or any of these people are killers. So just tell me what's really going on. Do you know where Desmond is or not?"

And then . . . he tells me everything.

Chapter Eight

Quinn

Even as I take a seat at a table surrounded by serial killers, I don't believe a word of what he said. And yet, his explanation makes the most sense. I guess I won't fully believe it until I see someone slain with my own eyes, which he assures me will happen at this dinner.

I don't know how I'll react if he's telling the truth. The rational reaction would be to run screaming for the nearest boat, but I wouldn't call myself a rational woman. Part of me hopes he's being honest and that I really have been sucked into the seedy underground. Maybe I can make my dark romance dreams a reality after all.

Not with him, though.

I've pretty much accepted that Aven isn't interested. Is it disappointing? Yes. But it's not surprising. He's on emotional lockdown, and I don't have the energy to expend on breaking through those barriers. If I want to get my kicks, I'll have to do it with someone else.

That shouldn't be hard, considering the other little

tidbit he offered me. As it turns out, I'm not only surrounded by serial killers; I'm serial killer royalty. Some murderous bigwig named Grantham Carter provided the other half of my DNA. I won't be able to use that to my advantage, however. Aven said I can't tell anyone until Jim says I can, and when Jim tells me himself, I'm supposed to act surprised.

No, my feminine wiles will have to do, so I scan the room in search of eligible men. I spot a few of them, but then those men join us at the table, and I realize they aren't so eligible after all. All three of them appear to be attached to the women seated near us—aside from Eve, whom I've learned is a lesbian fashion model on top of being a serial killer. I feel like I've been living under a fucking rock.

The excitement of it all dazzles me more than it frightens me. I mean, it frightens me too, but the adrenaline rush errs more on the side of thrill than chill. Killers surround me—if Aven is to be believed—and yet I'm untouchable.

Even beyond my fabled heritage, my safety is assured. Granted, that's only because Aven assures it, but still. It's a fucking assurance.

"Aven, who's the lovely lady on your arm tonight?" a beautiful blonde asks. She sits across from us beside a man in a pineapple-print shirt.

Aven introduces me to everyone, and I make a mental note of their names. Are these really their names, though? Seems kind of risky for them to trust me so fully when they don't know if I'm with the cops.

But then I learn that one of the women is an agent with the fucking FBI. How deep does this rabbit hole run?

I'm just excited to have other people to talk to for once. These humans are capable of more than one-word responses, unlike Aven. They're so friendly and outgoing and not at all what I'd expect serial killers to be. It makes me wonder how many people in my day-to-day life are doing unimaginable things behind closed doors.

But before we have much chance to talk, the lights in the conference room begin to dim, and Jim steps onto the small stage at the head of the event space. Conversations still as waitstaff tiptoe through the tables and fill glasses of water.

"Hello, Sinners, and welcome to Slaughter Park!" he says, and the crowd offers a small round of applause. "For those of you who have been with us for a while, I'd like to say welcome back. You'll notice a few changes this time around, such as our selections for Cattle, but we'll get into that shortly. For our newcomers, I'd like to go over our rules for these retreats."

I lean closer to Aven so that I can whisper into his ear. But as I get into his space, my thoughts leave my head. He smells so *good*. It's a mix of black leather and sea salt, and I just want to fall asleep with this scent in my lungs. It relaxes everything in my body.

My brain reminds me to ask the question before he notices me sniffing him. "The killers here follow rules?" I whisper.

He nods and points for me to listen to Jim.

"First and foremost, the only sanctioned targets on this island are the Cattle. They're easy to recognize by their attire. Cattle who have committed crimes against children wear pink. The rapists are in red, and our new category this year will take up the yellow robes. That's right, Sinners! We're killing animal abusers this go round!"

A cheer erupts from the crowd, and I have to cover my mouth to hide the giggle trying to squeeze out of me. I feel like I'm on some prank show. Any minute now, someone is going to pop out and point to the cameras. This can't be real life.

Jim grins and urges everyone to settle, and they do. He clears his throat and brings the mic to his mouth again. "I'm so glad to see the excitement for our new category at this retreat, but I must reiterate that only Cattle may be slain. If you take the life of a staff member or a Sinner, there will be . . . repercussions."

I want to ask Aven where I fall in all of this. When he explained what this retreat really was, he didn't say what part I'd need to play. Other than helping them lure Desmond into the open, I'm not sure what I'm expected to do. Will I have to kill someone?

God, I hope so.

It's no secret that I have dark fantasies. Everyone in my chat knows about my obsession with dark romance. But that's just what I've let them see. They don't know just how dark my heart gets. If they did, I'd probably attract the wrong type of client. My feed would be flooded with Desmonds.

But these people are different. If they really are killers, they follow a code. They're vigilantes, doing good in the world by ridding it of pedos, rapists, and animal abusers. I want to be part of this world.

And as the lights dim and Jim leads three hooded Cattle onto the stage, I might just get my grand entrance into the dark universe that is my birthright.

Chapter Nine

Aven

All things considered, the girl is taking this well. A little too well, maybe. I didn't expect her to start screaming her wee head off or anything, but she seems more intrigued than put off about the whole serial killer thing. Jim said the simulation predicted this outcome. I don't think his precious simulator could have predicted just how jolly she'd be, though.

Granted, we never ran a simulation where I told the lass her father was a prolific killer. That was probably a mistake on my part, but I figured it would help her adjust a little more. The last name comes with certain benefits, and I figured knowing those benefits would set her at ease. It certainly seems to have worked a trick. She doesn't appear frightened at all.

When Jim opens the dinner with a game, Quinn's hand is the first to shoot into the air when he asks for volunteers. We discussed what would likely happen in this moment. In most instances, the simulation predicted she would be interested in witnessing the killings, but that she wouldn't go so far as to participate. I guess we need to stop relying so heavily on that machine's predictions, because this woman is clearly the least possible outcome in any given situation.

Jim looks at me, silently asking what to do. I look back at him and offer no help. This is his monkey and his circus, and I'm just here to hold the tail.

"Well . . . come on up, Quinn," Jim finally stammers. He introduces her to the group, but instead of smiling and listening, the performer inside her rears its massive head.

Quinn snatches the mic from his hands and smiles at the crowd. "Hello out there," she says with a wiggle of her fingers. "As Jim said, my name is Quinn, but some of you might know me by a different name." She offers a wink.

A fucking wink.

What is she doing? If she tells everyone who her da is, Jim will send me out with a boot in my ass.

"That's right! I'm Daisy!" She lifts her heel and covers her coy giggle with her dainty little fingers.

I breathe a sigh of relief. She meant her cam-girl alter ego, not her Carter lineage.

"After the dinner tonight, I'll be hosting a private show in my chat room, just for the fellow Sinners. If anyone needs a little extra entertainment after tonight's dinner, you know where I'll be." She nibbles her bottom lip and shimmies her shoulders with another playful giggle.

The crowd goes wild after her announcement. Even the girls are tossing out wolf whistles and supportive applause. The men at our table only clap politely, but the unattached men are practically drooling. And I don't fucking like it.

None of this was discussed previously, and if there's one thing I cannae fucking stand, it's making decisions on the fly.

I look at Jim to gauge his reaction, but he's firmly in Camp Happy Face. And why wouldn't he be? What better way to bait Desmond into the open than by putting his prized painting on display?

The trouble is . . . she appears to be prized by pretty much everyone who isn't tied down. I glance around the dining hall and see dozens of male eyes dancing with wonder as they watch her swing her hips and answer Jim's questions. The girl is a natural on stage. She oozes sex appeal and sultry energy in that little purple dress.

My attention turns back to the stage as Gary, one of Jim's staffers, wheels a large table into the spotlight. A thick velvet covering drapes the contents, obscuring them from view as he positions the table in front of the three Cattle still awaiting their executions. In the center of the table is a perch. Once the rolling wheels are locked in place, the large white bird flies from offstage and lands in the center of the table, right on the perch.

"Everyone, I'd like you to formally meet Kenny," Jim says, and the bird flaps its wings and flares its crest. The screaming starts, so Jim drops his voice to a whisper. "I need everyone to use quiet voices for this fellow. You see, Kenny came from a home where his family neglected him. He was kept in a tiny cage, no bigger than he is. When he screamed in distress or boredom, they would strike his cage and scream back. He was the only survivor of a house of horrors. Twenty-three birds were found deceased at the hands of this man."

Jim snatches the yellow hood away, revealing a whimpering man who's had his thin lips sewn shut. Rivers of sweat plaster his greasy black hair to his forehead, and his eyes bulge when he sees the bird.

"That's right," Jim says. "We've brought Kenny's old

master to the stage so that he can finally pay for his crimes, and who better to serve up the revenge than the very bird he tortured?"

"Piece of fucking shit," the bird mutters in a very human-like voice. "Piece of fuck, piece of fuck."

Gary snatches away the table's velvet covering, revealing a line of gleaming silver weapons. His job finished, he exits the stage with a shit-eating grin.

Kenny's head bobbing resumes as he eyes the shiny assortment. He wiggles his wings and rocks from side to side, still repeating his creepy mantra. "Piece of fucking, piece of *fuck!*"

Quinn stands on tiptoes behind Jim, trying to see around him so that she can glimpse the weapons on the table. There are several options to choose from, including a machete, a revolver, and some sort of scythe. Before she can choose any of them, Jim steps forward and grabs the flashy revolver with a pearl grip. He wiggles the gun in the air, keeping the barrel pointed toward the ceiling. I'm not so sure he's that experienced with firearms if he's about to do what I think he's about to do.

But that's exactly what he's planning. As he places the revolver into a special holder at the center of the perch, the bird's crest rises. Its head tips to the side, and it studies the gun with increased interest. One scaly foot reaches toward the trigger guard, and my stomach lurches.

Jim places his hand over the guard and wags his finger at the bird. "Not quite yet, Kenny." He turns back to the crowd with a laugh. "We've opened a new division, you see. We don't just want to ravage the cruel humans who've abused these animals. We want to save the animals as well. Kenny is the first of a few animals you'll meet at this retreat. Through care and compassion, we've reduced his plucking and have brought him back to excellent health. We even desensitized him to gunfire to make this moment possible for him. For his final act on his healing journey, we're giving him the opportunity to destroy the very human who abused him."

The crowd whispers its approval, and Quinn quietly claps her hands behind Jim.

Ice Pick raises his hand from his table, and Jim leans closer to him. The mic barely picks up his timid question as he says, "But Jim . . . that bird ain't got any thumbs. How's he gonna shoot the gun?"

Jim tosses his head back and laughs, and the crowd offers a polite titter in response. "The weapon is designed especially for Kenny. There is minimal recoil, and he's trained to perform the action on command. Ultimately, it will be his decision, but when I say *bang, bang,* we'll see what he does. This gun has a state-of-the-art, hair-trigger—"

Blam!

The gun goes off, and everyone screams. Kenny flaps his wings and dances on his perch with his crest held toward the heavens. The Cattle looks down at his chest, where a red rosebud begins to blossom behind the yellow fabric. He screams through his nose as he realizes what's happened.

Kenny flaps his wings and looks . . . really fucking pleased. He retracts his scaly foot back to the perch and wiggles his wings as he bobs his head some more. His dark beak opens in what I can only describe as a smile as he keeps doing his happy murder dance.

I look at Quinn, the polar opposite of Kenny. The excitement has drained from her features, leaving behind a pale landscape of shock and uncertainty. Her fingertips quiver against her chest. Her mouth hangs open, and her eyes are widened to the point of no return. She doesn't take a breath, and neither do I. Not until a smile slides onto her face.

She peers into the crowd, somehow finding me in spite of the spotlights in her eyes. *Wow*, she mouths.

Excuse me, what? *That's* her response?

The dying man drops to his knees, and the hooded Cattle to either side of him cower and try to move away, but they're linked together by chains around their ankles. There's nowhere for them to go. The crowd falls silent as we witness the animal abuser's death, which takes entirely too long, which is exactly what he deserves. After five minutes of groaning, Jim finally snatches up the gun and finishes him off with a bullet to the brain.

Then he turns to Quinn. "Who's next?"

My blood runs cold because this was never part of the plan. Having her witness the kills was as far as this was supposed to go. She isn't meant to participate. Yet she's all smiles and eagerness as she moves to the table and plucks up a hacksaw with a chrome blade. And it's all my fault for telling her about Daddy Carter. Fuck me sideways.

"Pink is for the child abusers, right?" she asks as she eyes the cowering Cattle.

Jim nods, and she sidles up to the pink character. With a nibble of her lip, she grips the hood and yanks it off, revealing the shriveled face of an old man. He looks harmless, but many of them do. That's how they get away with it for so long.

Quinn doesn't even wait for the rundown. She doesn't need Jim to tell her what this vile monster has done to children. She grabs the man's gray hair, snatches back his head, and begins to saw his throat open.

His legs kick out as he tries to scramble away from the blade, but the chain catches and sends him to the floor.

Quinn is on him immediately. With his hands strapped behind his back, he's defenseless against her wild onslaught as she straddles his waist and starts sawing again. We can't see his face. We can't see the carnage. What we can see is the way his kicks grow weaker as a red puddle begins to spread across the stage.

When he stops moving, Quinn finally stands and faces the onlookers. She's all purple elegance and crimson wrath as she holds out the hacksaw and takes a bow. Red stains paint her fluffy dress, her pale skin, and her golden hair.

I've never seen a more beautiful sight.

Or a more terrifying one.

Quinn didn't need to wait for Jim's explanation of this man's crimes. She didn't even need to know he'd done anything wrong. She just needed permission. To kill.

My friends, I believe we've just witnessed the birth of a monster.

Chapter Ten

Aven

I brought my concerns to Jim after dinner, but he would hear none of it. He sees Quinn's hunger for blood and attention as a positive. Especially the attention bit. His thinking is that the enticement of her special stream for Sinners will be too much for Desmond, forcing him to show himself. Jim liked the idea so much that he went so far as to help her set up a stream to every single room in the hotel. In just a few minutes, she'll appear on channel four for anyone who wants to tune in.

How positively fucking lovely.

He even kicked me out of the room so that they could discuss what she would do during her stream. Me. Her fucking bodyguard. He expects me to keep her safe, but he isn't including me in the plans. I've let it slide tonight, but I cannae work in these conditions. I'll speak with him tomorrow.

For right now, it's time to watch my favorite program.

I flip on the television and turn to channel four. It just

shows a screen that welcomes me to the resort at the moment, but soon enough, Daisy's Room will fill my screen. But one screen isn't enough, so I pull out the laptop, too. With a few clicks, I'm seeing her room from angles no one else has access to.

Quinn sits on her bed, right in the center. She's traded her lavender cocktail dress for a silver-sequined bra-and-panty set. It looks like something a pop princess would parade around at a concert. I half expect her to raise that Hitachi Magic Wand like a microphone, but she just plugs it in and tucks it beneath a pillow.

As she moves to the mirror beside the bathroom, I switch cameras so that I can continue watching her. She eyes herself in the wide reflective surface, turning back and forth as she squeezes the poochy bit of skin at the front of her flashy panties. A frown slides onto her face as she tucks the skin behind the fabric. She's clearly displeased with her figure, but I find her perfect. That extra bit of softness around her midsection is a bonus, not a detraction.

I'm not supposed to look at her this way. She's my primary, and my focus should center on her safety alone. Why does she have to be so damned distracting?

When it's time for the show to begin, she hurries back to the bed and positions herself on the comforter. Once she's certain she's framed the shot correctly, she goes live. My television screen switches to a shot of her, banishing the darkness with all of her glittering attire.

"Hey, party people," she says with a wiggle of her fingers. "I'm so glad all of you chose to join me in Daisy's Room for the night. I'm typically used to a little back and forth, but chat isn't possible in this setting." She pushes out her bottom lip in a pout, and I get an instant vision of her on her knees, looking up at me as she makes that same face.

"Not to worry, though! I'm sure I can keep us all *very* entertained."

She shifts positions on the bed, going from lying on her side to sitting on her knees. As she leans forward, her breasts fill the camera. The tight top pushes them toward the heavens. I wonder what they'd feel like in my hands. Would she let me squeeze them until it hurts? Could I bite—

Fucking stop it!

I shake my head to clear my brain. But it's no use. I should be more focused than ever, but when she nibbles her lip and plays with her hair, I can't concentrate on anything aside from filthy thoughts. That is, until she says something that turns my blood to ice in my veins.

"Jim gave me permission to have a date with one lucky Sinner tonight. He'll choose the winner. All you have to do—"

Her voice fades as the hotel room door closes behind me. When that first sentence left her mouth, I was already on my feet. I grab my key from my pocket and try to open her door, but then I remember that I gave her the other key. The one currently in my hand only works for my room.

"Fuck," I say under my breath. Banging on her door won't do any fucking good. She's probably eating this up, knowing that she and Jim orchestrated this behind my back. They knew I'd never agree to this.

So I'll just take it straight to the man himself.

When I reach Jim's door, King is standing just outside. He acknowledges me as I approach, raising a hand and stepping in front of the door before I can knock it down. "Jim's simulation predicted correctly this time," he says with a sheepish smile. "I wasn't too fond of this idea myself, but he thinks it's the fastest way to draw Desmond out of hiding."

"And the fastest way to get the girl killed," I bellow into his smug British face. "She doesn't even know what sort of risk she's taking. Jim didn't need a predictive machine to figure out that I wouldn't be okay with it."

The door opens, and Jim's head pops through the opening. "That's where you're wrong, my boy. Now come in here and stop shouting in the halls."

I'd rather come into the room and throttle both of these men, but I bite my tongue and wait to hear his explanation. Even once I've heard it, I'm not satisfied.

The "special guest" was Quinn's idea, and both Jim and King warned her about the dangers. It's meant to bait out Desmond, but there's no guarantee he'll take that bait. He's smart, and he'll see this coming.

"It's some weird fantasy we're allowing her to live out," Jim says with a flail of his hand. "I was shocked she wanted to kill, but I'm even more shocked that she has a desire to sleep with a killer."

"So who's the lucky chap tonight?" I ask with a roll of my eyes. "Surely no one has tried to take this offer."

Jim winces. "As of right now . . . Ice Pick. He's called no fewer than three times."

I blow out a breath. At least we know he's harmless. He'll probably just sit in a corner and giggle the entire time.

The phone rings, sending Kenny into a wild flailing of wing flaps and screams. Jim hurries for the phone, leaving King and me in the main living area.

"What do you think about all this?" I ask.

His broad shoulders rise in a shrug. "While I don't like this risk, I can't deny that having her be such a willing bit of flash in the pan for Desmond is a benefit. He may not take the bait tonight, but if we keep trying . . ."

"How often do you expect us to put her in danger like this?"

"Until he makes a move that reveals who he is. We've narrowed it to three men, but he could be any of them."

"Or he might be none of them."

"He is," King says with a certainty that almost makes me believe him. "We've set this up too perfectly. There's a little bit of the equation we haven't let Quinn in on just yet, but once we have Desmond, we'll tell her everything."

"I won't keep any more of your secrets, so I don't want to know. So long as I have the information to do my job, that's all I require."

King nods. "I understand, but—"

"No buts."

Jim rushes back to the living area. "Aven, we've just had a call from one of the men we suspect may be Desmond, and he wanted to meet with Quinn, but he got nervous and backed out. That means Ice Pick is our only option for tonight. If the other men can see her interact, it might give them some confidence, so can you meet Ice Pick in the costume department?"

"You're really going through with this? You're sending in Ice Pick?" I cannae believe my ears. "Jim, he'll blow this entire thing out of the water. You can't do this."

King and Jim share a glance.

"No," I say. "Absolutely the fuck not."

"She wouldn't even know it was you," King says.

"And how will she think it's anyone else once she sees my face?"

King and Jim share another look, and minutes later, I'm headed toward the costume department to prepare for a date with Quinn.

Chapter Eleven

Aven

I raise a lime-green fist, but I can't bring myself to knock on the door. She won't even know I'm the one sucked inside this ridiculous Zentai suit, but I'll know. It's mortifying. I look like a demented Teletubby walking the halls of the hotel. And now I'm supposed to go in here and enjoy a private show from a goddess?

There was a time in my life where I wielded an ax and brought wrath down on anyone who looked at me sideways. My god, how far I have fallen.

I sigh into the shiny Lycra. It was the only way. The mask options didn't work because my arms and legs were still very much exposed. The tattoos give me away. Thankfully, there are a few men here who match my body type, so seeing this monstrous green mass shouldn't give her any clues. And I do *not* want her to know it's me.

Even aside from my self-imposed rules regarding keeping a safe distance from my primary, this goes against who I am as a person. I don't wear costumes. I don't play silly games. And I never pay for sex.

Technically, Jim is paying for the sex, but still. I don't like it. Which is why there will not be any sex.

That's what I keep repeating in my head as I finally raise my hand and knock. My dick doesn't want to listen, but he'll need to in this suit. The slightest bit of arousal will tear a hole through this flimsy green skin. I have nowhere to hide.

Quinn doesn't look the slightest bit nervous when the door swings wide. Her smile greets me, but my damned eyes drop to her breasts. They spill from that glittering top and practically beg for my mouth. That's when the suit begins to feel a little too snug.

I slip past her and head straight for a chair in the corner so that I can sit and hide the growing proof of my failure.

"Well, we're quite the eager beaver, aren't we?" she says with an adorable giggle. She closes the door and moves to the bed, where she takes a seat and pats the mattress. "Why don't you come over here and join me?"

I shake my head.

"Oh, not so eager now, hmm? Are you nervous?"

I shake my head again.

Quinn rolls her eyes with a smirk. "There's not a thing to be nervous about. I'm a beautiful woman, and you're . . . Well, you're here. I can't tell if you're attractive behind all that green fabric, but you're certainly muscled, aren't you?"

She bites her lip as she eyes my physique, and I'm crumbling under the weight of her scrutiny. Why do I feel the sudden urge to tense up and show her just how strong I am? What next? I'll pull out my new sneakers to show her I'm fast too? Jesus fuck.

But then again . . . no one aside from Jim and King and the little guy in the costume shop knows who's in this suit. Gary's too afraid to tell anyone my identity—I threatened to dent the other side of his skull if he so much as thought of leaking that information—and Jim and King both assured me they had no interest in watching her performances. If I want to go a little out of my comfort zone, no one will be the wiser.

So I raise my arm and flex.

Quinn's eyes widen as my biceps strain against the thin material. As she scoots back on the bed and a tinge of fear colors her green eyes, I remember that she thinks I could be her stalker. Her very large, very muscled stalker. I fold my hands in my lap and try to look less threatening, though I would think this getup would be the least threatening thing on the planet.

She grabs the reins again and clears her throat. The glimpse of fear fades as she pulls the Magic Wand from beneath the pillow. She drags it up her thigh and smiles at me again. "Do you want to play? Or would you just prefer to watch?"

This is a very dangerous question. What I want is to treat her like I treated my toys as a child. I want to play until something breaks. But I take a deep breath and motion for her to soldier on alone.

"That's okay with me," she says. She flicks the button on the side of the device, and it buzzes to life. "Could you show me, though? Can I see what I'm doing to you?"

As she lies back and drags the vibrating head of the device between her thick thighs, my mouth runs dry. I could get out my dick. She's never seen it in person—and aside from this, she never will—so it's not like she'll recognize it and attach it to me. Lots of men have dark pubes and a piercing straight through the tip of their dick, right?

Then she spreads those thighs and lets out a moan, and it's no longer up for debate. I reach between my legs and grab the delicate inner seam, then rip it apart. My cock practically plays a theme song as it springs from the fabric, but I still don't want her to see the piercing. I keep my closed fist over the tip, only allowing her to glimpse my stiff shaft.

"Fuck yeah," Quinn whispers, and she's looking right at me. Her wish to see my junk wasn't entirely meant to placate and is, at least in some sense, doing something for her. Her thighs quiver, and she bumps the button to make the device vibrate harder. "Stroke yourself. Make me come, just like that."

Keeping the piercing concealed, I fist my dick and stroke because I can't help myself. There is no denying how much I want this. Not just *this*, but *her*. Being around her day in and day out has been torture, and why shouldn't I get a little relief? So I stroke a little faster, all the while telling myself that this is just to clear my head.

No pun intended. I fucking hate puns.

She seems to be enjoying herself, so I keep going. While she rubs her glitter pussy with that massive masturbation mallet, I stroke my cock and try to forget that I'm wearing this asinine outfit. It's making this moment possible, so I should be grateful, but the shame is really killing the vibe here.

"I'm feeling pretty confined. I think I should really lose this top." She sits up and unfastens the bra, freeing her breasts. Her light-pink nipples make my mouth water the moment they turn my way. "That's so much better."

Yeah, lass. I agree. My dick does too, as it practically

swells in my hand as a spurt of pre-cum burbles out of me. It greases my palm, but I keep that piercing concealed.

"You could get more comfy too," she says, but I shake my head. "Aw, that's okay. If you're feeling a little shy, you don't have to remove your outfit. You can come over here and touch if you want, though."

She grips her breasts and lowers her chin to lick the top of one, and I have never wanted to touch something so badly. Taste it. Bite it. But I can't. This is as close to her as I'll allow because I don't trust myself to behave if I come any closer. Besides, I don't need to touch her to get myself off. Just being this close to her is enough.

I grip my shaft and speed up the tempo a little more. This is a dangerous game, and the sooner we reach the end, the better. Her thighs shake more as she grinds the vibrator over her pussy, and her breasts wobble with each rapid breath she takes. Before she can initiate takeoff, however, she freezes. Her thighs clamp together, and she grabs the remote from the bed.

"If you people out there in TV Land want more, you'll have to sign up for your own private session tomorrow night. Jim will have all the details." She offers a wink, then cuts the feed. The red light on the camera above the television blinks to darkness as she turns to me. "Um . . . if you can give me just a second . . ."

She stands to leave the bed and nearly falls. I jump to my feet to help her, but then I remember what I look like. I'm a giant green monster with his stiff dick swinging toward her like a weapon. But as she goes to stand again, I get a better look at her face. She's turned tomato red and begun to swell up like a biscuit in the oven. I can't even ask her what's wrong, as my voice would give me away.

"Don't go. I really just need a sec," she says as she stumbles to the bathroom. Before she can reach the door, she doubles over and grips her stomach. "On second thought, we might need a raincheck."

She needs more than a raincheck. She needs a fucking doctor.

"Jesus, why am I so itchy? The soles of my feet, my scalp." Her short nails claw at her skin as she scratches her stomach, and then I realize what's going on.

How the fuck do I mime "allergic reaction"? Where the fuck is Rose when I need her?

I move past her and begin digging through her bags on the sink. She goes to protest, but a sharp pain strikes her silent as she clutches her stomach again. My fingers graze Tylenol, some sort of bloat guard, and a few freewheeling Tums, but I see no Benadryl.

"Listen, I know this isn't exactly sexy, but I think I'm going to be sick. Could I ride this out in private? I must have eaten something that didn't agree with me."

A loud fart rips out of her. It startles the fuck out of me, and I send her toiletries scattering over the counter.

I turn back to her and nearly speak out of shock. In the span of a few seconds, she's swollen even more. If this keeps up, she'll choke on that fat tongue of hers and dash all fantasies of her wrapping it around my dick. I have to help her. And fast.

But as she stumbles against the bathroom doorframe and collapses on the floor, I realize I'm out of time.

Chapter Twelve

Quinn

When I open my eyes, my quirky German neighbor is the last person I expect to see, yet there he is. His silent lover stands beside him as he speaks to Aven. The woman holds an orange-capped stick in her hand, which she tosses to the floor when she sees that I'm awake. She tugs on the German man's arm and points down at me.

"Ah, the prostitute is conscious once more," he says. "Are we needed further, or may we leave now?"

Aven clears his throat and tosses a towel into my lap as I sit up and try to clear the fog from my head. "She's not a prostitute, pal."

"Technically, I am, but we prefer the term sex worker." I use the towel to cover my breasts. The evening's events come rushing back to me, and I remember why I'm shirtless. "Shit, how bad did I fuck everything up tonight?"

"We can handle it from here," Aven says as he begins ushering the elderly pair out of my room.

The woman stops and grabs the German's hand. She scrawls something on his palm with her finger, and he nods before turning to Aven.

"The epinephrine may not be enough. I am content to leave her to die, but Rose feels—"

"Content to leave me to die? Epinephrine? What the fuck is happening right now?" I look down and spot the pinprick bruise on my thigh. "That was an allergic reaction?"

"Aye, wee lass," Aven says, his voice a touch softer than he usually speaks. "When you went off camera, I came right over and found you collapsed on the floor."

I place my hand to my head as the room begins to spin. "I think I'm going to vomit."

Rose pushes a trash can in front of me, and I lean forward and retch. My entire dinner lands in the bottom, and let me tell you, shrimp scampi does not taste as good coming up as it does going down. The sight and smell are enough to make me gag until I only have frothy yellow bile to offer the trash-can gods.

Aven kneels beside me and pats my back. "That's it, lass. Get it all up and out. But what would convince you to eat shrimp when you clearly have a shellfish allergy?"

Rose passes a damp rag to me, and I wipe my mouth. "I'm not allergic to anything other than turmeric, same as my father. My mother said it was his parting gift before leaving my siblings running down her thighs."

Aven's brows pull together, but he turns back to the couple. "I'll get her down to the infirmary if she shows symptoms again. Could you be a friend and go ask Chef Maurice what he put in the scampi tonight?"

"No, we do not have any desire to be of future service to

you. We planned to try painting with our anuses this evening, and you are killing our vibe, as the children say."

"Seriously, Grim?" Aven opens his mouth to argue further, but I place a hand on his arm.

"Just let them enjoy their literal artsy-fartsy stuff. We can speak to the chef later."

"I am offended you would insinuate we would release gas onto the artwork." He scoffs. "It would ruin the composition! *Dieser Dummkopf!*"

Rose offers a polite, apologetic smile as Grim grips her slender arm and leads her out of the room. He slams the door as he exits.

I push the trash can away with a groan. This couldn't have gone any worse if I'd planned it. Not only did I blow my chance to make a serial killer come, but I potentially fucked up this entire mission. If that was Desmond, there's no chance in hell he'll be baited back to my room anytime soon.

But if that was Desmond . . . why didn't he kill me?

The toe of Aven's boot bumps against my foot. "You okay, pal? You scared me pretty good there."

"I thought we weren't friends," I say as I struggle to my feet. I nearly crash to my ass, but he steadies me. I snatch my arm away. "Stop being so nice. It doesn't go well with your mean face."

"Ach, I don't have a mean face," he mutters, and I'll be damned if he doesn't look genuinely hurt. "You said your mother told you the allergy came from your dad, aye?"

I nod.

"How is that possible if you're a Carter sibling?"

"I don't know. I probably got the allergy from her, and she made it up so that I'd never learn who my father is.

Which, to be fair, was the better call. The moment I found out, it justified my bloodlust."

"I never should have told you," he mutters.

I steady myself and wobble to the closet, where I pull a baggy t-shirt from my suitcase. This day needs to come to an end. I feel like shit. After sliding the soft fabric over my body, I pull off the flashy panties and crawl into bed, then cover my head with the pillow and pray for death.

"Could you cut off the light when you go?" I yell through ten pounds of feathers.

Instead of answering me, he sits on the edge of the bed and sends me rolling toward him.

"If you're going to be so big, could you go do it in your room?"

"For tonight, this is my room."

I toss the pillow away and bolt upright. "Like hell it is! I feel like shit and just want to sleep. How can I do that if you're just sitting here? If you want to be a creep, again, go do it in your room. You have fifty cameras on me at all times anyway."

He folds his hands in his lap and looks at the carpet.

"You're serious, aren't you." I say this more as a statement than a question. "You really mean to sit in my room all night. There is no way I can sleep if I know someone is watching me, Aven."

"And why is that? Because you're too worried you can't curate your image while you're unconscious? Newsflash. I couldn't care less if you snore and fart in your sleep."

"No, I'm not *that* self-centered."

His head slowly turns to face me.

"Okay, maybe that's part of the reason, but I seriously can't sleep if you're just sitting there on the edge of the bed like that. If you're going to stay in here all night, could you at least sleep like a normal person?"

He grumbles something under his breath, then walks around the edge of the bed and flops down on the other side. With his shoes on, I might add.

"Manners," I say, and I wiggle my fingers toward his boots.

More grumbles follow as he pulls off his boots and sends them crashing to the ground. With a huff, he folds his arms over his chest and lies back.

I click off the light and snuggle under the covers. The soles of my feet and palms of my hands still itch like fire, but I try not to scratch. I'd hate to give him a reason to rush me down to the infirmary and cut out even more of my beauty sleep.

But as I lie here, sleep won't come. I'm too worried about the plan Jim and I concocted and how badly I've bungled this shitshow. After tossing and turning for what feels like forever, I finally find a little comfort in the warmth behind me. I hope he doesn't notice when I snuggle a bit closer. If he does, he doesn't move away from me. I just hate that it has to be him. Why couldn't the Jolly Green Giant stick around and care for me?

Jim knows who my secret guest was. Would he tell me his identity if I asked? He wasn't Desmond, that much is clear. He was too shy. Too nervous. It was kind of cute.

With a smile, I snuggle into Aven a little more and imagine it's the big green monster. They're roughly the same size, though I think the stranger was probably stronger. Or maybe that's just me and my sour grapes. Aven didn't want me when I practically threw myself at him, so now I'm reaching for the next best thing. But Green Guy could be the better thing . . . and there's only one way to find out.

Chapter Thirteen

Aven

When the girl couldn't get Jim to give up her secret admirer's identity, she turned to me. She's begged and pleaded all morning, but I'll be damned if she ever learns I was the one in that ridiculous suit. Then she had the nerve to personally request another visit with him to make up for what went down. Yeah. I think not.

Jim suggested I take her into the park to enjoy some of the activities and get her mind off the stranger. He wants her to continue participating in the retreat as if she's one of us, and he seems completely unconcerned with the attempt on her life. And whether or not he wants to admit it, what happened last night was definitely a shot taken. We conferred with Chef Maurice and learned his scampi has never contained turmeric, which means someone else put it in her dish.

What I didn't discuss with Jim was the odd comment Quinn made about her father. It's still eating away at me, even as she and I walk the garden trail that leads us toward the amusement park. She couldn't have inherited an allergy from her father, because Daddy Carter has no known allergies. It's in his profile, which I've read from front to back. The FBI knows everything about him, aside from his current location and appearance. The man is a chameleon of sorts, and his last confirmed sighting was over twenty years ago. But the point still stands. That would have been in his file.

I've wanted to ask Quinn more about it, but an opportunity hasn't presented itself. For now, I plan to keep my ears open for anything else that raises the hairs on the back of my neck.

As we draw nearer to the amusement park's front gates, I spot Bennett, Cat, and Eve standing by the turnstiles and chatting. I'd hoped to avoid the others and keep Quinn sequestered from their nonsense, but it appears it can't be helped. Especially not when the girls spot us and come rushing over.

"Are you two here for the coaster demonstration or the popcorn-eating contest?" Cat asks when we meet them.

"Which were you guys attending first?" I ask.

A wide smirk slides onto Bennett's face. "The coaster demonstration, naturally. But I suppose you and your friend are headed off to the popcorn stand, huh?"

Quinn looks up at me. "Well, we hadn't discussed what we planned to do first, but—"

"But we're doing the popcorn-eating contest," I interrupt. "Off we go. Don't want to be late."

"Aven, cut it out," Quinn whispers. She snatches her arm from mine and returns to the other three. "I'd kind of like to see the coaster demonstration. Who doesn't love thrill rides?" She grins at me over her shoulder.

The last thing I want to do is spend time in a fucking group setting. I have to find a way to get her to come with me.

"Wasn't there someone you wanted to meet over by the popcorn stand?" I ask, hinting that I might actually reveal the identity of the green invader.

She tastes the bait and swallows the hook. "On second thought, popcorn does sound pretty good right about now. Maybe we could all meet up afterward?"

"Don't bet on it," Bennett mutters with a scoff.

"Of course we can." Cat kicks Bennett in the shin with the toe of her sneaker. It isn't a hard enough blow to hurt him, but it's enough to shut him up. "What he said wasn't directed at you. It's just that . . . See, Aven . . ."

"She's trying to find a nice way to say that I don't play well with others," I offer, "and she's right. I don't. I make no pretense otherwise."

Quinn offers a snarky glare my way before turning on the charm for Cat. "Well, I'm sure I can convince him to join us after the popcorn thing. He doesn't exactly have a choice. He's required to follow me around like my cute little guard dog." She reaches back to give my head a condescending pat.

I let it happen.

Why? I don't fucking know, but when her hand comes back and pats my head, I'd wag my tail if I had one. This little crush is getting out of hand.

Eve looks at her watch, then glances at me before saying, "Let's not leave it up to chance, honey. Let's make a plan. The next round of events isn't due to start until after lunch, so we'll meet at the pool at one and do the next game together."

"Okay, pal. We'll see," I say as I try to lead Quinn away.

"One o'clock," Eve shouts behind us. "Don't be late!"

Once we're through the turnstile and into the park proper, Quinn folds her arms over her chest and looks increasingly nervous. Her green eyes dart around, and the clang of a bell nearly sends her out of her skin.

"It's just the sound to let the bloke know he won a teddy." I point toward the game booths, where a staffer hands a cheap red teddy bear to Ice Pick. I try to get us moving again before he notices us, but it's too late. He comes rushing over with the bear tucked under his arm.

"Where are you two headed? The coaster or the popcorn?" he asks. "I'm headed to the popcorn event."

I nod my head and look around, checking our surroundings for anyone who might be watching Quinn from the shadows. "Yeah. Should have figured you'd be headed that way too."

"Here you go. I won this for you," Ice Pick says.

I look down, thinking the squat bald man is speaking to me, but it's Quinn's hands that he shoves the teddy bear into. She smiles sweetly at Ice Pick and hugs the bear to her chest.

"He's very cute. Just like you." She gives Ice Pick's nose a little boop with her finger, which is enough to turn his face the same shade of red as the bear.

It's harmless flirting, but she's very convincing. For Ice Pick's sake, I hope he knows that this is just part of her job. Making men feel special is what pays her bills.

But then she loops her arm in his and motions for me to lead the way like I'm some sort of guide for them. "Take us to the popcorn, Aven," she says with a flutter of her mascara-coated lashes.

I swallow the bit of jealousy roiling in my gut. This is fucking Ice Pick we're talking about, not some sex symbol.

She's as likely to make out with him as she is to make out with a sewer grate. Not that I care either way.

"Oh, wow!" Quinn says behind me. "You're so much stronger than you look."

I glance back just in time to see Quinn squeezing Ice Pick's doughy arm. Rolling my eyes, I face forward again. Nope, not bothered at all.

Ice Pick chuckles and says, "Thanks. I've been working out."

Like hell he has. I wake up an hour before Quinn each day just so that I can get down to the hotel gym and keep my physique in check, and I haven't seen his mustache on so much as a treadmill.

"After the popcorn-eating contest, we plan to meet up with some of the others at the pool. I hope you'll join us," Quinn titters in that sickeningly sweet voice. Great. Now she's trying to make this a fucking party.

"That's an invite I can't refuse," he says with a laugh.

Fabulous. Wonderful. I can't fucking wait.

My fists clench at my sides as I pick up the pace. The food booth is just ahead, and I want to get this shit over with so that I can steer her back to the resort. Seeing her all over Ice Pick is just pissing me off for no good reason, and I can't take much more of it.

"Aven, wait up!" Little footsteps pitter-patter behind me, growing closer once I finally stop walking. "What are you doing? Why are you being extra icy today?"

I search my brain for a reasonable excuse because the truth is too unreasonable. I cannae very well tell her I have a crush on her against my will and that seeing her paw at Ice Pick is crushing my soul.

"If you're all over *him*, Desmond might lose interest," I say without thinking.

Her slender shoulders nearly touch her ears as she shrugs. "Let him. I think I've found a new hobby I'd like to explore, and his name is Ice Pack." She looks over her shoulder and gives Ice Pick a little wave as he continues plodding closer. "My special green suitor will keep me safe. Hell, I might not even need you to protect me anymore."

"Green . . . ?" My lips slam shut. "You think *he* was the man in your room last night?"

She giggles and tosses her honey-colored hair over her shoulder. "Don't try to play dumb now. He's super shy, just like the guy from last night. You also hinted that someone I wanted to meet would be at the popcorn event, and then you said you figured he'd be there. I just put two and two together."

"This isn't a math problem, lass, but if it were, you've properly bungled it." I point toward Ice Pick, who's stopped walking to get something out of his shoe. "That man is about two feet shorter than your bloke, and I dare say a good many brain cells fewer. Not to mention that spare tire around his middle."

She swats my arm hard enough to leave a stinging pain behind. "Don't body shame," she whispers.

"It's the facts, lass. You don't know what he looks like. Hell, you cannae even say his blasted name."

"Yes I can," she says. "It's Ice Pack."

Now I nearly do laugh. "No, it's not. Ach, you can't even get this much right. It's Ice *Pick*, lass. *Pick* . . . like the tool."

The truth of my words hits home, and her shoulders sag. "What do I do now?"

"You start listening to me and stop listening to that warm spot between your legs. This isn't one of your books. These are real killers, and you aren't one of them."

She sets her jaw. "I beg to differ. You saw what I did last night. I took a life and didn't even bat an eyelash, and I'm more than ready to do it again."

"*I* saw it, sweet thing." Ice Pick finally reaches us and gives her bottom a smack. She jumps from the force. "You were beautiful. I watched you in the room with that green guy, too. Maybe Jim will give me my chance tonight."

"Oh. Maybe." Quinn smiles at him and tries to scoot a few inches to the left, but he scoots with her.

I could save her now. I could.

But I won't.

"Hey, hey, hey! Come on down to the Popcorn Palace!" a barker calls from the food stand. He's dressed in an orange-and-white striped suit. A wide-brimmed straw hat sits stiffly on his head as he motions us closer with a black cane. "You've heard of the store that lets you stuff your own bear to take home as a souvenir, haven't you? Well, we've got the next best thing! Come on in and check it out!"

Quinn looks up at me, a question written in her eyes. "I thought this was a popcorn-eating contest."

"It is. We just won't be the ones trying to eat it." Ice Pick heads for the stand, completely forgetting he was just competing for the fair maiden's hand. She's but a memory as the prospect of a kill looms so large.

For once in my life, I'm having the opposite problem. I've found something that holds my interest far more easily than murder. Not that these fabricated murders do much for me anyway.

I place my hand on the small of Quinn's back and urge her forward. She takes a few tentative steps before coming to a halt.

"Deciding we aren't so comfortable with murder after all?" I ask. "We could go back to the—"

She shakes her head and clears her throat, trying to hide the sudden fear on her face. She does a poor job, though. Trepidation is the prevailing emotion flicking through her eyes. "No, it's not the killing. It's that . . ." She shakes her head again, and her smile is more convincing this time. "It's nothing."

I lock this away in my head for later because it's definitely not nothing. It's something, and I plan to find out more.

Behind the popcorn stand is a small red tent. The barker leads the three of us inside, and we take a seat on creaky wooden benches in front of a small arena. Sawdust coats the asphalt, and the tent shields us from the spring sunshine. It's not nearly as grand as the main circus tent, but it's big enough for the small crowd that gathered for the demonstration. Grim and Rose sit in the shadows, along with two random men.

As the barker begins setting up for the show, the houselights dim. The low lighting allows me to study the unfamiliar men more closely. I recognize neither of them, though I don't exactly make a habit of memorizing serial killers the way Jim, King, and Cat do. One is tall and thin, with a ruddy complexion and reddish hair.

The other is built more similarly to me. He's tall, bulked out, and a deep scar runs down his cheek. Tattoos darken his arms, matching his dark hair and eyes. Bright grays speckle the short sideburns at his jaws. Deep crow's feet crease the sides of the eyes, which would fit with Desmond's current age. He also looks mean.

Psh, I'm meaner.

The barker finishes setting up two machines in the center of the arena. Each is a large glass box filled with buttered kernels of popped corn. Thick hoses protrude from the sides and connect to two special chairs positioned between them. Two red Cattle are led to the chairs and strapped down.

"Welcome to the popcorn-eating contest," the barker yells toward the crowd, though I use the term lightly. This is more like a gathering. "This is an elimination event. In each round, you'll guess which Cattle will choke first . . . literally!"

He pauses to give us a chance to laugh. When we don't, he pushes ahead.

"We'll tell you a little about the Cattle, and two of you will step up and start the machine behind the one you think will die first. The loser is eliminated, and the winner moves to the next round. Which two of you will go first?"

Quinn's hand shoots into the air, but I pull it down. "Wait and see what the gimmick is," I whisper.

"Gimmick?"

As the barker brings down the two men I don't recognize, I explain to Quinn that Jim sometimes sets up little traps and loopholes in the games. If you want a leg up on the competition, you don't want to go first. She nods, then turns back to the game, genuinely interested in the murder that's about to take place.

The barker positions the men behind the Cattle. The red-suited bloke on the left thrashes against his restraints and tries to turn his head as a mask is lowered over his face. The Cattle on the right just starts crying.

"I almost feel sorry for him," Quinn whispers. "He's done something bad, though, right?"

"Aye, that he has. He's wearing a red jumpsuit, which means he's sexually violated someone. If you want to know their crimes and pick your victim personally, Jim has a book of them."

"Just knowing they deserve what's coming is enough for me," Ice Pick chimes beside her. "Course, they could do nothing and I'd still cut 'em up if the mood hit me right."

Quinn's eyes light up. "Oh, then I'm afraid it would never work between us after all," she says with a pout I almost believe. "I prefer killers who are a bit pickier about their victims."

She means it as a way to brush him off politely, but she's politely brushing me off as well. I'm not like Jim and the rest of the crew. In this way, I'm more like Ice Pick than I care to admit.

"Did you mean that?" I whisper. "About preferring killers who choose their victims carefully?"

"Honestly? I don't know," she says with a wrinkle of her nose. "There's still some honor in it then, you know? But I'm trying to let him down easy."

I nod my head and try to focus on the event.

The workers have managed to get the rowdy Cattle's mask over his face. The barker warns them to stay very still as a blade in the mask whips across their lips to cut the stitches away. The Cattle on the left stays very still, yet both chins swim in a fountain of blood seconds later. At least their pained screams are silenced as the hoses are screwed into place inside their mouths.

The barker pats the side of one of the popcorn machines. "These devices are primed to pump popcorn into their mouths at a rate of about five kernels per second. Once activated, the machines won't stop until the Cattle do." He steps forward and taps the wrist strap on one of the chairs. "When the heart stops beating, a light will flash above his chair, and the machine will cut off, declaring our winner."

"It's so exciting," Quinn says. She grips the edge of the bench seat and wiggles her butt. "I can hardly sit still."

I turn my head so that she doesn't see me smile, but that was the most adorable thing I've ever seen a woman do. I want more of these cute little Quinn moments. They're like drugs to me.

And much like drugs, indulging in these moments would be my downfall. There is no Narcan for an overdose of Quinn.

So, I turn back to the event and try to focus once more. The men start their machines, and popcorn begins to flow through the tubes. Every second, the crowd is greeted with a loud whoosh as more kernels are shoveled down the line. Each time it happens, the Cattle jerk as if they've been shot. How fast is that tube pushing the popcorn?

Quinn tugs my arm and points to the Cattle on the right. "Jeez, look at his throat!"

Sure enough, his throat begins to bulge as the man does his best to swallow the kernels whole. With the wide hose crammed between his teeth, chewing is an impossibility. His legs strain against the metal straps pinning them down, but it's no use. There is no escaping this concession from hell.

About three minutes in, one of the machines begins to hiss. The barker steps forward and mashes a red button built into the side, and the Cattle jerks a bit harder with the next push of popcorn. After two more pumps, blood begins to ooze from his nostrils.

Not wanting to lose, the skinnier Sinner rushes to his red button and gives it a whack. Just like the other machine, his contraption begins pushing the popcorn with more force. The Cattle won't be able to work the popcorn into the right position for swallowing it now. Not that his plan was working too well to begin with.

Our attention turns back to the bleeding Cattle, but

seconds later, the buzzer and flashing lights declare the other guy the winner. His target must have had a heart attack or something, because he slumps in his chair without a sign of distress . . . other than the popcorn being forced from his nostrils. I guess the machine didn't shut off like it was supposed to.

Despite losing, the Desmond prospect stays by his Cattle and stares into his face as the lights begin to go out. All those sharp kernels have sliced and diced their way into an artery, judging by the way the blood leaks from his nose. When the buzzer finally sounds, we're all bored.

"That took longer than I expected," Quinn whispers. "Maybe we should have picked the roller coaster after all. Is it too late to swap activities?"

I ignore her and watch the loser. He looks into the audience like he's searching for someone, and I bet I know who. She's seated right beside me.

"I'll be right back," I whisper to Quinn. I'm not sure if she hears me because I'm on my feet and moving toward him as he makes his way to the winners' area as Grim and Rosie go to take their turn with the popcorn machines. I just want a quick chat with him.

But as I turn and look back at the stands, I realize Quinn is no longer seated beside Ice Pick. She's waited for me to turn my back, then taken the chance to run. My suspicions are confirmed when I spot the tent flap dropping back into place. If a game of hide-and-seek is what she's after, I'm happy to oblige.

Chapter Fourteen

Quinn

I make it as far as the Pirate Plunder ride in Dead Man's Cove before the urge to hide overwhelms me. Aven is probably hot on my heels, and the sooner I conceal myself, the more likely I am to remain undetected. There are no crowds to slink into, so I choose the next best thing and dive into the foliage beside the ride's queue. Then, I wait.

Several minutes pass before Aven strolls by. His head spins on a swivel, turning every direction but mine as he considers which path I might have taken. After checking a signpost, he heads down a side street that will lead him far away from me.

Perfect.

Once he's gone, I unfurl myself from the shrubbery and begin plucking bits of greenery from my hair. When I feel icy fingers wrap around my arm, I turn toward the figure with a raised fist, certain it's my damned bodyguard.

But it's not Aven holding my arm in an iron grip. It's Jim.

He steadies me on my feet and lowers my raised fist. "Where's your security detail run off to?"

"Probably to go fuck up someone else's good time," I grumble as I pull a final twig from my shirt. "You said I could have some fun for the rest of the trip, but he's seriously killing the mood, Jim. He tricked me into going to the lame popcorn thing, and—"

"Lame?" Jim frowns and looks genuinely hurt. "I thought it was exciting and fun."

"Oh, it was so exciting and fun," I say, trying to cover my blunder. "It's just that Aven wouldn't let me participate, and I got bored."

Jim sighs and releases my arm so that he can cup his chin. "Yes, he's concerned about your mental welfare, I'm sure. Going from Normie to Sinner is a bit of a leap, and no one wants you to regret your decision."

"Regret? I don't know the meaning of the word."

"I'm serious, Quinn. For once, I'm very, very serious." He stops rocking. "Would you like to see something very not lame?"

"Practically dying for it," I say.

He smiles at me, then raises his walkie to his lips. "Scotland's package is with me. Let him know so that he doesn't worry. And prepare the simulation."

With that, he offers me his arm, and I take it.

After a golf cart picked us up and ferried us to the hangars I saw when we first arrived, we went inside and ended up in this large white room with an egg-shaped chair in its center. I've never been to the back lots of a theme park before this impromptu excursion, but I doubt many of them have a room like this. In front of the chair is a single concave wall of glass.

A beautiful, dark-haired woman with striking blue eyes approaches Jim. I recognize her as one of the girls who sat at our table the night before, but I can't place her name. She gives me a polite smile before pulling him aside and whispering, "Do you really think this is wise?"

Jim waves her off and pulls her closer to me. "Frankie, this is Quinn. She's part of the project King and I have been working on for these past months. Since she is the subject of our little simulation, I figured it might be good to let her see it."

Frankie turns and offers her hand, which I accept with a firm shake. "Nice to meet you," she says. "Has Jim explained what you'll see?"

"I guess. He said I'd see some predicted outcomes of some events."

Frankie glares at him. "Right. Some *events*. And what *events* did you want her to see?"

"I didn't have anything specific in mind." He rolls his hand through the air. "Maybe show her what would have happened if she'd gone to the roller coaster exhibition."

Frankie shakes her head and walks off as Jim takes my arm and leads me to the egg chair. When he motions for me to sit, I do. The white cushions practically grab me in a comforting hug as I sink into the pillowy fabric. It's much more comfortable than it looks.

"Now sit back fully," he instructs. "Let the seating immerse you, and don't take your eyes off the screen." He motions to the curved glass wall. "Frankie just needs to feed the device a little data, and it will spit out some scenarios for you."

As he steps away, the lights click off overhead. My senses are dulled by the chair, meaning all I hear and see is whatever is in front of me. The concave glass lights up then, and the chair begins drifting closer with a grating whine. I grip the edges until the ride comes to a stop way too close to the screen. While my mother wasn't in my life for very long, I can still hear her telling me to scoot away from the television before I ruined my eyesight. Which didn't happen often, as being homeless doesn't exactly put you in front of televisions very often. Still, her voice fills my head.

Little memories of my mother continue to haunt me in this place, but I welcome her spirit. I feel closer to her now than I have in a long time. A reunion seems an impossibility, but with all this money I'll make at the end of this, I can probably pay a pretty good investigator to find her.

Speakers in the chair play a soft tone as the screen comes to life. It's almost like the opening scene of a movie. The camera pans over the park and comes to land behind two people: me and Aven. It looks like it could have been shot while we were walking to the park, but I never saw a camera behind us.

"This is all simulated video," Jim says through the speakers. "None of that mucky generative-AI mess, though. Our program is state-of-the-art! Spared no expense. You'll find that all human renderings have the correct amount of fingers, and no one's head will turn into a cabbage if it's bitten off by a dog."

"Is the cabbage thing a common problem? Because that seems oddly specific," I say, but Jim doesn't respond. He just keeps going on about how they hired actual artists and used extensive human motion-capture research to feed the sim machine instead of stealing from actual human workers.

On the screen, Aven and I begin walking again. The camera follows us to the roller coaster, where the simulation once again pauses.

"Quinn, at the coaster event, you and Aven would have been required to choose the red team or the blue team. No other information would have been provided. Which team would you have chosen?" Before I can answer, he interrupts me. "Don't say it aloud, dear girl. Just have the answer in your head."

I'd pick the red side because it all but promises blood.

I nod to let Jim know I have my answer locked in.

The simulation picks up again. A faceless barker approaches and asks which team we're on. Sim Quinn answers before Sim Aven has a chance to open his mouth.

"*I'm picking red,*" she says.

The hairs on my arm stand up. How did it know that?

Jim pauses the simulation again, freezing Sim Aven as he looks at Sim Quinn. Is that really how he looks at me? There's a hint of admiration in his eyes. And something else. I don't have time to dwell on it, though, because Jim's currently getting annoyed with me for ignoring him.

"Sorry, what was that?" I ask.

"Did it get it right? Would you have picked the red side?"

I bite my bottom lip and nod. "Yeah. That's what I was thinking."

Despite the egg chair's soundproofing, I hear Jim's joyous shout and clapping hands from here, even though his mic is off. I'm glad he's so overjoyed about this outcome. Meanwhile, I'm just getting more curious—and nervous.

"Let's try another one," Frankie says through the speakers, and even she sounds a little excited about this. "You'll be given the option to ride the coaster. You'll be allowed to choose where you sit. Each coaster car has four seats—two in front and two in back. There are six cars to a train. Are you riding, and if so, where are you sitting?"

I close my eyes and think about it. "Is it one of the original coasters?"

"The only original I kept in the park," Jim says. "Steel Tiger, one of the most diabolical hybrid coasters ever created."

A smile eases onto my face. I can't help it.

That was my mother's favorite ride at the park, and I just made the height requirement on that last visit. I'd had a nice little growth spurt that summer. When Mama and I were standing in line, she told me all about the best places to sit on each coaster in the park. For Steel Tiger, you wanted to sit in the very last row on the last car. That way, every time you went down a hill, you had the force of the entire train pulling you down.

"I know exactly what I would say," I tell Jim as I open my eyes. "Roll the footage."

The people jump to life on the screen again. Another faceless staff member approaches and asks if we'll be riding the coaster. Once again, Sim Quinn jumps in to answer before Aven can open his mouth. Am I really this much of an attention whore?

But I'm not paying attention to whatever Sim Quinn says on screen. My eyes remain on Sim Aven. He's watching me again, but not in the way I imagine him watching me in real life. In my mind's eye, he's perpetually rolling his eyes and grumbling about anything I have to say, and that's when he's even listening. Sim Aven, on the other hand, listens to me speak as if I'm saying the most interesting thing he's ever heard.

I'm starting to think this simulation is just creating another fantasy for me to lose myself in, but then it happens. The shift. The simulation captures the moment perfectly. As Sim Quinn turns to Sim Aven to ask if he wants to ride with her, the admiration fades as quickly as if someone dropped a curtain of indifference over his face. His gaze cuts to the side, and he shrugs.

"Whatever the lass wants is fine by me, pal," he says to the worker, and Jesus fuck, they nailed the accent.

Sim Quinn huffs and trots her happy little ass toward the back car, last row. I will have them know I do not walk like that. My hip swing is *not* that dramatic.

The screen freezes again, right on an unflattering angle as Sim Quinn is climbing into the coaster car. She's bent over with her ass facing the camera as Sim Aven stares a hole through her khaki shorts.

"Did it get it right again?" Jim asks, and I confirm.

"Now let it play!" I shout toward them. "I want to see what would have happened next!"

Initially, what happens next isn't that exciting. We ride the coaster, and Aven keeps his eyes clenched shut the entire time. I'm all smiles as the cars whip us right, left, and upside down. By the end of it, the smile has turned upside down, and I'm crying, which is totally embarrassing. God, I am such an ugly crier.

It's also probably totally accurate. Because I would have been thinking about my mother.

Sim Quinn and Aven exit the ride, and the former tries to cover her tears as the latter tries to figure out why she's crying. The three people we met earlier—Bennett, Eve, and

Cat—come over to find out what's wrong, but as Aven tries to shoo them off, I slip out through the exit. The camera stays with Sim Quinn, but Sim Aven joins her moments later at the bottom of some stairs.

"Maybe it's best we don't do the event. Why don't we head back to the resort and grab a bite?" Then Sim Aven steals my breath as he wraps his arm around my facsimile and actually tries to comfort her. "I don't know what all this fuss is about, lass, and you don't have to tell me. But if you want to talk, I've ears enough to listen."

Tell him, I urge in my mind. *Tell him how badly you're hurting. Let him in.*

But it's a very accurate simulation, and I already know what my copy will do before she does it. Still, it's a slap in the face when she pulls away and tells him he wouldn't understand.

How can he when you won't tell him anything?

Fuck therapy. This little egg chair is giving me more insight into my psyche than I bargained for.

Sim Aven grabs Sim Quinn's arm to prevent her from running off again. She stumbles from the abrupt stop, then tumbles backward into his arms when he grabs her. As he rights her, they're looking right into each other's eyes. A fire burns there, glowing right between them, so hot I can nearly feel it myself.

Kiss him, you fool!

And by god, she does. She grabs that big hunk of man and just goes for it, leaping onto him and mauling his face like a mountain lion who hasn't eaten in a month of Sundays.

The image freezes on the screen, and I sit forward with a shout. "No! It just got to the best part! Don't stop it now!"

Then the chair spins around, and the lights come on.

Frankie and Jim are tucked away in a little booth with the simulation characters displayed on large screens behind them. The *kissing* simulation characters that represent me and Aven.

And right behind Jim stands Aven.

Chapter Fifteen

Quinn

The golf cart bumps over a rock and almost sends me into Aven's lap. I grip the long metal rod that runs into the roof so that I don't go the other way and fall off the side. Not that I would have, anyway. Not with my guard dog back on duty. I shrug off his protective hold that feels more like a joke now.

"Was it really the best part?" he asks, rubbing salt into the festering wound.

I cover my reddening face with my hands. I scream.

"It wasn't that it was us," I say. "It was like watching a movie with actors or something."

He doesn't say anything. He just smirks and admires the passing scenery.

"And I would never have kissed you, just so we're clear," I add.

"Sure you wouldn't, lass."

"I wouldn't! That simulation didn't get everything right, anyway. If I'd seen a faceless man, I'd have screamed."

The cart comes to a stop near the start of the park, and we climb out. The driver gives us a wave and speeds away. My stomach waits until the vehicle's whining fades completely before uttering the most fart-like growl I've ever heard.

"I didn't bust ass," I say. "My stomach is growling because I'm hungry."

Again, my abdomen chooses the silent moment to make itself heard.

"Sure you don't need the bathroom? Sounds like you might. Serves you right for running off."

God, I don't know how I ever thought kissing him would be an enjoyable activity. On second thought, at least it would shut him up.

Aven shoves his hands into his pockets and looks around. "We still have a bit of time before we're supposed to meet the others. What are you hungry for?"

"About three heavy sedatives, a long vacation, and competent oral?"

"Fresh out of that, I'm afraid. We've got something that passes for Italian on this stretch of street, though."

I wasn't kidding about the competent oral. Ever since seeing my virtual self mauling him on the big screen, I can't stop thinking about that kiss. I could practically feel it. Now I'm imagining him kissing other parts of me.

"On second thought, maybe we should head back to the hotel. I'm due for another show soon anyway," I offer. "I can always order room service."

He nods and starts toward the hotel. "Aye, room service is fine, but I'll be the one bringing it up to you straight from Chef Maurice. We cannae take any big risks with your health, lass."

Right. Desmond.

I shudder as we pass through the gates and turn toward the garden trail. Sometimes I almost forget that while I'm busy becoming a predator, I'm still prey for someone else. He's here on this island, stalking me from every shadow. Even so, the thought of them finally unmasking him and ending him makes me feel more panicked than the thought of him catching me.

Because either way, it will all come to an end.

These people are letting me into their world right now because they need me. Once my usefulness runs out . . . Well, I haven't fully considered what that might mean. Will I be killed as well?

I glance up at Aven.

Something tells me no. Not that he wouldn't be the first to take up a weapon against me if Jim gave the go ahead, but I don't think Jim would. When they say they want to protect me because of who my father is, I believe them. But that doesn't mean they'll let me hang around once I've served my purpose, not even with my lineage.

"I've never really belonged anywhere," I blurt.

Aven stops walking and turns to face me. "What's that?"

That simulation is getting to me, because discussing my feelings isn't exactly a very *me* thing to do, but if I want them to keep me around once this ends, I need to let my guard down.

"I know you're worried about my mental state after killing that guy last night, but I want you to know I'm okay. Maybe better than okay because for the first time since . . ." I stop myself before I reveal too much. My mother is a secret thing I keep tucked away, and no matter how badly I want to connect with him, she isn't a bargaining chip to be used as a way to garner favor. "For the first time in a long time, I feel like I finally fit in."

He studies me for a moment, and deep in his dark eyes, I see it. That hidden flame. That ember he refuses to let shine. But the light winks out as quickly as it sparks to life. "Can't say I'm familiar with that feeling myself, but what makes you want to be part of this?"

"It's the way some of these people interact. It reminds me of a family." I shake my head and laugh. "Not the boring kind of family that I grew up in, though. We were meant to be perfect children who never talked back or stepped out of line."

Aven's jaw clenches. "Were they abusive to you or the other children?"

"No, not in the slightest. The Parkers are wonderful people. They're just . . . wonderful people." I shrug because I don't know how else to explain it.

But I don't have to. He nods because he gets it. Wonderful people are wonderful, but they're boring for mentally divergent individuals such as ourselves.

It's in these little moments of connection that I feel most afraid. The mean back and forth is somehow easier for us than the connection.

The garden path opens up, and we take a right into the pool area. Cat and Bennett give us a wave as we pass. They're reclining on loungers and watching Eve and Ice Pick chicken fight with another couple in the water. I really don't know how Eve balances him on her shoulders.

"We should join them," I say. "We did tell them we'd meet them here, and we kind of no-showed."

"Because someone ran off."

"Because someone else was being a buzzkill."

"Because someone else was—"

I hold up my hand. "We will be here all day. We will take this back to Adam and Eve if we don't stop right now."

He huffs and turns back for the hotel. "I'll meet you back down here in ten. Don't dawdle."

Chapter Sixteen

Aven

By the time I get down to the pool, it really is a party. All of the usual suspects are in attendance, so I take the opportunity to introduce Quinn to the entire sordid lot. Hell, she's related to three of them, so she might as well get to know them. Her eyes brighten every time she hears the last name Carter.

Keeping the secret of her lineage has weighed heavily on me since she mentioned wanting to belong to something. She belongs more than she realizes. Sure, she knows the truth, but she can't do a damn thing with it until Jim tells the rest of the group.

Once the girls have finished gushing over Quinn's figure in a teal one-piece swimsuit, the lady of the hour spreads a towel over a lounger and reclines among her admirers. She's safe as houses with that crew, so I wander over to the hot tub to join the men.

Ezra, Bennett, and Ice Pick recline low in the water,

while Maverick sits on the edge and dangles his feet in the roiling spray. Grim and Rosie rest nearby on sun loungers. Per usual, they're nude, so my gaze doesn't linger very long.

"Grab a cold one and join us," Ezra calls.

I don't drink on the job, so I shake my head, but I'll join them in the hot tub. I slide into the water and position myself across from them so that I can still keep an eye on Quinn. She's in her element, surrounded by women who are just as silly as she is.

"Don't you think beach weddings are a little overdone?" Bennett says to Ezra, and I see that I've walked into a very awkward conversation. One that I hope they don't include me in. "I get that's what Kindra wants, so you're kind of bent over a log, but it's so cliché."

Ice Pick adjusts in the water, sinking a little lower. "Shit, if I could convince a woman to marry me, I'd let her pick whatever she wanted. I hate that I blew my chance with Quinn."

"Chance with Quinn?" Ezra says with a laugh. "That's Aven's territory."

"Shit, I done it again," Ice Pick mutters.

I sit forward and shake my head. "Ach, she isn't my anything. I'm just keeping an eye on her. You know the score."

"Yeah, I know how that one goes," Maverick says. "One minute, you're just doing a job. The next, you're making space in your nightstand for her sex-toy collection."

"Jim got me too, but it's not all bad," Bennett says. "His next business venture should be a matchmaking service."

"Yeah, well, not me." I shake my head again to really drive the point home. "Once we get paid, I'm moving on."

The men share a look.

"I mean it. Once I have the funds to . . . to get back to Scotland, I'm gone."

I nearly fucked up and mentioned the real reason for the money. The debt I need to pay. It's not something I want to talk about with anyone, least of all them.

"What's in Scotland? You got some hot piece of ass to get back to or something?" Bennett asks.

"More like a nice piece of green land." I shrug. "A little place to keep all to myself. Aye, I think that sounds like my slice of heaven."

Ezra smiles and adjusts his glasses, which have fogged with the heat. "Sometimes I miss England."

I dip below the surface, putting an end to the conversation. He's trying to relate, but he doesn't get it. Wanting to return to Scotland isn't just a passing fancy or wild whim. It's a need that claws at me. It's never having felt at home here. No matter where I stop to rest, I never feel like I've found my place.

When I surface again, they're already laughing about something else. I turn my attention back to Quinn. She and the girls have swapped the loungers for the pool steps. She sits on the top stair, her arms draped over the shiny metal railing that runs through the center. Smiles and laughter come easily for her among the women, and it lightens my heart a bit to see her so relaxed.

My light heart lasts only until a dark shadow falls over the women. Two men approach them, and I recognize them from the popcorn tent. It's that skinny guy and the bulky older man. The one who might be Desmond.

I nudge Ezra with my foot to get him to turn around and look at what's happening behind him.

His brows screw up, and he scoots away from my

outstretched toe. "I don't care if a man wants to love another man, but I don't wish to play footsie, Aven."

I roll my eyes and grit my teeth. "No, you numpty. Look behind you."

All four men turn and look. Bennett springs out of the water the moment his gaze lands on the men, but Ezra grabs his wrist and snatches him down again.

"Sorry, old man," Ezra says to me. "We don't know you all that well, so I wasn't—"

"You can apologize for assuming his sexuality later," Bennett growls. "Right now, I want to know why those two jackoffs think they have any right to talk to our women."

Maverick clears his throat. "Probably because the women aren't our property and can speak to whomever they please. If they want those guys to fuck off, they'll tell them. Frankie isn't afraid to say what needs to be said."

"Neither is Kindra," Ezra says with a shudder.

"I cannae hear anything over this damned jabbering," I say.

All four of us shut up and lean toward the pool, trying our best to listen to whatever they're saying.

"Just wanted to see if any of you ladies wanted to join us for a drink at the rooftop bar tonight," the smooth-talking older bloke says. Then he flashes a smile that's all charm and zero threat. The threat lies in his eyes.

Kindra holds up a hand, showing off her ring, and the other women give their excuses as well. Relationship, relationship, lesbian . . . silence. Quinn doesn't have a ready excuse, and now she's staring at him as he waits for her reply.

I rise out of the hot tub, and no hands reach out to stop me. That's wise of the men. I'd just drag them with me, all the way to those pool stairs. Nothing will stop me from getting this creep away from Quinn.

"Hey, pal. Anything I can help you with?" I say as I approach.

He and the women turn toward my voice. The girls look relieved, but the hulking asshole just looks annoyed. He holds his hand toward me as his skinny friend takes a step back.

"The name's Nathaniel Graves. My friends just call me Graves, though." His hand waits in the air, held toward me like an olive branch.

I accept it, squeezing with all my might as I give it a shake. "Pleasure, Nathaniel. My name's Aven Slade."

"What do your friends call you?" the skinny guy asks with a laugh.

"Don't have any." I pin him with a smile. "But back to what I was saying. Is there anything you men need that I can assist with?"

"We were simply seeking a little female companionship, but I fear these women are unavailable. I apologize if I've stepped on any toes." The older man shoves his hands into his khaki pockets. "This is my first time at one of these events, and I'm unaware of the customs."

"It was an honest mistake," Quinn says, and my hackles rise. What is she doing? Why is she coming to his aid? "I'm technically available, but I have plans tonight. If you want a drink with me, you'll have to bid at the auction."

Everyone's head turns toward her, including mine, because what does she mean by *auction*?

"Not sure if you saw my show last night, but it will be similar to that. Just tune in after dinner for all the details if you want a chance to spend some time with me." Quinn nibbles her bottom lip. "Privately."

The man smiles down at her. "After dinner, you say? I just might do that."

She gives him a little wave, and he and his friend head toward the hotel. I'm all but forgotten as the girls start gushing about her cam-girl career. Meanwhile, the gaggle of empty-headed ninnies has completely forgotten we're talking about a practical Normie spending the night with a Sinner.

"I hate to spoil your excitement, but do you think this is wise, Quinn?" I pin the lot of them with a glare.

Eve waves me off. "Honey, let the girl have a little fun. You'll be right across the hall if shit starts to go south."

I turn to look at her, confused why she seems to know more than she should.

"Jim briefed us all this morning about the stalker situation," Cat offers. "He explained that she's a cam girl who's dealing with a stalker, but she's also exploring becoming a Sinner."

"And you think all of this is just okay?" I ask.

"No, I agree with you about tonight's auction being dangerous," Kindra says, always the voice of reason. She looks at Quinn and takes her hand. "If you're at all nervous, we'll all pitch in and make the high bid. Then you can just hang out with us all night."

Quinn squeezes her hand. "I appreciate that, but this is my purpose, isn't it? To bait him into the open?" She turns to me, and her eyes have never been greener. "I want to do this, even if it's risky. You think that's him, don't you?"

I nod. "Aye. I do, lass."

She takes a deep breath and sets her jaw. "Then I say we catch him. No matter what, we have to let him win the bid."

Once again, I had no idea this was the plan. Hell, I don't

even know if *Jim* knows this is the plan. Knowing Quinn, she came up with this harebrained scheme in the moment, and I hate that it's so fucking brilliant. No matter how much it terrifies me—or enrages me—I have to let Nathaniel/Desmond get the winning bid tonight. It all but guarantees he'll take his shot and try to spirit her away, which gives me the right to take his sorry life.

All I need is a reason, and he'll give me that tonight.

Chapter Seventeen

Quinn

I took dinner in my room with Aven, Jim, King, and Frankie. Part of the reason was so that we could ensure no one slipped anything dangerous into my dinner, but the other part was so that we could discuss my plan and the myriad risks associated with it. Surprisingly, no one bitched at me for coming up with something on my own. Not even Aven.

But now, I'm alone. As I prepare to auction myself to the man who wants to kill me, there is no one here to save me. Sure, Aven is directly across the hall, but he won't have time to rush into the room and prevent my demise if the winner pulls out a knife and decides to field dress me on the bed. Knowing this, Frankie took a moment to teach me a few self-defense moves. She even gave me a knife that belonged to Kindra. I test its heft in my hand before I tuck it under the mattress.

"Are you ready to do this?" Aven says through the

speakers, and his voice comforts me. He's here, even if he's not.

"Almost," I say. "I need to change into something a little more alluring if I want to get any bids."

"You'd get bids if you wore a shower curtain," he mutters, and I smile.

With shaking hands, I pull a see-through babydoll teddy from my bag and slip it over my body. The emerald fabric makes my eyes pop.

"Ach, don't wear my favorite color, lass," he whispers, and I realize he doesn't know his mic is still hot. "This is bloody torture."

I smirk to myself and glance at the clock. It's a quarter till six, meaning I still have fifteen minutes to fuck with him. Pretending I'm oblivious to his grunts and groans, I keep going.

"Should I go with these?" I ask myself as I raise a pair of six-inch black heels. "Hmm . . . maybe a kitten heel would be better?" I pluck a shoe with a shorter heel from the small assortment I brought.

"Yes, anything but those stilettos," he mumbles overhead.

I bite my cheek to stave off the smile as I lift the shoes with the break-neck heels. "Yeah, definitely these."

He lets out a groan. "You're killing me."

I sit on the edge of the bed and fasten the straps around my ankles, all while he laments about how miserable I make him. For the following ten minutes, I practice poses and all of those glorious little sounds that drive men crazy. It's no different from an actress rehearsing her lines before a take, and my lucky audience member certainly appears to enjoy bearing witness to last looks.

It's all fun and games until I glance at the clock and

realize we're about to go live. Sweat collects on my palms and forehead. Shows don't usually make me this nervous, but I've never put myself up for auction before. What if Desmond actually bids and wins?

Or worse . . . what if no one bids at all?

I think I'd rather be murdered and remembered fondly than be alive to realize that I won't be remembered at all. That I'm unwanted. That the entire reason I'm a cam girl is because I crave the feeling of being loved that was taken from me when my mother abandoned me at an amusement park almost twenty years ago.

Jesus Christ, I am seriously overpaying my therapist.

"Your mother didn't abandon you," I whisper to myself. "Something happened that night."

And when I get this money, I'll use it to find her and tell her that I forgive her for everything.

"Everything okay?" Aven asks through the speakers.

I shove down the real emotion and force the fake emotion onto my face. With a smile, I look toward the ceiling. "Just peachy. Ready to start whenever you guys are."

"Jim and King just called. They'll cut the feed to all rooms but mine once the auction is won. If at any point you want this to stop, you just need to say the safeword."

"Who the fuck picked pineapple?"

"It's a long and very weird story. I'll tell you all about it later."

"If there's a later," I say with a shudder.

"There will be, lass." There's a pause before he says, "I won't let anything happen to you."

The weight on my chest doesn't lighten. I should feel safe, so why don't I?

"Okay," I say. "I'm ready."

The light on the camera above the television turns red,

and the screen fills with a shot of me right now, reclining on the bed. I give the camera a seductive wave and sit up, then scoot to the edge of the bed so that the viewers get a better angle of my cleavage.

"Hello again, you dirty perverts. Last night was a lot of fun, but tonight, I'd like to spend more time with one of you. In fact, I'd love it if we could hang out *all* night." I nibble my lip and giggle. Is it obnoxious? Yes. But for some strange reason, men love a woman without a thought in her fucking head, and I'm in the business of giving them what they want. "I can't be expected to choose just one of you, though, so Jim has been kind enough to allow me to auction off my evening. Best of all, all proceeds will go to local animal shelters, so you're supporting a good cause."

This was initially a sore spot for me. I wanted the proceeds for myself. After all, I'm the one putting my life on the line and my legs in the air. Then Jim showed me videos of some of the animals they've saved, and I'm a sucker, so I caved.

I uncross my legs and cross them again, giving the viewers a classy flash of what they want. "The bidding is simple. We'll start off at five hundred and move in increments of the same. If you want to put in your bid, simply call the number on your screen."

A phone number glitters to life at the bottom of the television. All I need now is a rotating display featuring gaudy sweaters, and I'm fucking QVC. For just the low, low price of five hundred dollars, you too could spend the night thrusting your dick between Quinn Parker's legs. But wait, there's more! Call now, and she'll even let you fuck her face!

God, what have I become?

The number at the top of the screen shifts from zero to five hundred, and the shame recedes. Money may not buy happiness, but it makes me forget I care faster than a Valium on an empty stomach. And this isn't even *my* money!

Then I notice the names on the screen. They're supposed to be secret so that no one can tell who's bidding, but with tags like Ice Man and Fashionista, it's pretty obvious who's fighting for my platinum pussy.

Still, that doesn't stop the excitement from rising as the ticker rolls toward two grand. Unfortunately, that's where it stalls. Worst of all? I haven't seen anyone who could be Desmond. The bids are limited to fifteen minutes, so I need to get them going again. I change positions and lie back so that I'm draped across the bottom of the bed. I arch my lower back and "stretch" as I sigh as sweetly as I can.

"This bed is just too *big* for me. Do you know how *hard* it is to sleep all alone? Can you imagine just how badly I *long* for someone to share it with?" I place my finger into my mouth and suck. "I can almost taste how much fun we'll have together."

Another brief bidding war breaks out, but the ticker stops again when it reaches five grand. Not even my poses and pouting can push the number any higher. I can only hope this is like eBay, and all the serious bidders are waiting to snipe. At least a few more contenders have joined the fray. Fashionista—Eve and the girls, I assume—dropped out around three thousand, but "Ice Man" is still beating out newcomers Dark Knight and Gravedigger.

Could Gravedigger be Nathaniel Graves, aka Desmond, aka the creepy guy from the pool? It makes the most sense. But if that's the case, Ice Pick needs to back off and let him take it.

Minutes tick down as I writhe on the bed and try to entice more bids, but no matter how sweetly I speak, no matter where I let my fingers wander, the ticker doesn't move. Ice Man remains the high bid.

"Come on, boys," I plead. "Do me for the animals! Whoops! I mean, do *it* for the animals. Five grand isn't enough to help that many homeless pets. Show me just how *badly* you want this."

I spread my legs and smack my pussy with a moan, and the number jumps a few more times. I'm more than pleased to see the total climb to ten grand, but when I see that Ice Man is still in the lead, I want to scream. What is he doing? He has to let Desmond win!

As we rush headlong into the last thirty seconds of the auction, I've all but given up hope. Then the ticker shifts once more, and Gravedigger finally takes the top spot. My fingers unclench from the comforter, and I breathe a sigh of relief. One way or another, this part of the torture is about to end. Either I'll finally put an end to my stalker, or I'll spend an evening living out my BookTok fantasies with a murderer.

Then the ticker rolls over once more in the last second of the auction. It seems we had a sniper after all, and it's none other than Green Guy.

Confetti sprays on the screen, and the CGI bits of ticker tape briefly obscure me from view. I take the momentary interruption to compose myself and school my face. I don't know how to feel. Rather, I don't feel how I *should* feel. This outcome should have left me disappointed and frustrated, but it's excited me instead. The devil you know is better than the devil you don't know, and I happened to be very intrigued by my little green friend the other night.

No, I'd say this isn't the worst outcome, though Aven, Jim, and King will probably disagree.

The confetti fades, and I'm back on the screen in all my

sultry glory. I smile at the camera and lean forward. "I just want to say thank you to everyone who participated, and to the winner of the auction, I'll see you soon."

I wiggle my fingers, and the camera shuts off. I flop back on the bed with a groan.

The phone on the bedside table begins ringing, so I scoot backward and yank the receiver to my ear.

"Terribly sorry that this hasn't gone to plan," Jim says into my ear. He doesn't even give me a chance to greet him before launching into an explanation. "Our final bidder was very . . . adamant. We tried to dissuade him, but he seemed to want an evening with you very badly."

"This could work in our favor. Men tend to want something more when they've been denied it. This might force Desmond to make a move."

Jim sighs into the phone. "Yes, well, for your sake, I hope his desire *doesn't* overwhelm him and force him to act."

"Wouldn't that be ideal?"

"For us? Yes. But despite what you believe, your safety is important to us. We don't want any harm to befall you."

Because I'm a Carter . . .

"You're important to someone who is important to me, and I refuse to let harm come to you." Fabric shuffles on the other end of the line, and someone says something to Jim. It's a male voice, but I can't make out the words, though I hear the lilt of an accent. It must be King. "I've just been informed that your guest is on his way to your room, but he's coming by here first. Try to relax and enjoy your evening, and remember that you'll have complete privacy from prying eyes."

"Wait!" I shout before he can hang up. "Aven will be

watching, won't he? I get that we don't think this guy is Desmond, but that doesn't mean I'm not at risk."

"Oh, yes. Aven will be paying *very* close attention," Jim grumbles before the line disconnects.

I set the receiver back in its cradle as Jim's words linger in my head. *Because you're important to someone who is important to—*

A knock on the door pulls me out of my thoughts. I stand and smooth the front of my teddy, then head for the door. No matter what happens tonight, I trust Aven will keep me safe. He hasn't let me down yet.

Chapter Eighteen

Aven

The door swings open, and Quinn smiles up at me. "I was hoping it would be you," she says, and the sincerity in her voice drives a knife through my soul.

She's falling for the green stranger, not *me*. Not *Aven*. If she knew who was hiding behind this monstrous green unitard from hell, she wouldn't be so eager to invite me into her room.

But she doesn't know, so she's more than eager. She practically wrenches my wrist from my forearm as she yanks me into her lair.

I stumble to a stop inside and head for the chair. That little seat in the corner means safety. It puts distance between us. The arms on the sides will prevent her from straddling my waist and pulling my soul from my body like some sex-starved succubus. I'm genuinely scared.

But before I can plop my ass onto the cushion, she reaffirms her iron hold and guides me toward the bed. The girl

127

wants to fuck a killer more than she wants to take her next breath, and if I hadn't taken that final bid, she might have gotten either outcome. Or both.

It was stupid of me, but I couldn't help myself. In those last thirty seconds, I called Jim and told him he could take a cut from my bonus. Hell, I told him he could take the entire thing. Not so that I can sleep with her, of course. I just want to make sure she's safe, and I don't think letting her spend the night with Desmond would have netted that result. Jim didn't like it, but he's also a fair man. He allowed the final bid at zero hour, and I won an evening with the girl.

Now what?

I may not have thought this far ahead, but I can tell what she has in mind. As I sit beside her on the edge of the bed, her hand traces soft, lazy lines up my forearm. Goosebumps rise beneath the millimeter of nylon fabric separating me from her touch, and my cock strains against my boxer briefs and pokes through the embarrassing hole I ripped in the suit during my last visit.

Quinn notices, and her hand moves toward my crotch. I want her to grip my dick, but not like this. Not under false pretenses, when she doesn't know whose dick she's grabbing. I jump to my feet before her slender fingers can grace my manhood.

With a shake of my head, I show her the tablet in my hand. I knew I'd need some way to communicate other than head nods and hand signals. There's no telling how long it took Grim and Rose to learn to speak the way they have, but we lack the time and patience. I pull out the Apple Pencil and scrawl a note on the screen.

I JUST WANT TO SPEND TIME WITH YOU. NO SEX

Quinn reads the message and sits back a bit. Her shoulders sag, and while I've seen my share of disappointment after I've turned a woman down, I've never seen someone represent the emotion so fully. Her lower lip pokes out, not in that fake pout I've seen so often, but in a genuine show of hurt.

I erase the message and think of something that might ease the ache a bit.

COULD WE CUDDLE?

I almost jotted "lass" at the end, but I caught myself and popped the question mark into place instead. When I turn the tablet to face her, some light returns to her eyes.

"Sure, we can do that," she says. Quinn shuffles around until she's lying on her side, then looks back at me. "The activity requires both of us to participate, though."

Shit, she's right. I'm just sitting here watching her. It's what I'm used to doing. I'm not accustomed to participation where she's involved.

I recline on my side and try not to think of the way the lime-green hood smashes my nose against my face. At least she can't see me. No, she can't see me . . . but she can feel me. As her ass eases toward my lap, I scoot my hips away from her.

"Oh, come on," she titters. "I don't bite. Not with that end, at least."

She takes my arm and bands it around her waist, then rams her soft ass against my stiff dick. I close my eyes and suck in a deep breath, but it doesn't help. My lungs fill with the toasted-vanilla scent that is so uniquely hers. Her hand takes mine and raises my eager fingertips to her chest, and against my better judgment, I let it happen.

"See?" she whispers. "This feels good."

Fuck, fuck, fuck. It does.

I damn near whimper when a moan eases out of her. My fingers aren't moving over her nipple, but they don't need to. She's forcing them over that tight bud, squeezing and pinching and teaching me the pressure she needs. She wants me to take over and give it to her myself. I want that too.

But I can't do it.

I pull my hand away and place it on her hip. This isn't right. Even aside from her being the primary, everything about this is wrong. If she knew it was me, she wouldn't want my hands all over her, and continuing to touch her like this feels dirty in a way I can't abide.

Quinn sighs and rolls over to face me. Her hand goes toward the suit's hood, and I pull back.

"Relax," she says with a playful roll of her eyes. "I wasn't going to unmask you. I just wanted to caress your cheek. Like this."

When she reaches out again, I let her hand land on my face. Her thumb slowly strokes my cheekbone as her head tilts to the side.

"I don't care who you are or what you've done," she says, and I struggle to stop the Backstreet Boys chorus from bursting out of my mouth. I've never seen the girl look quite so serious, and I need to listen to whatever she's saying, tits and catchy songs be damned.

I grab the tablet from the nightstand and write another note.

IF YOU KNEW MY IDENTITY, YOU WOULDN'T WANT
ME TO TOUCH YOU. I SHOULDN'T HAVE COME HERE.

There. Now I'll just make my exit. I just needed to know she'd be safe, and I've done that. When Quinn tells this story tomorrow, no one will even know it was me. Well, except for Jim and King, but they won't say anything if they like breathing air.

I go to stand, but Quinn grabs my hand.

"I meant what I said. I don't care who you are." Still gripping my hand, she sits on her knees. "Listen, let me level with you, Green Guy. This is as much for you as it is for me. I've spent the last ten years of my life masturbating to the thought of some unhinged psycho chasing me through the woods and ravaging me once he catches me. This is as close as I'm going to get, and you aren't taking that away from me. I don't care if you're Jim, Eve, or that asshole across the hall. I don't even care if you have a massive knife or a massive cock in those boxers. One way or another, I'm getting impaled tonight!"

She can't see it, but my jaw drops. I mean, technically, the lass *did* say she doesn't care if I'm the asshole across the hall . . .

I shake off her hand, get to my feet, and turn to face her. With my fists clenched at my sides, I finally see that beautiful fear in her eyes again. She scoots backward on the bed, a nervous smile playing at the edges of her mouth. She smooths her hair, trying to look calmer than she is, but it won't work. I've seen what I do to her, even in this non-threatening suit.

"That's more like it," she whispers in spite of her fear. "Which is it, though? Are you going to kill me or fuck me?" She sends her hair flying as she shakes her head. "No, don't tell me. I want it to be a surprise."

God, she is so fucked. And so am I.

I drop on top of her and wrap my hand around her

throat. Her legs kick out as she tries to fight me off, but I just tighten my grip as genuine panic takes hold in her frantic gaze. Using my hips, I force my way between her trembling thighs until my rock-hard dick presses painfully against her. Only our damned undergarments stand between us.

Her fingers find my hand, and she digs her nails into my flesh, desperate to claw me off of her. Still, I refuse to release her. I look into her face as the light dims. I grind myself against her, reminding her that she asked for this.

Just before she passes out, I let go and pin her arms above her head so that she can't scramble away. She gulps air, her breasts rising and falling at a rapid tempo as consciousness slams into her.

"Fuck," she cries. "At least we've established that you won't kill me."

I nod. *Good girl*. She gets it. Maybe we aren't so far off from that telepathic-communication thing after all.

Her head is still swimming as I wrap my hand around her slender throat again. This time, I apply a blood choke, robbing her brain of everything it wants. The impact hits much faster, and the lass practically trembles with fear when I release her.

"What the fuck was that?" she whispers. Her eyes somehow find mine beneath the mask. "God, I'm shaking. It felt like balancing on a knife's edge between heaven and hell." She licks her lips and smiles. "Do it again."

My fingers find their home around her throat, and I squeeze. My cock practically throbs against her; I'm so turned on. She struggles against death this time, and her hips rock her glorious mound against my cock. It's not enough. I want more.

I release her and rip the boxers open. I'll need a new underwear budget after this trip, but no matter. If destroying my entire wardrobe gets me closer to the girl, I'll learn to do without. I lean forward and slide my iron dick through her panty-covered slit. I know right where to aim—that dark spot in the emerald fabric. She's soaked.

Quinn's eyes dance as I release her again. Her head rolls to the side, and she smiles as I drag my cock through the mess she's created. I never knew a man dressed in a big green condom could do it for a woman, but here we are.

"I know we're all disease-free here, thanks to Jim's rigorous medical tests, but if you're worried about pregnancy, the condoms are in the drawer." She motions to the nightstand. "I have an implant, so I'm not concerned. But it's up to you."

I'm not sure where I expected all this choking and thrusting to lead, and I don't know how I didn't expect us to get to sex eventually, but my mouth still runs dry now that we've reached this crossroads. I have a decision to make.

But as I look down at the woman beneath me, I know there was never any choice in the matter. Even if my mouth were to form the word no, my voice would offer a resounding yes.

I drag the head through her wet heat, and she grinds against me. She's practically begging me to split her in half, but that isn't what I want. While I love to see the fear in her eyes, and while I would love to administer a little pain to the brat, what I want more than anything is to see her face when she comes. Not that fake shit she does for her viewers, but a real orgasm that is brought about by my hand. Or cock. Or tongue. The lass can take her pick.

Especially with the way she's looking up and whimpering. Her hands fall to her tits, and she pinches her nipples as she begs me with her eyes. She doesn't even know what she's asking for, but she wants it. She wants it so fucking bad.

As I draw her panties to the side and slip my dick between her pussy lips, her eyes widen. "Are you . . . pierced?"

I nod.

"Like, how pierced?"

I take her hand and guide it toward my cock, finally allowing her to touch me. Her fingers search until they wrap around my girth. Her thumb finds the piercing through the head of my cock, and she strokes it as she nibbles her bottom lip.

"Will I be able to feel it?" she asks. "I've never been with a pierced guy before."

With her panties still pulled to the side, I drag the piercing through her slit and grind the metal nub against her clit. Her eyes roll in her head as she grips the comforter.

"Fuck, I can definitely feel it," she says through a moan.

I pin her arms above her head again, and she closes her eyes and braces herself. I have the pleasure of watching every expression she makes. Behind this mask, I'm free to explore her all I want.

As I stroke and tease her, I revel in each sigh, each nibble of her lip. I live for the way she whimpers and writhes. I'd die for the way her heat feels on my skin. I'll probably die once it's taken away, but I can't think about that right now. For tonight, she's my only thought.

My cock throbs along with the beat of my heart, and I can't take it any longer. I lean forward and sink inside her. Despite the monster dildos I've watched her cram in this perfect cunt, she's as tight as a bigot's asshole in a prison shower. Tighter, maybe. I hold still, afraid to move inside her.

She reaches between us and grips the base of my cock, then squeezes for all it's worth, and I damn near fill her right then. I cannae be a minute man now! To stop her from squeezing, I give a few gentle thrusts that rock her breasts beneath the gauzy green material.

This position gives me too much visual stimuli, so I grab her thighs and rotate her onto her side. She lets out a squeal as I complete the maneuver and slide in behind her until my green suit melds with her skin. I tuck an arm under her right thigh and raise it as high as I can, giving me a straight angle to sink into her again. And I do.

And it's fucking heaven.

Her pussy clamps down again, and I realize I'm not the only one struggling to fend off a premature explosion. She isn't just tight; she's already on the verge of an orgasm.

Not one to miss an opportunity, I reach for her pussy and stroke her swollen clit as I thrust. I start slow, ratcheting the pace and pressure until she's about to break my dick off inside her. Just when I think I can't take another second, it happens. Quinn Parker comes all over my cock.

I feel like I'm in a dream as her eyes roll and her mouth contorts. She tries to keep quiet by gritting her teeth and breathing through it, but I fuck her harder and force the pleasure out of her. She cries out finally, gripping the comforter as a light sweat slicks her chest.

When she's finished convulsing against me, I pull out of her and grab the tablet.

Quinn sits up, frantic, her golden waves falling around her face like she's some sort of starlet. In a way, she is. After this, she'll star in my fantasies until the day I die.

"Where are you going?" she asks. "Don't you want to stay the night? You didn't pay ten grand to make me come."

I pull the pencil from its holder and scribble a message on the tablet.

ACTUALLY, THAT'S EXACTLY WHAT I PAID FOR.

I exit her room, leaving her confused on the bed. As much as I want to spend a night with my arms wrapped around her, it's a risk I can't take. I've risked enough as it is, and I've already got the next risk in mind.

Chapter Nineteen

Quinn

When I wake up the next morning, I find a surprise on my nightstand. At some point during the night, someone snuck into my room and left a simplified, teeny-tiny cell phone. It can't call out, and it refuses to connect to the internet, but I'm pleased to learn that it's capable of texting the only contact in the device.

Green Guy.

I feel like a giddy schoolgirl as I flop back on the pillows and read the first note from him.

I want to see you again.

I kick my feet and squeal. My brain tries to conjure images of us on our wedding day, but all I see is a hulking green man in a tux. If I want to marry him, he can't stay hidden forever. My fingers type out a reply, but my brain won't let me send it.

I nibble my bottom lip and consider what I'm asking. Pressuring the guy isn't a very good look, and it makes me seem superficial. Truth be told, I don't give a shit what he looks like. If he's a disfigured mess beneath all that fabric, it won't bother me a bit. When I'm with him, it just feels right. The sex, at least. We can work on the actual connection later.

Not wanting to scare him off, I delete the message and type something else.

My heart skips a beat when the bubbles pop up on the bottom of the screen. Somewhere in this hotel, maybe even just a few doors down, my crush is doing exactly what I am. He's hovering over a phone and waiting for a reply. It's torturously romantic.

I flip the television to the day's itinerary. There are several events going on this morning, including another coaster demonstration before lunch, followed by a few events scattered around the park afterward. Dinner is set in the grand dining hall after a show in the circus tent. Since I'm forced to take my meals at the hotel now, sneaking away shouldn't be too difficult. I'll just say I'm heading back to eat. I've lost Aven once before, and I can do it again.

With a smile, I stretch and climb out of bed. This is going to be a good day. Not even Aven can dampen my good mood when he knocks on my door a few minutes later.

He's dressed in a pale-green t-shirt that brings out the golden flecks in his dark eyes. I hate the way it hugs his muscles. Also, I hate that I'm still so attracted to him when I should be focused on the man who actually wants me.

I should also be thinking about the stalker—you know, the whole reason I'm on this impromptu vacation—but I can't seem to think of anything other than exploring this dark fantasy. If I want to earn that money, I'll need to buckle down.

I let Aven into my room, and he takes a seat on the chair in the corner as I finish brushing my teeth.

"What's the plan for the day?" he asks.

I rinse my mouth and come around the corner, pulling my hair into a high ponytail. "Are you giving me carte blanche?"

"Within reason."

I study the television again. "Let's do the coaster demonstration. We missed it the other day, and I'm curious to see what it's all about."

"You dinnae get enough from the simulation?"

My cheeks blaze red. I'd almost forgotten about that simulation . . . and the kiss. Reminders about my crush on Aven are the last things I need right now. My pussy and I are firmly in camp Green Guy.

Right?

Right.

I wave my hand through the air. "Or we can do something else. Doesn't matter to me."

He nods his head and sits forward with his elbows on his knees. "Aye, we could do whatever you'd like. If that's the coaster demonstration, then that's what we'll do. But I've seen where your mouth has been, so don't expect a kiss."

Pushing my arms into a light jacket, I roll my eyes and head for the door. These lips are reserved for the man in green.

I'm grateful to see the ride operators have faces when we arrive at the coaster. Even so, I make choices that differ from those I made in the simulation. Wouldn't want to give Aven the wrong impression after that little comment he made.

In reality, I chose the coaster demonstration because I figured Desmond would be there since he chose the popcorn-eating contest yesterday. It's not that I want to see him, but if I want to help them catch him, then I need to pull my weight. That bonus from Jim is the shortcut to riches I've been praying for, but I only get the additional money if I help them bag their prize.

And sure enough, as we approach the boarding platform—to get into the front coaster car, not the back—I spy the man of the hour preparing to board the final car. I tug Aven's sleeve, and he stops, nearly causing me to ram into his back.

"Do you need to piss again?" he asks.

I shake my head. "What? No, look over there."

I point toward the man and his skinny friend, and Aven turns to look at them. He nods and turns back to me.

"Aye, I see him. Clever lass." He ruffles my head and fucks up my ponytail. Asshole. "Do you feel up to tugging the line a bit?"

I nod and smooth my hair. Jim and Aven have really latched on to the fishing euphemisms, but I guess it works. Tugging the line means enticing Desmond to act, which is something we haven't fully tried yet. What we've been doing is more like dropping the line in the water without letting him get a nibble.

God, now I'm using fish talk. Gross.

"Yeah, I think it's time," I say.

I raise my hand and wiggle my fingers at the men. The skinny one spots me first. He punches his older friend in the arm and turns him toward me. "Nathaniel" waves back, and the pair start heading our way.

"What do I do?" I whisper as I keep smiling at the approaching men. "I didn't think this far ahead."

But Aven doesn't respond.

Not wanting to look behind me and show too much dependance on another man, I take a step forward and nearly fall into the older man's disgusting arms. He doesn't even bother to reach out and catch me as I steady myself on the queue railing.

"First day on those beautiful legs?" he asks with a sly smirk. His gaze eats up my body, lingering for entirely too long on my thighs.

I giggle and swat his chest. "Oh, Nicholas. You're so funny!"

He simultaneously preens under the attention and bristles because I got his name wrong. It was intentional. Men like you more when you make them feel small and inconsequential. Some men pay heavily for it.

"It's Nathaniel," he says, "but you can call me Desmond."

He whispers this last as he takes my hand and brings it to his lips. It was so quiet, I can't even be sure I heard it.

I'm in such a state of shock that I turn to Aven for reassurance.

But he's no longer there. The sun has set, and my shadow is nowhere to be seen.

"Would you like to join me in the last car?" Nathaniel—fucking *Desmond*—asks. "I hear it's the best seat."

I would rather lie at the bottom of the first hill with my legs spread wide as the coaster train barrels directly into my asshole. But, as so many women have before me and so many women will after me, I smile and nod to appease the asshole in my life. Such is our lot.

Cold sweat slicks my palms as I allow him to lead me to the end of the train. Flashes of memories break through, of that last ride with my mother and the way it felt to have her protective fingers wrapped around mine. It wasn't like this. There were genuine smiles and laughter, not this plastic grin to smother my fear. When I held my mother's hand, there was *never any* fear. Holding this man's hand brings it out of me in spades, though.

I glance behind me again, searching for Aven. Surely he's still watching from somewhere. He wouldn't leave me in this vulture's scaly hold.

I try not to study Desmond's face too closely as we wait to board, but I can't help it. He's becoming a silver fox, as patches of gray creep into his dark sideburns, but he lacks King's charm and allure. I'd say it's just that King has the benefit of that sexy accent, but Aven's accent doesn't help *him* at all.

Okay, that's a lie. Aven's accent is the stuff that orgasms are made of.

Why are you thinking of him right now? He didn't even stick around to keep you safe.

Desmond's ice-blue eyes stare down at me. He'd be

attractive if he didn't have that creepy air hanging around him. I've read enough dark romances to know he lacks the sliver of soul required to become a leading man. He'd be the villain.

I glance behind me again, but I only see a few more Sinners as they file in for the ride. There's Grim and Rose, and Ice Pick waddles in right behind them. The familiar faces put me more at ease, but the one face I want to see still isn't there.

"I think your little friend was jealous. He took off. It's just us, princess." Desmond's words settle around my lungs and squeeze. That isn't a threat. It's a promise.

My spine stiffens, but I slide my arm into his. I won't let him beat me, even without my scary-dog privilege. "Wouldn't want it any other way, Desmond. It's nice to put a face to the name after all this time."

"Nice?" He chuckles, and the sound is like gravel in his chest. When he bends lower and breathes against my ear, his warm breath does the opposite of giving me goosebumps. My skin wants to recede inside itself. "Aren't you terribly afraid?"

Yeah, I am, and if I didn't care so much about my image, my weak-ass bladder would release and I'd be pissing myself right now. He can't know that I'm scared out of my mind, though, so I offer him a playful roll of my eyes as I turn my head and whisper right back, "I'm not the one who should be afraid."

He laughs again, right as the gates open for us to board the ride. I allow him to load first, mostly so that he doesn't enjoy the same view of my ass that Sim Aven had. Desmond doesn't get that honor. Now, if I'd had a nice explosion brewing in my gut, I'd have crop dusted him and not felt bad about it, but my bowels have chosen the freeze response. I almost feel numb as I sink into the seat and pull the lap bar over my thighs. It clicks into place and holds me down.

I look over at Desmond. He smirks at me and goes to lower the lap bar, then shakes his head and moves to get out of the seat.

"Where are you going?" I ask, panicked. Did I fuck this up? Did he sense how terrified I am and decide it's not worth it, it's too easy?

Before he fully exits his seat, he flops back down and turns to face me. "I won't be riding this with you today, Quinn. I've had fun playing our little game of hide and seek, but now I'm bored. You know who I am, and I've known who you are for a very long time. So let's play a new game, hmm?"

"What do you mean?" I pull on the lap bar, but it's already locked in place. I'm trapped. "Watching me rub my cunt for a bunch of randos on the internet doesn't tell you anything other than whether the carpet matches the drapes."

I yank on the lap bar again as he rises to leave. I can't let him get away. Not when he's suddenly being so open. God, why can't I get other men to open up like this?

Speaking of other men, Aven may not be where I can see him, but he's watching. He has to be. There's no way he'd leave me to my own devices at such a crucial moment. I might act like I know what I'm doing, but I have no clue what these buttons do, and the machine is starting to smoke.

Desmond stops and places his hands over mine. "Stop all the fretting and enjoy the coaster. We'll have plenty of time for conversation later. Don't you worry." Before he reaches the exit, he turns to me with one parting shot. "Oh, and the person who told me the last seat on the train is the best? That was your mother."

As he turns with a laugh, I shout for the ride attendant to cut me loose, but it's useless. The ride music has already started, and it drowns out anything I say. Desmond slides into the shadows with a gentle wave, and then he's gone.

Chapter Twenty

Aven

The coaster flies by on my left, and I spot Quinn's golden ponytail whipping through the breeze. She zips by too quickly for me to see her face, but I note that the seat beside her is empty. As I'm processing this, the man who I believe to be Desmond comes strolling out of the ride exit. He stops at the top of the stairs and turns to watch the coaster barrel down another hill.

I tuck myself beneath the stairs before he notices me. After a tense few seconds of silence, his boots clank overhead, and then he's gone.

I pull myself from the hiding place, confused. Why isn't he riding with her?

What happened?

I turn and watch the coaster as it comes around another turn, clipping the Cattle positioned on the edge of the track. A spray of red coats the passing car as both of the figure's arms and one of their feet disconnect and go flying. The body flips through the air with a scream before slamming onto the track with a silencing splat. I'd laugh if I weren't so concerned about Quinn.

Seconds later, brakes hiss, and feet clomp on the ramp as everyone exits. Ice Pick is all smiles as he totters down the stairs. A splash of crimson coats his bald head. He gives me a wave and a thumbs-up as he keeps walking, muttering something about riding again once they set up another body. Grim and Rose follow close behind him, and the skinny guy —the one that always seems to be hanging around our Desmond suspect—brings up the rear.

But where the fuck is Quinn?

I push past them and hurry up the stairs. That's when the phone in my pocket buzzes with an alert. I stop at the top of the stairs as I free the device. I can see Quinn now. She's still seated in the last car, looking down at the phone in her lap.

> I know this isn't very attractive, but I'm scared and I don't know what to do.

My heart squeezes in my chest. I never wanted the girl to be scared. When I left her alone on the platform, I did so because I figured I'd just be in the way. This wasn't supposed to happen. She was supposed to ride this stupid coaster with him, then entice him back to her room. After that, I'd kill him and deal with Jim's consequences. I'm not waiting any longer for him to hurt her.

I type out a reply and hit send.

> It's okay to be scared. I get scared all the time. Where are you?

She can't know it's me. I have to pretend I'm oblivious to the situation, though I'm not entirely pretending. The reasons for the man's departure and Quinn's tears are very big unknowns.

I hide my device and hurry to her side. When she sees me on the platform, she shoves the phone into her pocket and swipes the tears from her cheeks. I'll pretend I didn't see the cell, but I don't think I can ignore the discomfort on her face.

I offer her my hand, but she gets off the ride on her own.

"No, don't try to help me now. You weren't here when I actually needed you, so there's no need to make an effort at this point. You just left me alone"—she glances around—"with a fucking *murderer*."

She whispers this last part, but it could have been a shout with how she delivers it.

"Quinn . . . we're all murderers. Including you now."

She hears the sense in what I say, and that just pisses her off more. With a grunt, she pushes past me and starts down the stairs. I try to grab her arm to stop her, but she just shakes off my hold.

"I thought I was being helpful," I say as I hurry after her.

She stops at the bottom of the first flight and rounds on me like a madwoman. Fire jumps in her eyes, and I take a step back to avoid getting burned. "Helpful would have been you standing there when he fucking admitted he was Desmond. Helpful would have been grabbing his arm and asking him what the fuck he meant when he made a fucking comment about my mother!"

"He admitted he's Desmond? What did he say?" The rest of her words finally slam into me, and I'm confused once more. "Wait, what does your mother have to do with any of this?"

Her small hands form clenched fists at her sides, and

she screams internally before bursting into tears. Just standing there, she looks so small. Fragile, even, like if I reach out to touch her, she'll shatter into pieces and cut me.

It's a risk I'll have to take. I can't just stand by and watch the lass fall apart like this. Not after what we shared last night—even if she doesn't know it. Despite the alarm bells blaring in my head, screaming how this is the most dangerous thing I've ever done, I step forward and wrap my arms around her.

"Get off me," she mumbles against my chest. "I hate you. And despite these shitty tears, I'm not trying to kiss you!"

Her fists wallop my sides, but the puny blows don't deter me. I don't loosen my hold on her, and eventually, she relaxes against me and begins to cry harder.

"There, there," I whisper. "Tell me what happened, lass."

She pushes away from me again, and I let her this time. She smooths the hair from her red, tear-stained cheeks and looks up at me with a quivering chin that threatens to break me. If she looked small before, she's practically minuscule now. I step forward to take her into my arms again, but she takes a step back with a shake of her head.

"No, you don't get to pick and choose when to support me. You don't get to run off and leave me like my mother left me, Aven."

She bursts into a fresh wave of sobs as she turns and eases down the last set of stairs. It would have been quite the dramatic moment had she not missed the first step and basically tripped her way to the bottom. Can the girl not even have a dignified exit?

Instead of feeling angry with her, I just want to make something go right for her. I follow her out of the station, keeping a few steps behind to give her some space. Her little sneakers pound the pavement as she swipes the tears from her face and tightens her ponytail. Despite my long strides, she's putting more ground between us. Anger is her great motivator, I guess.

As we near the park entrance, I slow even further. The only thing that way is the hotel, so I don't feel the urgent need to keep her within arm's reach. My heart rate slows a tad, but it picks up again when she glances back.

To make sure I'm still behind her.

I wince. I cannae help it. God, I was a feckless bampot for leaving the wee lass alone with him. Now I've either given her a complex or so firmly solidified an existing one that she'll be in therapy for the rest of her years. Ach, what have I done?

When she's finished glaring at me, she stomps her way through the exit turnstile. That is, until she spots a group of familiar faces just outside the gates. Her posture shifts from pissed-off She-Hulk to the infamous sway and soft curves that I've grown to think of a tad too fondly. The soft lilt of her head reveals more of her cheek, which is raised in a gentle smile. She's back to playing pretend for an audience.

She's painfully beautiful, and after last night, I'd do anything to keep her smiling. Bearing witness to the perfection that was her at her most vulnerable . . . Fuck, I can't even think of words. It was something beyond beautiful or heavenly. Fantastic is too fake, and there was nothing fake about that orgasm.

Okay. Thinking about that moment with Quinn was a terrible idea when I'm about to walk into a group of people who do *not* need to see the way my dick is straining against my shorts. I have an image to maintain, and "the boner guy" is the *last* thing I want to be known as. Asshole? Aye. Feckless prick? On occasions such as these, yeah. But not the boner guy.

I push through the turnstile, purposely ramming the metal arm against my cock as hard as I can. I anticipate the pain, which is meant to help deflate the raging—and incredibly inconvenient—erection. What I don't consider is that, as the stiff bar travels up the length of my concrete cum-gun, the damned steel will inevitably collide with the metal balls sitting on either side of the head of my dick.

My linen shorts don't dampen the distinctive *clink-tink* as the arm rips my soul from my body. The pain is exquisitely horrific, and I nearly pass out on the spot. Worst of all, I don't even know if the damned pain has accomplished its purpose. I grit my teeth as heads turn my way. I'm doing my very best to raise my cheeks in a smile.

I also raise my hand and open my mouth to say I just bumped my arm, as everyone is now looking directly at me, but my voice refuses to register to the human ear. The tuning-fork vibrations continue running up and down my dick, and now I'm not even sure the piercing is still attached. For that matter, I cannae even be sure my godforsaken dick is still attached because I cannae even *feel* my godforsaken dick.

Just that gnawing, grating, searing, never-ending pain.

White haze clouds my vision, and I'm fairly certain I'm about three seconds away from kissing the concrete. That's when an angel steps in front of me. A halo surrounds her golden ponytail . . .

I blink away the tears birthed from my pain, then look down at Quinn. Her eyebrows pull together, and she glances back at the group before stepping closer to me and putting her arm out. As her fingers wind around my wrist,

I'm reminded of the way she let me hold her down last night.

Fuck! You cannae think of that!

Fresh pain shoots through my cock as it either tries to harden again or reaches the apex of hardness. Is that piss, blood, or sweat running down my leg? Hell, maybe it's come. I'll never know because I refuse to look down and see what's going on below my abs.

Quinn cocks her head. "Are you okay?"

I raise my arm again and clear my throat. "Yep, just hit my watch on the metal—" My voice cracks when I try to say *arm*. God, the pain is too much.

With a growling grunt, I lean over the metal banister, peer down at the red mulch, and vomit every ounce of protein shake I guzzled before she woke up this morning. Some of it comes out my nose. I'm sure the lass will find me irresistible when she spots all the stomach contents on my damned face. Now I'll never make her like me more than Green Guy.

You are Green Guy, you numpty.

As I grip the metal banister for my life and blink away the fuzzy haze of slowly receding pain, a soft touch lands on my shoulder. I'm too ashamed to look, but I know it's Quinn. Her smokey-vanilla scent breaks through the protein powder, traveling straight to my gut and soothing the tumbling torrent.

She licks her lips and looks toward the group. "Bennett, could you and the other guys—"

I wave her off and stand upright before she can finish that sentence. "I'm fine, pal!" I shout toward the group.

Someone starts walking toward us, and I see that it's Eve.

I turn toward Quinn. "Ach, call off the cavalry, lass," I whisper.

"Will you come back to the hotel with me and have a . . . a talk?"

"Fine," I whisper. "Just make them go away."

She puts on that blinding smile and turns toward Eve. "Thank you, but he looks a bit better now. He has more color in his cheeks." Her bratty little fingers reach up and give my cheek a pinch. "See?"

Eve halts, and aye, I'd pay good money to have a framed picture of her face just as it is now. The entire group is busy gawking because they've just witnessed this wee lass reaching up and pinching the resident asshole's cheeks. And what is the resident asshole doing?

Letting it happen.

Aye. And that's how I know I'm in trouble.

Quinn hooks her arm through mine, but motherly concern crosses her face when she looks up at me. After pulling me to a halt with my back facing the others, she hurries to remove her jacket, then hands it to me. As discreetly as she can, she motions to my mouth and chin. She wants me to use her attire to clean the puke crust from my face. Five minutes ago, she was throwing a toddler-sized tantrum, and now . . . she's making a sacrifice for my honor.

I can't turn her down. It would hurt her pride, and Christ knows that's a tender spot for that lass. I know another tender spot for that lass, but it's in my heartless chest. So, I take the jacket and use it to clean up my face.

"Let's get up to your room," she says once I've tidied up. "We really need to talk."

Those words have never meant anything good before, and I don't think that's about to change now. Swallowing the knot in my throat, I nod and follow her lead as she smiles and heads toward the hotel. I can't muster a smile, but at least I can walk upright now. The pain has receded, and I'm assured by the gentle throb against my balls that my dick is still intact and is very much soft and sad.

Just like I'm going to be at the end of this assignment if I don't find a way to overcome this obsession I have with Quinn. Either overcome it or allow it to overcome me. I don't know which outcome terrifies me more.

Chapter Twenty-One

Quinn

I've almost calmed down by the time we get into his room and close the door. I'm still pissed, and I plan to hang on to that vile emotion for as long as possible, but the hurt has subsided. The memories have retreated back to their hiding places in my brain, and I can probably get through this without crying again.

Probably.

Not that I have a choice. Aven needs to know this information if I want him to have any chance of helping me.

As he closes the door and enters the room, I pace in front of the window and try to think of how to begin. I suppose the beginning is best, but I don't know exactly where that is. Where does my story even start?

I turn to face him before I lose the nerve. "My mother disappeared from this theme park twenty years ago, and I haven't seen her since. Desmond is somehow tied to her disappearance. He has to be."

"Hold up, lass. How are you sure he's Desmond? Just

because he said it doesn't make it true. Now that more people have cottoned on to your mission, some of that sensitive information could have slipped."

"I just know, Aven."

Aven purses his lips and nods. "Aye, that's confirmation enough. But where does your mother factor into this?"

"That's just it. I don't know." I sigh and sit on the edge of the bed. "He said my mother was the one who told him to sit in the last coaster car. That tracks because that's the reason I wanted the last car. It was one of the last things she said to me that night."

"Do you think he was there the night your mother disappeared?" He steps closer and kneels in front of me, taking my hands in his and peering into my eyes. "Think, wee lass. Wrack that bonnie brain of yours and see if he's in there."

I close my eyes and try to recall what I can from the night, but it's too hazy. The memories fade like a fart I've held in too long. Maybe it works the same way. Maybe I've hoarded these memories for so long that my body has absorbed them into my bloodstream to be parted out and forgotten.

My eyes pop open. "I had an upset stomach after eating the popcorn. My mother was worried that they'd doused the kernels with turmeric to enhance the color. That's why I was anxious when we first got to the popcorn event."

"That would explain how he knew about your allergy."

"It all makes sense," I whisper. "If he'd been following us around and hunting my mother, he'd have heard all of that. When she told me about the cars, the turmeric allergy . . . Aven, he was there."

"Aye, lass. I think so too."

When he smiles up at me, I almost feel bad for throwing

a fit earlier. Almost, but not quite. But it's not really fair to him.

I blow out a breath. "I'm sorry for how I acted earlier. It just brought up a lot of emotion. All these years, I've been told that my mother abandoned me, that she just wanted to get rid of me. When I was scared and I looked and you weren't there—"

My voice catches on a lump of emotion, but I swallow it. No more crying.

"Lass, look at me," he whispers.

Against my will, my eyes jump to his. His dark irises draw me in until I feel like I'm under some sort of spell. The anger dissolves further as he licks his lips and speaks with such a husky whisper that I fear my panties will melt.

"I will never abandon you. That is a promise. For as long as you are under my care, I will do whatever it takes to protect you."

The bubble pops when I'm reminded that I'm still a job to him. I'm still "under his care."

I'm still a paycheck.

I pat his hand and offer the warmest smile I can muster. "I know you will. I just have to accept that I'm not as strong as I pretend to be. Aven, I need your help. Desmond has to pay for whatever he's done to my mother."

"Aye, I'm way ahead of you. I'll hunt him down and take care of it right away."

I hold up a hand. "No, not yet. For starters, I want to be the one to kill the piece of shit. I also want a full confession about my mother before he dies."

He lets out a low whistle and rises to stand. "That's a tall order for a wee lass such as yourself. Confessions from men of our ilk might require a little torture. Do you have the stomach for it?"

"No clue," I say with a shrug of my shoulders. "I've never tortured anyone before."

He winks at me, and my heart stops. "Then I think I know what we should do to pass the time. Give me a tick to speak to Jim."

The golf cart stops and spits us out in front of the circus tent. Aven steps down first, then turns and offers his hand. I nibble the inside of my cheek to stifle a smile as I slide my fingers against his warm palm.

As he helps me off the seat and through the entrance gate, I can't help but reflect on the change I've seen within him. I can't say that I mind it, but it's kind of throwing me for a loop here. He's been softer in both the way he speaks and the way he approaches me. I've caught that look in his eyes, too. The same one I saw in the simulation. And now, he's showing genuine care for me as he leads me into the circus tent.

If I'd known opening up to someone about my mother would have brought me closer to them, I'd have done it so much fucking sooner. Again, I'm paying my therapist entirely too much money. Take it from Quinn Parker. If you have a miserable, shitty life, just go to a murder retreat and become a serial killer. Fucking one of them is optional, but I highly recommend it.

A pit forms in my stomach as I immediately think of Green Guy. We aren't exclusive or anything like that. I don't even know his name, for fuck's sake, yet I feel an attachment to him. I also feel a gnawing guilt for harboring this nagging crush on Aven. Is it really so wrong to admit that I haven't squashed these silly feelings?

It certainly doesn't feel very good.

The icky feeling fades as I slide my hand into my pocket and feel the tiny cell phone. This is nothing that can't be cleared up with a little communication. I'll be honest with Green Guy. If my desire to explore something with Aven would make him uncomfortable, then I'll keep it platonic with my guard dog. If Green Guy is open to letting me explore other avenues…

Now I just need to sneak away long enough to figure this out.

I glance up at Aven, then at our surroundings. A blinking sign points the way toward the restrooms, and a metaphorical light bulb clicks on over my head. I grab Aven's sleeve and give it a tug.

"Hey, I really gotta piss," I whisper. My typical bathroom habits make this lie seem like a truth. Being cursed with a Barbie bladder isn't the worst, I guess.

He stops walking and looks around. "I think I saw some restrooms over there. Would you feel better if I waited just outside your stall?"

At first, I'm baffled by this suggestion, but then I realize he's unsure just how long his leash is. After my embarrassing come apart earlier in the day, I guess I can't blame him.

"Um, no," I say with a shake of my head. "I can handle this much on my own. But if you'll wait just outside the restroom, that will make me feel better."

He nods once and moves me in front of him. "Lead the way, lass."

"You wanting to enjoy the view?" I give my hips a playful wiggle.

"Ach, I'm simply trying to keep you in my sights," he mutters, but the bite is gone from his voice. All that aching softness has buried the sharp tones. That raspy, heavenly softness.

Fuck, I've got to text Green Guy.

"I'll be right back," I say before rushing off to the restroom. God, he probably thinks I have diarrhea.

Oh fucking well. Before I sink any further into this rabbit hole that Aven's creating, I need to make sure it's okay with my leading man. After all, he's shown me that he's willing to put me first. He paid good money just to get me off, and that tells me everything I need to know about him. A: He has money. B: He's willing to do what it takes to please me.

Does a girl need anything else?

Well, actually, she does, and it just so happens that Aven is the other half of the puzzle. He has the looks. Those devilish smirks and that seductive wink. He's protective of me, and he takes what I say to heart. He was prepared to stand outside the stall and hear whatever unholy sounds came out of me, just so that I'd feel safe. He didn't just listen to me. He *heard* me.

Granted, I was snarling and gnashing my teeth, but still. He heard me.

And I don't know that I've ever been heard before.

I slip inside the stall and lock the door. My fingers are shaking, but I don't know why I'm so nervous. What's the worst that can happen? Green Guy says he isn't comfortable with me pursuing anyone else? *Oh no, the serial killer who wants to make me come is obsessed with me and wants me all to himself!* Like, what? What BookTok girly doesn't secretly fantasize about this?

But if there is one thing I look for in a romance novel,

it's a loyal lead. It sounds outlandish, but I've accepted that this trip is more than just my violent awakening. I'm also living out a sexual fantasy for a week. I'll go back to my normal life eventually, and I'll be a few hundred thousand dollars richer, which gives me time to build back all the subscribers I've lost. Life will go on. For now, I'm going to live it up.

And maybe, if I'm a really, really good girl for my male lead—whoever he is—I'll get invited back for the smutty sequel. A girl can dream, can't she?

But first, I have to get through this chapter. I take a deep breath and type out a message.

Chapter Twenty-Two

Aven

With the way she trotted off, she either needed a lavatory very badly, or she's already planning to sneak away to see her secret lover. Odd as it sounds, I'm more disheartened by the second prospect, which makes no sense. I cannae be jealous of *me*.

But that's the long and short of it. Aye, I've gone and made googly eyes at her all day. After what she shared with me last night, I couldn't help it. Then I've been a proper gentleman all afternoon. After what she told me about her ma, I couldn't help it. That moment was more precious to me than when she let me make her come.

Because she opened up to me.

The hard me.

The gruff, asshole me.

She opened up to a brick wall, and that takes a level of courage I can't help but admire. And desire. After hearing her story, I want to help her fill in the blanks until she's satisfied. If she's never satisfied, I want to keep trying for the rest of my natural life.

God, I'm fucked.

The phone buzzes in my pocket, and I nearly scream from the shock, despite expecting this. With a sigh, I pull the tiny cell from its hiding place and read the message from Quinn.

> Sorry about earlier and the lack of response. I can't text when my guard is on duty. Everything is fine now, though.

Hearing her refer to me as her guard hasn't bothered me before, but now that she's talking to another guy, it feels very dismissive. Like I'm just some object in her life. Why would she withhold my name from him?

Why does it matter, dumbass? You are the other guy!

Oh. Right.

Before I can type a response, the phone buzzes again.

> Speaking of my guard, that's what I wanted to talk to you about.

I hold my breath as I wait to see what she'll say about me.

> I'm pretty sure he has a thing for me. How do you feel about that?

She's pretty sure *I* have a thing for *her?* Ach, the lass has lost her mind. It's been the other way round, and I just happened to get caught up in it myself. A man can only deny a siren's song for so long when she keeps singing so prettily.

> If you're uncomfortable with that, I'll tell him to stop.

Like hell she will! The lass can try, but I'll just chase her harder.

> I really don't want to damage... whatever this is.

I finally realize I've just been standing here having an argument with myself while the wee girl worries in a bathroom stall. There's no reason for me to be jealous of her feelings for another man when I'm both of them, and I've got to remember that.

Even so, it won't hurt to push her toward me just a bit. The real me.

> I'm not the possessive type. If you want to explore something with him as well, you have my blessing.

I hit send, even though the entire message is a lie. She'd have the opposite of my blessing if this were really coming from me, as I'm a very possessive man when I want someone all to myself.

> Really? And you'll still meet me tonight?

> Wouldn't miss it for the world.

I'm still staring down at the tiny screen, waiting for a reply, when Quinn appears behind me. Before she can spot the familiar device, I shove it into my pocket and offer her a smile.

"All good, lass?"

"Better than good," she says with a cheeky smirk. "Now, where is this torture practice you've set up for me?"

I motion for her to keep moving past the seating area and into the performance space. My brain is still back at the bathrooms, though. I'm still reading those messages and wondering what they might mean.

As we step into the center ring, a spotlight clicks on overhead and brightens the space. I shield my eyes and look toward the control box.

"Thanks, pal," I say to Gary.

He grins and gives me a thumbs-up. Jim sent him ahead to set things up for us, and I can only hope he's done as I've asked. Gary's not the brightest man I've met, and he's been even less so since he took that bonk to the noggin on the pirate ship. Still, he's a good bloke, and he's the sort I'd share a beer with if I were the sort to share a beer.

Beneath our feet, the sawdust begins to vibrate. Quinn grips my arms to steady herself as heavy-duty chain-link fencing rises from the floor circling the center ring, caging us within. The zoo-grade fences click into place with a groan once they've reached their full height.

Just tall enough to contain a tiger.

Gary hurries from the control box and disappears into the backstage area. Moments later, the red curtains part as he appears again, pushing a wheelchair toward us. The man in the chair screams and tosses his head from side to side as he tries to tip over. Gary just grits his teeth and keeps pushing.

"See his yellow jumpsuit?" I say to Quinn.

She nods. "He's an animal abuser."

"Aye, lass. That he is." I grin to myself. She's a quick study, that one. "He ran a little roadside zoo in the Midwest. Well, he ran it until Jim discovered how he'd been keeping the poor beasts. He'd remove the monkeys' teeth so that tourists could pose with them without being bitten. The larger animals were forced to perform, and when they wouldn't—or couldn't—he'd use intense pain and starvation as a motivator."

"Stop," Quinn whispers. "I don't want to hear anything else."

I nod, because I don't want to *say* anything else. I may be heartless where my fellow man is concerned, but I have a genuine affection for animals. My early yearning for blood never involved helpless creatures. Always humans.

Always the creatures who are more heartless than I.

Gary opens the gate and wheels the man to the center of the ring, where Quinn and I stand. The man looks up at us, terrified.

"What's going on here? I demand to know why I'm being held hostage!" He pulls against his arm restraints with a grunt. "You can't keep me caged like this!"

"This is an interrogation," I tell the man before I turn to Quinn. "The first time Jim visited this piece of shit, he discovered a very neglected shack at the back of the property. Inside that shack was an even more neglected cockatoo that Jim hoped would help Kenny feel more comfortable."

"There's nothing wrong with keeping the bird in a different building," the man says with a roll of his eyes. "It did nothing but scream from sunup to sundown."

I backhand the idiot in the chair, which sends the entire thing tumbling over. When I've righted it again, I grip either arm and lean into his ugly face. "You can't take a social being and shove it in a box by itself and expect it to remain silent. You're proof enough of that."

The man closes his mouth. Wise decision. I'm about

three seconds from killing him myself, and then Quinn would miss out on all the fun.

"Bring out the tools," I say to Gary, and he hurries off to retrieve a selection of torture devices. I can't wait to see what Quinn picks first.

Minutes later, he rolls a table into the ring. Quinn glances up at me, and I motion for her to make her selection. She nibbles her bottom lip and moves down the line, touching everything with her delicate fingers at least once. Finally, she settles on a whip.

"Aye, good choice," I say with a nod. "Why'd you pick it?"

"If we want to extract information, we'll need to keep him around for as long as possible." She raises a hammer. "If I just whack him in the head with this, we'll never get anything out of him."

I bend lower and place my mouth beside her ear so that the asshole can't hear me. "Don't think about the kill. Think about different ways of inflicting pain. Sometimes death is a final act of kindness on our parts."

She considers this, then swaps the whip for the hammer. My dick is already getting hard before she takes the first swing to his shin.

"I thought you'd go for the fingers!" I shout over his screams. I can't remember the last time I smiled so widely. "You're brilliant."

"It just came to me," she says. "I thought about how bad it hurts to get whacked in the shin, and voilà!"

"Aren't you supposed to ask questions?" the man wheezes through cries of pain. "Isn't that what an interrogation is? You ask questions, and if I don't answer, *then* I get tortured?"

"Oh, shit," Quinn says with a giggle. "Guess I forgot that part. What are we trying to find out?"

I turn to Quinn. "The bird. When Jim arrived to seize the animals, the bird was no longer present. Despite scouring the property, the poor cockatoo was nowhere to be found."

"And no one thought to just *ask* me?" the man screams.

I shrug. "This seemed more fun."

"The bird is at my cousin's place in Texas. I'll give you the address if you'll just let me go."

"Way to suck the fun out of my day." Quinn's shoulders drop.

"Don't lose heart yet, lass. I'm sure he knows something that he doesn't want us to know." I pluck a golf club from the table and toss it to her. "You've got a pretty good swing, if I remember correctly."

She tests the weight in her hand before drawing back and whacking his other shin. A glorious howl springs out of him, and tears stream down his cheeks.

"Oh, shit," Quinn says with a giggle. "Forgot to ask a question again. Hmm . . . tell us your darkest secret."

"I slept with my brother's wife. Twice." The man gulps and peers up at Quinn through tear-filled eyes. "When I was sixteen, I set a trash can on fire and burned down the neighbor's barn. It was an accident, and no one got hurt, but I never told anyone."

Quinn sighs and tosses the golf club to the floor. "It won't be this simple with Desmond. This is pointless."

I take her shoulders in my hands and look down at her. "Hey, no getting discouraged now. Let's finish him off and try another one."

"What's the point? These men are wimps." She motions to the whimpering man who likely sports two broken tibias.

"If I want to know what it's like to really work something out of someone, you'll need to provide someone who's a little more . . . hardened."

I sigh and nod. The girl is right.

"Get Ashwin ready," I shout toward Gary.

Little bug-eyed Gary is all smiles and giggles as he retreats behind the curtain again.

"No," the asshole in the wheelchair whispers. His head begins to shake as he chants the word louder. "No . . . no, no, *no!*"

"Who is Ashwin?" Quinn asks.

I point toward the curtain as Gary grunts behind a large crate on wheels. The large metal cage creeps closer and closer. "*That* is Ashwin. He's a three-year-old Bengal tiger who has been abused by this piece of shit since the day he was born. We are here to witness his final performance before he heads off to a sanctuary in Nepal."

The man in the chair thrashes until he tips himself over. I give his head a solid kick with my boot, which dazes him. Blood mixes with the sawdust beneath his head as I bend to untie his arms and legs. Once he's free, I hoist him over my shoulder and drop him near the edge of the ring, right beside the fence.

"Come on, lass. Ashwin's not the friendliest toward humans, as you can imagine." I hold out my hand, and she takes it. It's a comfort to me when it shouldn't be, but I tuck that emotion down in my gut. I can explore feelings later.

The front-row bench has been set up just for us. I lead Quinn to the red blanket covering the creaky wood, and she takes a seat. She plucks up a red-and-white container of popcorn and studies it.

"No turmeric, so it's safe to eat," I say. "I checked."

She smiles to herself before settling in with her snack.

Seconds later, the lights dim until only the spotlight on the center ring remains. I asked Gary to choose a common circus song for the main event, just to really set the mood. Unfortunately, something got lost in translation, as "Circus" by Britney Spears begins blasting from the overhead speakers.

"Oh my god, I love this song!" Quinn squeals. "It's our own private performance!"

As the bonnie lass starts swaying and rolling her hips to the music, I'm entranced. Bright lights flash and zip overhead, casting her in a rainbow of allure. She takes a piece of popcorn from the box and drags it from her lip down to her tits before popping it into her mouth.

God, make me that popcorn, and I'll never ask for any—

A loud bang pulls me out of the trance, and I turn toward the sound. The tiger is sick of being in that cramped crate, and he's banging around inside. I don't blame him. In just a few minutes, he'll have the most fun he's had in his life, and then he's off to live out his days in a jungle, just as God intended. No more cages for the poor bastard after today.

Gary wheels the crate up to the gate and locks it in place. About this time, the animal abuser comes to and realizes what's about to happen. He totters to his feet, still dazed from the knock to the head. Gripping the chain link, he begins to climb.

"Shit, he's escaping!" Quinn shouts.

I tap her shoulder and direct her attention to the top of the cage, which is beginning to close, clamshell style, with a top made from nylon netting. We didn't want to use barbed wire. The last thing we want to do is harm the animals any more than the harms they've already known. But we also don't want to have an escaped monster on our hands, and that includes our human victims.

"The netting will keep everything contained," I tell her, and she nods her head in approval.

Right as the chorus starts and Britney commands all eyes to the center ring, Gary raises the gate on the tiger's crate. The great orange beast shoots from the darkness and heads straight for the greasy man making his way up the cage wall. Black stripes quiver within the orange fur as the fatal missile connects with its target. Claws poke from the massive paws and disappear into flesh.

"He's killing me!" the man screams as the tiger pulls him down from the wall.

"We know!" Quinn shouts back at him. She tosses her head back and laughs.

It even earns a laugh from me.

"Jesus fucking Christ!" Quinn screams.

My head jerks toward her, terrified she's somehow been injured, but she's just staring back at me.

"What?" I ask, feeling my body to be sure I don't have a second head growing somewhere. "Is something on me?"

"No. I just haven't heard you laugh like that before. It's nice." She gives me a playful nudge with her shoulder and goes back to watching the mauling.

Yeah, it was kind of nice, wasn't it?

I return my attention to the event as well, but it's almost over. The man hardly struggles beneath the tiger. He just kind of groans and spits blood while the animal lies on top of him and pants. Ashwin is clearly pleased with himself, as he should be.

Britney's voice fades out just in time for us to hear the powerful jaws close around the man's skull with a *crunch*. His legs jerk a few more times, and then it's over.

Quinn sighs and drops her head to my shoulder. "That was fun. What's next?"

I close my eyes and enjoy the feel of her being so close. It won't last long. She plays like she's an open book, but the lass is just as closed off as I am.

"Did you fall asleep?" she asks.

"No, lass. Just thinking about you torturing someone."

I don't mention that the person she's torturing is me.

"Did you have someone in mind? Any criminals you need to get intel out of?"

An idea strikes me, and I smile. "Aye, I might just. Let's go check out Jim's little book."

Chapter Twenty-Three

Quinn

Aven and I sit at a table in Jim's suite, hovering over a binder full of criminals. Jim sits on the couch with Kenny, the massive white cockatoo. He pets the bird's head and speaks softly against its beak, and as the bird closes its eyes and listens, it's the sweetest sight I've ever seen. The fact that someone once abused this animal is beyond my understanding.

Jim catches me watching them and smiles to himself. "They have problem-solving skills, you know," he says with a sad smile. "The cockatoo's cognitive abilities could be compared to that of a young school-age child. Terribly, terribly smart animals, the cockatoo."

"Seems like you two have developed a bond," Aven says. "Might not need that other bird after all."

Jim shakes his head. "Kenny and I have a bond, that's true, and I plan to keep him around, but the other bird still needs us. So many do."

"Aye. We can't save them all, but we'll save the ones we

can." Aven flips to the back of the book, and yellow suits fill the pages. His finger drags over the faces until he stops on a man. "Terrence Brickle . . . Was he the one with the lemur colonies that magically disappeared?"

Jim stands and delivers Kenny to his perch. "Yes, and we still haven't discovered their location. He seems to believe we'll have to let him go eventually. He fails to realize we aren't the authorities and are under no such compunction. His release is inevitable, but only his release to Satan himself. Until I know the whereabouts of those animals, we have to keep him alive."

He pulls a few cashews from his pocket and offers them to the bird, who accepts one with a gentle squawk. Jim pops the remaining cashews into his own mouth. The bird bobs his head in approval and goes back to munching.

"At least we can save the other bird. Our team is en route as we speak." Jim palms a few more cashews, then stuffs them into his pocket. "Maybe I'll set up a bird sanctuary on Devil Horn Island." He turns to the bird. "You'll like it there. Very warm. I'll spare no expense."

"Let the wee lass have a crack at the lemur bloke," Aven says. "The other egg broke a little prematurely."

"We can save the lemurs," I say with a crack of my knuckles. "Give me a few minutes alone with this guy, and I'll get the location out of him."

"Someone has developed quite the bloodlust," Jim says as he rocks on his heels with a pleased smile. "Are you handling the mental aspect well? I have psychologists on staff if you need to speak with someone."

"Oddly enough, my time here has been more therapeutic than the eons I've spent with my therapist. I think it's time to cut ties with her."

Jim gets an odd look in his eyes, like I've nearly touched

a hidden live wire, but he recovers and smiles at me. "Yes, well, if you change your mind, just let me know. For now, I'll get an area set up so that you can practice your torture skills."

I tuck that look into my back pocket for later. Right now, it's time to enjoy my new hobby.

"Of course, it might be fun if we turn it into a game," Jim offers.

"No need to turn it into a group activity," Aven counters.

I shrug and turn to face Aven. "I don't really mind if others are there. So long as Desmond isn't invited."

We filled Jim in on the Desmond situation before we started going through his big book of bad people. Aven wants to take out Desmond immediately, but Jim says we have to wait. As long as he hasn't been witnessed trying to take my life, we aren't allowed to act, and no one saw him put the turmeric in my meal the other night.

"I'll speak with King and Frankie regarding the Desmond information," Jim says, "but I can assure you he won't be at this event. The invitation will be extended to our insiders only."

I look back at Aven. "I'm fine with that."

With a sigh, he relents. "Aye, call them in, then. If it's what she wants, make it a game."

Jim practically explodes with joy as he flitters off to begin preparing. Meanwhile, I'm exploding with excitement. I get to torture a piece of shit *and* rescue endangered species. I'm living the fucking dream, and I don't know what could make this any better.

But then I feel the phone in my pocket, and I remember what's to come tonight. What started out as a horrible day is turning into one of the most exciting days of my life.

After taking lunch in my room, Aven and I join five other teams of two outside the Pirate Plunder ride. It's only once we arrive that Jim explains what we'll be doing.

"Everyone, listen up. The game is simple. You'll need to ride rides to get clues, and the clues will eventually lead you to your target. The first team to extract information from their target will be declared the winner. If both members of your team refuse a ride, your team is out of the game."

Cat raises her hand. "Bennett and I don't do water rides."

Jim pulls a notecard from his breast pocket and runs his finger down the paper. "Then you'll last as long as round three."

Cat and Bennett start grumbling to each other, as do most of the other pairs. They're likely trying to figure out who is willing to ride what and if this is just an exercise in futility.

I turn to Aven. "I'm not afraid of anything, so we won't have any issues there."

"Aye, me neither," he says, but I distinctly recall the way Sim Aven closed his eyes on the coaster. Not to mention the way he ran off when Desmond offered to ride Iron Tiger with me. Maybe his fear of heights had something to do with it.

I glance up at Aven again, but his face is a stone mask. He shows no emotion.

"Let the games begin!" Jim raises a starting pistol and fires it into the air, and the entire group rushes to get on the ride.

Pirate Plunder is a large ship that swings higher and higher until it eventually goes upside down. It's not my favorite ride at an amusement park, but it's also not the worst.

I slide onto the long bench seat, and Aven presses in against me. His shorts ride up a bit, making it so that our exposed thighs touch. Heat rockets through me, and I pretend I don't notice. I don't want him to move away or lower his shorts. I'm thirsty for something more from him, and I'm desperately grasping at whatever I can get.

"Sorry about that, lass." He pulls his shorts down and squishes in tighter as Kindra, Ezra, Eve, and Ice Pick join our row.

Motherfucker.

Cat, Bennett, Frankie, Maverick, Grim, and Rosie fill the row in front of us.

Another few rows of bench seats face us on the opposite end of the ship. As we're buckling safety belts and double-checking the lap bar, staff members begin popping a few Cattle into those seats. Oddly enough, the staffers buckle them in. I figured they'd let them fall right out, but no, they lower the lap bar, too.

"I don't like these sorts of rides," a woman in a yellow jumpsuit says. Her hands are fastened behind her back, but her legs are free. She tries to stand, but the lap bar holds her in place. "Let me off!"

The red Cattle sitting in front of her turns in his seat. "Would you shut the fuck up for once? We're strapped in. It's not like we'll fall out."

The woman struggles against the lap bar again, realizes he's right, that she couldn't get out if she wanted to, then settles in her seat again.

A ride attendant raises his thumb, signaling that they're

ready to run the ride, and another attendant nods and fires back the same signal.

"Oh, one more thing!" Jim calls. "Your first clues are hidden on the Cattle. Happy hunting!"

A loud buzzer sounds, followed by a *click* that I can feel in my feet. I tug on our row's shared lap bar, afraid it's come undone, but it's still firmly in place. A breath of relief shudders out of me as the massive ship begins to move.

We slide backward first, which is forward for the Cattle. When the ship gets a little lift, it drops and goes the other way. My ponytail flies away from my neck, and I grip the lap bar with a squeal and a smile as my stomach drops. Gravity pulls me down, down, down, and then we're moving backward and rising again, a little higher this time.

On the third pendulous swing, the Cattle lap bar rises. The click I felt in my feet was their side of the restraints coming undone, not ours. With their hands buckled behind their backs, they can't even hold on for dear life.

I laugh and turn to Aven, but he isn't looking at me. I don't think he sees anything as he stares at the dipping horizon and grips the lap bar with every ounce of his inhuman strength. The soft vinyl gives under his fingertips, and his knuckles blanch.

I wiggle my hand beneath his and give it a squeeze as the ship starts to rise again. His hold on the lap bar relaxes as he turns to look at me.

"Are you having a nice time?" he bellows over the rush of wind and creaking gears.

"Aye!" I shout with a smile.

My use of his native tongue seems to undo something inside him, and the fear in his eyes slips away, if only a little. He manages a smirk before the ship goes into another dive.

His face contorts, and he grits his teeth as the vessel takes our stomachs.

At the apex of this lift, one of the Cattle loses his fight with gravity and tumbles out of his seat. The ride starts its backward swing on our side and sends his body flipping all the way to the back of the ship. He lands on the platform, giving us the perfect view of his fatal disfigurement as we rise and rise and nearly go upside down. His legs twist at unnatural angles as he wriggles below us, and one of his arms is definitely broken. It won't matter, though, because the ship swings over him and silences his screams.

Kindra raises her arms and lets out a squeal, and Ezra does the same. I want to as well, but Aven is struggling, so I stay quiet and just keep squeezing his hand.

The ship swings the Cattle side into the air again, and they *are* upside down. The moment is brief, but gravity manages to pull one of the men from his seat. He tumbles toward us, then smacks the central mast running through the ship's center. His skull breaks open and sends part of his brain into Ice Pick's lap. Ice Pick swipes the tissue off his thighs as if it's just a bit of mud.

When we head backward again, I know what will happen. I can already see it in my mind, and Aven will miss it if he doesn't open those beautiful brown eyes. I clench his hand and lean closer.

"Don't be afraid," I say, just loud enough for him to hear me. "I'm right here with you. If you fall out, we go together." I raise our clenched hands to drive the point home. I won't let go.

He doesn't argue with me for once. He doesn't try to be Billy Badass and pretend he isn't scared. Instead, he just nods and opens his eyes.

The ship flips upside down and stalls. Three more

Cattle are sent screaming to the platform, but the woman is the final holdout. Her face burns red with the effort of clenching the seat with her legs, but it's a battle she won't win. Before the upside-down stall ends, her legs lose the fight, and down she goes.

Splat!

Everyone lets out a cheer, and I raise mine and Aven's hands as the ship flips all the way around. When I look over, I'm happy to see his other hand raised as well. He still looks absolutely terrified, and he isn't cheering with us, but at least he's trying.

Two of the bodies go flying from the force of the ship's return to land. After another turn, the ride slows and comes to a stop, and we all pile out of it. Working together, we pull mangled bodies from beneath the ship and dig through their pockets for a clue. We each find what we need, then separate into our little duos to read our secret messages.

Aven holds ours close to his chest and whispers the words. "If it's a key you wish to find . . ."

I roll my hand through the air, urging him to keep going, but he just holds the paper toward me.

"Ach, that's all it says. See for yourself."

Sure enough, it seems we've only been given part of the clue.

"Damn you and your dirty tricks," Eve shouts toward Jim, who looks pleased as punch as he rocks on his heels and laughs.

"Might want to figure out who has the missing pieces to the two puzzles," Jim says.

"Who has last words that rhyme with 'find'?" Aven asks.

Frankie, Maverick, Ezra, and Kindra all raise their hands, and we hurry to form new groups. When we put all three clues together, it makes a full clue.

You might go into the mine
If it's a key you wish to find
Or maybe it is just behind

"You tore down the mine train coaster," Maverick says to Jim. "That's no fair. How are any of us supposed to know where it used to be?"

"I know where it was," I say.

Aven looks at me, and he's about to ask how, but then he must remember what we discussed this morning, because a knowing look shines in his eyes. I nod at him, hoping he doesn't say more. He doesn't.

"Lead the way, then," Kindra says. "They're already getting a head start over there."

I turn, and sure enough, the other six are already setting off to follow their clue. We'd best get a move on. The mine train was on the other side of the park, and right behind it, we'll find the next ride. There's no telling what sort of calamity waits for us back there, but we'd better hurry if we want to win.

Chapter Twenty-Four

Aven

The second clue was on a small drop-tower ride. We had to strap ourselves into the death machine with a group of Cattle, then sort through their scattered remains once they were ejected from their seats at the bottom. At least we were able to split into pairs after that. Now we've all been directed to the log flumes.

As the larger group reconvenes at the third ride, I'm feeling a little more confident. I survived Pirate Plunder, and I didn't shit myself at the top of Death Tower—and yes, that's the name Jim went with. The log flume is a kiddie ride. This should be a piece of cake.

"Welcome to River Styx, a log flume for the dead and dying," Jim says with a cackle.

"This doesn't look anything like I remember," Quinn says as she eyes the dark entrance. A towering fiberglass Grim Reaper holds his scythe over the opening and coaxes us inside with a malevolent skeleton grin.

Jim pats the figure's cloaked arm. "We took the old

flume and completely revamped the theming. Most of the track is the same, though I had our engineers add a little oomph to the last drop. It's a doozy!"

My mouth begins to dry out. What's with human beings and wanting to be flung at the ground at the highest speeds possible? I cannae take it anymore.

I pull Quinn aside as Jim and Cat discuss the ability to wear ponchos during the ride. It's embarrassing enough to tell Quinn I want to sit this one out, and I don't want the rest of the group to hear.

"Do you think you could take one for the team, lass?" I whisper. "I, uh . . . I'm not the biggest fan of getting soaked."

I know it's a lie. She knows it's a lie. But she lets me tell it.

"Don't worry a bit," she says with a squeeze of my hand. "I've got this. However the Cattle are killed, I'll get the clue for us."

We turn back to Jim as he begins explaining how this game will work.

"You'll board the ride in your pairs"—he turns to Cat—"sans ponchos."

Cat grumbles.

"Once the ride begins, you'll have until the final drop to murder your Cattle rider before the ride photo is taken. Any teams whose pictures feature Cattle faces will be disqualified, as will anyone who doesn't dispatch their Cattle before the final drop."

I glance at Quinn, who seems unperturbed by this plan. Isn't she the slightest bit concerned she won't be able to make the kill? What if the Cattle overpowers her?

"So, who's up first?" Jim asks with a devilish grin.

Kindra looks around and asks the question most of us

are already thinking. "Are we supposed to use weapons? Or does the ride have some sort of—"

Jim holds out his hands. "Please, no more questions from the press. All will be revealed once you're inside."

Kindra rolls her eyes and grabs Ezra's wrist, then drags him into the darkness beneath the Grim Reaper's weapon. "Come on, Ezra. We might as well get this . . ." There's a brief moment of silence before she shouts, "Jesus fucking Christ!"

"I don't like the sound of that," Frankie says. She glances up at Maverick, who wraps his arm around her shoulder and pulls her closer.

Bennett offers the same comfort to Cat, and even Eve does her best to soothe the worry on Ice Pick's face. Grim and Rose are busy discussing it in their own way, but they both seem more excited than nervous.

And here I stand, ready to let the girl go it alone because I'm afraid of a little log flume.

I don't wrap my arm around her shoulder, but I find her hand and give it a squeeze. "Changed my mind, lass. I'm coming with."

"Are you sure?"

I nod before good sense catches up with me.

When Jim calls for the next group a few seconds later, I'm glad when Quinn doesn't jump at the offer. She lets Cat and Bennett have that honor. Once Jim has confiscated their ponchos, he sends them through the door.

"Jim, you fucking suck!" Bennett shouts toward the group a few moments after he's disappeared.

Now the curiosity is getting the better of me. I lean closer to Quinn. "Maybe we should go next and get this out of the way," I whisper.

"I think you're right," she says with a gulp.

Jim calls for the next group, and I step forward. I take Quinn's hand, pretending it's more for her sake, but the lass and I know the awful truth. I'm fucking terrified.

We slip under the scythe, and the darkness continues. Candles line a dungeon-like passage for a few feet, and then we're met with a wall of water. It cascades from the ceiling in a thin curtain, and there is no way to continue without getting drenched.

"I'm not walking through that," Quinn says, and I'm inclined to agree. The point of a water ride is to get wet . . . on the ride. You aren't meant to be drowned going into it. She looks up at me. "I'm not wearing waterproof mascara, Aven."

"Me neither."

She grumbles and takes a step forward, and I'm right behind her. A scream squeezes out of her as frigid water douses her entire body, and I damn near let the same sound out of me. Who the fuck designed this shit to be the same temperature as fucking Neptune?

"We will all get you for this, Jim!" Quinn bellows. She rips her hand from mine and starts swiping water from her face.

I pull off my shirt and hand it to her, but she waves me off.

"What's the point? You're as soaked as I am!"

Looking down at the dripping shirt in my hand, I realize she's right. I start laughing. I cannae help it. Seems doing the chivalrous thing is beyond my ken, even when I'm trying my damndest.

The worry eases when she starts laughing too. She swipes the shirt from my hand and wrings it out, then opens it and presses it to her face. She holds it there, doing gentle motions with her fingers to smooth away the makeup runoff.

"Wouldn't it make more sense to scrub?" I ask. "Doesn't seem very effective to just drape a wet cloth on your face and hope for the best."

"Bad for the skin," she mumbles into the shirt. "Pulling and tugging like that will give you wrinkles."

"Oh no, wouldn't want any of those," I say with a roll of my eyes.

When she's satisfied, she shoves the shirt back into my hands and starts walking again. Despite the low light, I can see that she got the job done, even if her methods make no sense.

My arms want to recoil inside my body as I shove them into the icy shirt and follow her. It's somehow colder now.

"Aven, what is that?"

I look up. Quinn's outstretched finger points to a tiny boat in a channel of water beside the loading platform. A few identical boats line up behind it, each with a faceless, robed Charon figure perched at the back.

"That would be the ferryman, come to take us to our afterlife," I say.

Quinn shakes her head, and her soggy golden ponytail flops against her nape. "No, not the boat. *That!* In his hand."

I look again and realize she isn't pointing at the boats. She's pointing to the ride attendant standing beside the loading dock. In his hand, he holds a shiny metal garrote.

"That's what we'll have to use to kill her." I nod toward the Cattle in the front of the boat. She's a gray-haired elderly woman, so it shouldn't be too difficult. "It's a garrote, used for strangulation. You slide the wire around her throat and use the handles to provide pressure. Would you prefer I do it so that we can make it quick?"

Quinn scoffs and rushes forward to snatch the garrote

from the attendant's hand. "Do you think I'm not strong enough? Because I'm a girl?"

Before I can answer, she drops into the seat, drapes the garrote over the woman's neck, and starts pulling. The woman's feet kick out, and her eyes go wide. Her mouth opens in a scream, but Quinn is putting her all into the metal wire, and no sound escapes.

"I'll kill . . . this animal-abusing cunt . . . before . . . the ride . . ." Quinn grunts and struggles as the woman flails against death. "Bitch, sit still!"

Quinn gives the handles a sharp tug, and the wire slices through skin as the woman turns her head sharply to the left. Blood spurts from a severed artery and soaks Quinn's legs.

"Oh, fucking gross," she says as she tries to scoot away.

The ride attendant holds up a finger. "Um, one final rule. If the Cattle dies before the ride starts, you're disqualified."

"Shit," I say as I hurry to drop into the seat behind Quinn. She didn't need me after all, but it's too late to back out now.

And as the woman keeps bleeding all over the place, it's almost too late for anything. It's more of a nick than a full severance of the artery, but it's enough to keep the blood pulsing out in violent jets. I motion for the attendant to get us rolling before she meets the actual Angel of Death. It's not until the boat dips forward and we drift into a black tunnel that I remember what's to come.

"Oh, wow," Quinn breathes as the woman gurgles in front of her. "Look at that."

The tiny boat bobs into a scene straight from a movie set. An animatronic Grim Reaper stands on the shore, beckoning us forward with a skeletal finger. Naked branches stretch toward the ceiling from the trees surrounding the water. We have no choice but to move closer as the boat carries us downriver.

"Who goes there?" a deep voice bellows from overhead, and despite the audio treatments the clip received, I can still tell it's Jim's voice. "Who dares venture down the River Styx?"

The boat comes to a stop in front of the massive animatronic, and a speaker hidden within Charon responds. "I bring more souls for the underworld."

Was that . . . *King's* voice? How did Jim get that priggish bastard to run lines? He's the only bloke I consider more standoffish than myself.

The animatronics continue their bit, but I can't focus on what they're saying. Not with the way Quinn keeps wiggling around in front of me and bumping against my blasted cods.

"Lass, watch where you're swinging that ass of yours."

"Aven, I think she's dead," Quinn says.

She shifts in front of me, and I see that the woman has slumped back against her. The freshet has stopped burbling from her neck as well.

"Do we just dump her out of the boat?" she asks, panicked. "I haven't ridden this in a long time, and I don't remember where the big drop is."

"Trying not to think of that part myself," I say as the boat starts moving again.

And it's picking up speed.

The nose dips into a rougher section that twists and turns through another scene. It's more like rapids here than a gentle log flume. We're bumped and tossed through a forest, where animatronic demons dive from above and screech overhead. Large jets intermittently blast pillars of fire and sweat-inducing heat.

I glance around, looking for any other bodies, but it's hard to see anything with how fast we're moving. A small world this ain't.

"Aven, she's too heavy," Quinn says with a grunt. "We'll have to switch places so you can dump her out."

"Aye, but let's wait for a quieter section," I say.

The boat begins to slow as we turn into another dark stretch, but then I hear the click of the ride's internal mechanism engaging with a chain lift. A breath later, we're going up a hill.

"Is this the big hill?" I ask.

Quinn shakes her head and struggles to get away from the dead woman, who's fully reclined against her at this angle. "There's a smaller hill, then more rapids. I think. It's been so long that I can't remember."

"Could we use this hill in our favor to hoist her out?"

But we're out of time. The clicking stops, and down we go. My stomach climbs into my throat, despite the drop being far less frightening than the measly drop tower. Quinn doesn't even bother raising her hands and enjoying it. She's too busy trying to get away from the dead body.

The boat eases to a stop again, and we're greeted by the Grim Reaper once more. This animatronic stands beside a large glowing tree. Lanterns hang from the naked branches, providing an eerie yellow haze to the scene.

"You're nearing the point of no return," Jim Reaper says in his booming voice. "Death lies just beyond those gates."

The boat turns on a track and points us toward a large set of looming metal gates. As they begin to slide open, I tap Quinn's shoulder. "It's now or never, lass. Let's switch places."

"I don't know if I can," she whimpers. "It's so unsteady. What if I fall out?"

The boat eases forward.

"Turn in your seat. You don't even have to stand. You go under me, and I'll go over top of you. That way, you're always safely in the death machine."

"Oh fuck, don't call it that," she whimpers as she wobbles to turn in her seat.

The boat jerks forward again and practically launches us through the gate and into the next set of rapids. These are much more violent than the first set, and the girl is getting tossed around like a rag doll in front of me. Her tiny hands grip the sides of the boat as she tries to steady herself, and the dead body, now pressing against her back rather than her front, isn't helping matters.

"Hold me around the middle, and don't let go, whatever you do," I bellow.

Quinn's arms stretch as far as they can around my waist, and I lean forward to try to work the body free. Swapping places is all but impossible, so we'll have to make do in this awkward position.

We drop down another small hill and barrel through another set of rapids in a blacklight forest. A massive demon head pops from a tree trunk and sprays mist from its nose with a deafening sound. Quinn screams and buries her face in my lap. This would be more welcome under different circumstances.

Fake lightning flashes overhead, and I spot a pink-clad body draped over the iron fencing lining an upcoming section. The man's head has nearly been sawn off.

"Bennett has definitely been here," I say as I try my best to hoist the tiny dead woman from our boat. It would be a lot easier without the terrified lass screaming bloody murder against my ball bag, but no matter.

With a final grunt, I manage to get the woman out of the boat. She lands in the water, and I worry her body will fuck up the ride mechanisms, but Jim has already thought ahead. A staff member rushes from some unseen hiding place as we pass by, and he fishes her out of the water.

"Think you can turn the right way round again?" I ask Quinn. "I'm not sure how safe it is to—"

The boat clicks again, and I'm nearly laid on my back as we start up what has to be the final lift hill. Before darkness fully enshrouds us, I spot a disembodied head resting at the base of a tree. Why didn't we think of that? Sawing off the head might have been easier than shoving the body out.

But my thoughts turn to Quinn and what risks she's taking by going over this final hill in this position. Instead of gripping the sides of the boat, I grip her.

If we go, we go together.

"Aven, I'm scared!" Quinn screams against my crotch.

I do something uncharacteristic of me, but I'll be damned if it doesn't feel like the most natural thing once I've done it. I raise her and kiss the top of her head and reassure her. "Aye, lass. Me too."

Her grip remains steadfast, but I feel her relax against me.

"Here, get closer," I say. "You can't turn around like this, but you can straddle my lap so that I can hold you better."

Quinn nods and carefully positions herself as the boat continues to rise. She straddles my waist, and if we weren't soaked, freezing, and fearing for our lives, I'd definitely have a hard-on with all of her sweet softness pressed against me. Her arms wrap fully around my neck and link at the back, and I wind my arms around her waist and do the same.

And yet the damned boat keeps climbing.

"When does it stop?" Quinn screams.

She isn't trying to make this worse for me, but she's pouring gasoline on my panic fire. I'm asking the same thing in my head, simultaneously wishing for this to end and hoping it never does. Holding her like this feels incredible, despite what's to come.

The clicking stops, and the boat's nose levels off. As we're brought to a flat position and dropped into a slow stream, the boat drifts into another dark forest scene, though this one has a different vibe. Instead of ripping past terrifying demons, loud noises, and flashing lights, we slowly glide through trees decorated with twinkling, soft-glow bulbs that mimic fireflies. Soothing, melancholic music plays in the background.

"Maybe we still have time to move. Before the drop," she whispers.

Her head pulls back a bit, putting our faces dangerously close together. She licks her lips and looks at me in the dim light. She doesn't try to sit the right way around, though this would be the opportune moment. No, the lass just stares at me as if she badly needs to be kissed.

She isn't the only one, so I do what I can't as Green Guy. I grip her face in a gentle hold, and I press my mouth to hers.

The world slips away as our lips meet. We're both tentative at first, both asking, *Is this really okay?* It's not, but that doesn't stop us from saying fuck it, even if it's cautiously. This act is somehow more intimate than the moment we shared in her bed. Her nails dig into my shoulders as I deepen the kiss, and I caress her cheek with my thumb in the same way she caressed mine when I was Green Guy.

Games and amusement parks are all but forgotten as we

float on a high of our own creation. Quinn's hungry hands pull me closer, demanding more. I want to give her all of me, but it's hard to do in these cramped quarters.

She whimpers into my mouth, and the sound hardens me instantly. Feeling my need beneath her, she rocks her hips and grinds down on me. I pull away from her greedy mouth and tip my head back with a groan.

The boat bumps against the sidewall as it drifts around another turn, and the spell breaks. Quinn freezes and looks down at me, breathing hard.

"Shit, what are we doing?" she says.

And she's right. Fuck, she's right. Why would I do something as stupid as kissing her?

There's no time to consider our mistake, however, because Jim Reaper appears again.

"The drop!" Quinn screams. She wraps her arms around my middle. "The boat will stop one more time, and then we'll go down the drop. I remember now. Fuck, I'm such an idiot."

Aye, and so am I. Instead of sucking the girl's face off, I should have demanded she right herself in the boat.

"Do you have time to turn around when we stop?"

She shakes her head.

I wrap my arms around her again and refuse to let go, come what may. She might regret that kiss, but her safety is still my priority. Maybe even beyond a paycheck at this point, and maybe even if the feelings aren't reciprocated. Hell, maybe it's best they aren't.

The boat stops, just as Quinn said it would. The Jim Reaper animatronic bends at the waist suddenly, nearly dropping on top of us, and we let out a scream as he says, "Don't forget to stop by the gift shop on your way out of hell!"

We drop.

"Oh shit!" I scream as we barrel down a pitch-black tunnel. We go down and down and down for what feels like forever, and then we finally level off in a blast of sunshine.

My arms remain around Quinn as a deluge of water consumes us. Are we dead or alive when the boat stops? I don't know. My eyes are closed, and my fingers have never clutched anything as tightly as I clutch the wee lass to my chest.

A smattering of applause greets my ears, and I open my eyes. Quinn's head pops up, and she peers around.

"Oh my fucking god, get me out of this boat," she grumbles as she scrambles off my lap.

Kindra offers her a hand, and I join her on the platform. Everyone looks like they've been swimming against their will.

"We have to get the next clue once everyone else has arrived," Ezra says. "Jim's orders."

Quinn shakes her head and starts walking toward the exit. "I think I've had enough of Jim's games for the moment."

She doesn't wait for me to join her. She doesn't even pause to see if I'm following her as she hurries toward the exit. A sinking feeling fills my innards, and I hope against hope that the kiss hasn't done more damage than I realized.

Chapter Twenty-Five

Quinn

Black eyeliner smudges at the corner of my eye for the third time, and I throw the stupid pencil at the wall with a scream. If I weren't planning to impress a man, the liner would glide right on, but *no*. Now it wants to play up and make me look stupid.

Men, Quinn. Plural. Because you're a whore and you don't know which man you want most.

That's the long and short of it. Kissing Aven was a horrible decision, not because it was a bad kiss. No, that would have made this simpler. Instead, he had to go and make me forget my fucking name. That's how mind-scrambling his kisses are.

I close my eyes and lean my forehead against the mirror. This was supposed to get easier, not more difficult. I had hoped that he'd be a bad kisser or that he had horrible breath or, at the very least, I wouldn't feel feelings and hear bells ringing when his lips pressed against mine.

Then there's the whole loyalty issue once more. Green

201

Guy was fine with my proposition to pursue both men, but will Aven be so willing to share? Something tells me his answer will be a laugh and a resounding hell no.

You gotta call things off with Green Guy, my inner voice whispers.

That seems like the best call. He's nice and all, but at least Aven can talk to me *and* fuck me. I'll break the bad news to Green Guy tonight when we meet.

Feeling a little more self-assured, I open my eyes and drag the pencil over my upper lid again. This time, the line ends in a delicate point, just as it should.

"Perfect," I whisper with a smile.

Voices rise outside my door, and I turn toward the sound as someone knocks. I'm not expecting any visitors, and Aven isn't due to pick me up until six. I still have thirty minutes.

Curiosity and trepidation mingle in my chest as I rise and go to the door. Peering through the peephole, I spot Frankie, Cat, Eve, and Kindra. Eve holds a large purple garment bag, and Cat has what looks like an entire MUA studio trailing behind her in a massive black case. A hot-pink hairdryer hangs from the handle.

I open the door and offer the girls a smile. "What's all this about?"

"Jim decided to give us a dress code for the show," Kindra says with a nod toward the garment bag. "Once that was set, Cat decided we needed makeovers."

Cat jiggles the case's handle. "Before I decided to go into nursing, I had a budding acting career. I miss doing everyone's makeup."

I motion to my face. "I only got as far as primer and eyeliner, so my canvas is fair game."

"And what a lovely canvas it is," Eve says. She eases

past me as I open the door wider to let them in. "Have you ever considered modeling? You have the facial structure for it, though my agency would make you lose about fifty pounds."

"Fifty pounds?" I look down at my thick thighs and stomach pooch. While I'd love to ditch the latter, the former more than makes up for it. "I think I'll stick to the pizza and chocolate shakes."

"I don't blame you, honey. I was blessed with the metabolism of a hummingbird, so I can eat whatever and maintain my physique." Eve admires her figure in the mirror, as she should. She's a knockout in a long powder-blue gown and strappy silver heels that lace up her sculpted calves. The color practically glows against her umber skin.

Cat is just as flashy in a hot-pink number that makes her blue eyes pop. The playful, flared short skirt paired with the tight, glittery bodice works well with her figure, and her bright blonde hair falls around her head in loose starlet waves.

"Why aren't you in a dress?" I ask Frankie.

She grimaces, then laughs. "I don't really do girly shit. I'm more comfortable in a power suit with flowing legs than a dress."

Frankie strikes a pose in her suit. The black legs puddle around pointed black shoes with a kitten heel. A black blazer sits just right on her frame, giving focus to her feminine lines without turning her masculine. Her slicked-back ponytail finishes off the look.

Kindra tugs on the short hem of her purple-sequined cocktail dress. "Jim didn't get the memo that I hate dresses too. Ezra picked this one out."

"I can tell," I say with a laugh. Her full ass nearly peeks

from the bottom in the back as she turns, and her tits spill from the top.

Kindra shrugs. "What can I say? He loves to torture himself through dinner, then have dessert back in the room."

We break into peals of laughter at that, though my laughter is merely polite. I'm too jealous to be genuinely happy for any of them. With the exception of Eve, they're living out my dreams; they're all in stable, committed relationships with unstable, non-committal men.

"Sigh. Someday my prince will come," I say with a wistful look out the window.

"Looks like you damn near had him coming on the log ride," Eve says with a smirk.

"Oh yeah!" Cat says as she begins opening her case of wonders. She moves the chair from the corner to the middle of the room and motions for me to have a seat. "I'd almost forgotten about that. Were you trying to fuck him on the ride?"

I sit down with a shake of my head. "Um, no. We were trying to change positions so that he could pull the dead bitch out of the boat, but we got stuck."

Frankie and Kindra share a look and sit on the edge of the bed as Cat starts to work on my face and Eve fiddles with my hair.

"What was that look for?" I ask Frankie.

She fusses with the edge of her ponytail. "Are you . . . attracted to Aven, perchance?"

Fuck, I don't know how to answer that. Also, he could be listening. Yeah, I kissed him, but his pride is big enough to overflow the Sphere in Vegas. He doesn't need an ego boost.

Sensing my hesitation, Kindra fills in the silence. "We

only ask because Jim played matchmaker on the cruise, and we have a sneaking suspicion he's doing it again with you and Aven. We just want to be sure you're comfortable and that you don't feel pressured since we're all . . . you know."

"Serial killers?" I say.

"Yeah, that." Eve pats my shoulder. "We're overjoyed that you're joining the club, but we want to be sure it's fully on your terms."

Cat stops applying eyeshadow long enough to shudder. "Especially the bit about baiting that one guy. He gives me the creeps."

"Desmond," I mutter.

"What's his deal, anyway?" Frankie asks. "We know a little, but Jim and King won't give me access to either of your files. Or Aven's, for that matter."

"There's a file on Desmond? And *me*?" My eyes widen, and Cat grumbles as I fuck up her eyeshadow work. "Sorry," I say before closing my eyes again.

"Yes," Frankie confirms. "There are files on everyone, and I have unrestricted access to all of them, save the few I mentioned. So please, fill in the blanks."

For the next thirty minutes, I answer questions and get the girls up to speed on the Desmond situation, from how it started to where we are now. Eve and Cat keep busy with the beauty treatments, but all four women listen with their full attention. I haven't had a dish session since high school, and I'd be lying if I said it isn't making me a bit happy. No one tells you how difficult it is to make—and fucking *keep*—friends as an adult.

Once they've finished dolling me up and I've finished telling them tales, Eve passes the garment bag to me. I unzip it with glee because who doesn't love dressing up? Well, besides Frankie and Kindra. Green velvet fabric spills from the bag the moment it's open.

I hold the dress against my body, and the girls fall silent.

"It's perfect for you," Cat finally whispers.

Eve smiles. "Aven did well."

"Aven?"

"We wanted the dress to be a surprise," Kindra explains. "We didn't know what colors, cuts, and fabrics you liked best, so we went to Aven and had him pick your attire for the evening."

Frankie leans forward and runs the sleek velvet between her fingers. "It's no wonder that he knew what would look best on you. We didn't realize you two knew each other for months before the retreat."

"Enough talk. Put it on!" Cat says with a clap of her hands. "We'll turn around if you prefer privacy."

A knock at the door interrupts us, and Frankie goes to answer it.

"Give her twenty more minutes," she says. "She's just getting dressed, and then she'll be down."

Aven's voice drifts across the distance. "Ach, it's a fucking dress, not a puzzle. Twenty minutes?"

"Beauty takes time!" Cat shouts. "Go wait in the lobby with the other men. We'll keep her safe."

Aven's grumbles fade, and Frankie closes the door. "Someone's in a foul mood. What do you see in him, anyway?"

"Yeah, he's an odd choice. He was so closed off on the cruise," Eve says. "We could hardly get two words out of him."

"For starters, he's not exactly bad to look at," I say. "He's actually got a sweet side once you get to know him. Plus, as you mentioned, we knew each other before this."

The girls nod.

"Yeah, it was the same for me and Bennett," Cat says. "We were stuck together in a cabin for one night, and that was all it took. I didn't even want anyone to know I was fucking him because I was afraid they'd give me shit."

"And you were right," Kindra says with a laugh.

While I have them here, I might as well pick their brains a bit. I've been going stir-crazy, keeping all of this to myself. There are only so many times I can have a conversation with the mirror before someone calls the padded wagon.

"There's someone else, too," I say, and four very interested sets of ears practically swivel my way. "The guy who won the auction the other night. I kind of . . . liked fucking around with him."

Eve and Cat join Frankie and Kindra on the bed, and Kindra rolls her hand in the air, urging me to continue.

I raise the dress. "Shouldn't I put this on first?"

Eve snatches it from my hands and drapes it over the bed. "That dress isn't going anywhere, honey. Now give us the hot tea."

I sit on the chair and tell them about Green Guy. I leave out the bit about the cell phone and our plans to meet tonight, just in case Aven is listening, but I let them know we have plans to see each other again. The girls can't seem to get enough. Each time I have an answer, they have another question.

"He could be anyone," Frankie says. "Do you remember any tattoos or piercings? I can scour the files and figure out your secret lover's identity."

Damn, I wish I'd thought of that myself. "His dick is pierced. Right through the tip."

Cat, Kindra, and Frankie let out low moans of approval.

"Gotta put something on it to make it more appealing," Eve says with a shudder.

"Like pussy is much better to look at," I say with a laugh, and we all burst into giggles because it's true. No matter the gender, genitals are fucking weird.

Frankie checks her watch and rises to stand. "I'll scour the files and get back to you tomorrow. Until then?" She shrugs. "Just see how you feel with each of them. No need to make a snap decision now."

The other girls stand, and Eve takes my hands in hers. "No matter what, follow your heart. Whether that leads you to Aven or Green Guy, we're here for you."

"Thanks, Eve." I look at the other girls. "Thanks, all of you."

The girls leave me alone to dress. Now if my thoughts would just leave me alone, I'd be doing well.

Chapter Twenty-Six

Aven

Standing outside the lobby elevators, I wait for Quinn to come down from her tower. The other hens clucked through here about ten minutes ago. If Quinn doesn't appear soon, she can forget seeing the show. Jim waits for no one.

The numbers above the elevator stop at the top floor. That has to be Quinn. I hold my breath and count down as the numbers tick closer to the lobby level.

Five . . .

I'll need to talk to her about that kiss. There's no avoiding it now.

Four . . .

Apologize first. Come right out with it so that nothing has to be awkward.

Three . . .

Fuck me, why are my palms so sweaty?

Two . . .

Okay, she's almost here. I'll give her a quick apology and tell her it won't happen again.

One . . .

Unless she wants it to. But surely not, right?

The elevator lands with a gentle *ding*, and the doors glide open. All thought leaves my head as she steps out of the elevator and smiles up at me, dripping in that gorgeous hunter-green velvet.

"You're stunning," I say as I offer my hand.

"Aren't you glad you gave me that extra twenty minutes?"

"Ach, you didn't need it." I give her the spin I denied her when she wore the purple dress, and her grin widens. "It's a lovely color on you."

"I hear it's your favorite." She gives me a cheeky smirk and pulls me toward the others near the lobby doors.

"I never told you that."

"Oh, look. There are the girls." She releases my hand and flutters toward the group before I can press her further.

As we approach, I'm pleased to see Jim got the word out in time. All the men—aside from him and King—are dressed in black long-sleeved dress shirts and pants. It was the only way I could make Quinn's meeting with Green Guy possible. There won't be time to rush back to the resort to change into the green suit, so I needed to make sure I could at least blend in with everyone else. The long sleeves cover the tattoos, the gloves in my pocket will cover my hands, and Jim has assured me a mask will be waiting for me at the circus tent.

But instead of heading toward the circus tent, Jim explains there's been a change in plans and we'll be having dinner first. Quinn's gaze leaps to mine.

"Not to worry," King says when he spots the nervous

look in her eyes. "You and Aven will join Chef in the kitchen, and you'll monitor the preparation yourselves." He places a firm hand on her shoulder and gives it a squeeze. "We won't risk your health."

That seems to settle the girl, though it doesn't settle me. This just puts more time between now and when I get to ravage her. I was more than eager to play Green Guy and slip into the role she prefers. Now I have to spend even more torturous time looking at her in this dress when all I want to do is rip it off her.

We follow the group into the park. The sun dangles on the edge of the horizon, dancing on twilight. A full moon already hangs nearby in preparation for the night to come. Thoughts of Quinn's skin painted by that haunting glow have my blood racing already.

The night I snuck the phone into her room, I secretly stole a trophy for myself—the smutty book on her night-stand. I flipped through it a bit, and I was intrigued by one particular scene where a masked man chases his love interest through a forest before fucking her into the dirt. Quinn really seems to like these stories, and I think I might like them a little myself. They've certainly given me some ideas, and the moonlight only fuels my fire.

Jim and King lead us to Jeff's Grand Dining Hall, which is named after Jim's absentee son. The restaurant is themed after a grand castle dining room, with large wooden tables placed end to end. Wrought-iron chandeliers hang from the ceiling, providing moody lighting. As everyone else takes their seats around the tables, Quinn and I head for the kitchen.

This is nothing like the ship's pristine silver galley. Black metal and dark woods prevail here. Even the workers don black attire, so it's no shock when Chef Maurice starts screaming at me.

"Where is my lamb? I can't be expected to make a meal when my protein is nowhere to be found!" He pulls off his black chef's hat and throws it on the floor. "I can't work under these fucking conditions!"

"Hold your tits, pal," I say. "We're just here to make something for the lass to eat."

He blinks and realizes I'm not one of his do-boys. "My apologies. The pantry is that way." He points toward a large metal door. "Please don't fuck my poultry. Or fruit."

Quinn looks up at me, but I just pat the small of her back and urge her forward.

"Long story," I whisper. "I'll tell you all about it later."

We enter the pantry, and Quinn starts picking through the ingredients. When she's done, she takes them back to the kitchen and sets them in front of Chef Maurice.

"I'd like a chicken curry," she says, "but no turmeric. I'm allergic."

Chef Maurice closes his eyes, takes a deep breath, and blows it out through his nose, causing his thick mustache to wiggle. "As I told Jim, you must prepare your own dish. I don't have time."

"But I don't know how to cook," Quinn says.

"Then I suggest you learn. It's a very useful skill." With that, Chef gives us his back and returns to his hunt for the missing lamb.

I pick through the ingredients she's dropped onto the table. She's gotten some of the shit right, but I've never prepared a curry that uses sushi rice. I leave behind what she needs and take the rest back to the pantry. As I'm going through the other ingredients, she realizes what I'm doing.

"You . . . know how to cook?"

I nod. "Aye, lass. My mother worked at a pub as the head chef for most of her life. Until her death, actually."

"I'm sorry to hear she passed."

"Do you want more or less heat?" I raise some pepper options.

Quinn offers a small smile. "You don't want to talk about that, huh?"

"What? Heat levels? After the kiss, I figured you made it clear that you wanted heat levels to stay pretty low, but I figured I'd ask."

I give her a smirk and hope she'll choose the topic of her dinner over the depressing subject that is my mother's death. It's a shameful secret I keep tucked tight. After all, her death was my fault.

"You aren't getting out of this that—wait, what? What are you talking about?" She grabs my arm and spins me to face her. "What did I make clear, exactly?"

"After the kiss," I say, trying to help her remember. "Your exact words were, 'Shit, what are we doing?' Not exactly what a bloke hopes to hear after he kisses the lass he fancies."

Her jaw drops, and she starts to laugh.

"Ach, no need to pour salt into my wounds. I can't help admiring you still, but I'm keeping my lips to myself." I turn back to the shelf and lower the basmati rice to the tune of more of her laughter. "If you're just going to make fun of me, you can make the curry yourself. I'll show you where the turmeric is."

She shakes her head and grips my hands as she quiets. "No, you don't understand. When I said that, I meant we shouldn't have been kissing instead of making sure I was safe." Her hand rises to my face, and she runs her thumb along my cheek as her jovial smile shifts to something much softer. "Aven . . . I loved kissing you."

"Really?"

"Yes, you big idiot. Really." She rises onto her tiptoes and places a gentle kiss on my lips. "*Really*, really," she whispers.

"Then why'd you run off afterward? I didn't even have a chance to talk to you because you locked yourself away."

Her hands smooth the dress shirt over my chest. "The kiss was incredible, but . . . it complicates things for me. I just needed time to think."

"And did that time clear anything up for you?"

She blows out a breath and averts her gaze with a shake of her head. She looks like the weight of the universe presses her feet to the earth. I'd give anything to lift that weight and help the girl fly. Maybe as Green Guy, I can give her some peace.

I place my finger beneath her chin and lift her face to mine. "Hey . . . none of that, now. Tonight should be about having a good time. Now that we've cleared the air, nothing but smiles. No stress, yeah?"

She finally smiles again. "Yeah."

We gather a few more ingredients, then head back to the kitchen. It's empty when we return. I guess Chef found his lamb.

I set to work on Quinn's dish, but I take time to teach her how to do a few things, like how to cook the rice without turning it into risotto. By the time we've finished, I've made enough curry for four plates.

"Guess I'm not too good about estimating portion sizes," I say as we survey the large quantity of food. "I usually just cook a mess of something and eat on it until it tastes off. A bachelor's life and all that."

Quinn shrugs and dips her finger into the sauce, giving it a taste. "It's incredibly good. Maybe someone else will want some too. It smells amazing."

I know something that smells a touch better, and it's right in front of me. I lean a little closer to get a hit of that sweet vanilla scent.

"Are you . . . smelling me?" she asks.

With a scoff, I lean back. "No. That would be weird."

"Yes, you were." She spins to face me. "You were just smelling my hair, and don't try to deny it."

"Ach, maybe a little sniff. I like the way your shampoo smells."

Quinn bats her eyelashes and smiles up at me, easing my embarrassment. "It's my body spray, actually, and thanks. I put it *every*where."

"Is that so?" I step a little closer, sensing the teasing tone in her soft voice. My hands go to her hips, and I ease her into me. "Maybe you can let me follow my nose, huh?"

"Okay, Toucan Sam," she says with a giggle.

She lets out a squeal as I lift her by the waist and place her ass on the wooden prep table. If Chef Maurice were here, he'd be screaming about sanitation, but there's nothing to stop me as I step between her gorgeous thighs and kiss her.

Quinn's hands burrow through my hair. Her nails drag along my scalp and send tingles down my spine. For the first time, I feel the butterflies everyone always talks about. My abdomen quivers with expectation each time her tongue brushes against mine. The little whimpers I swallow from her needy mouth only fuel my hunger. She hardens me to the point of pain, and she hasn't even tried.

"God, I want you," she whispers against my lips.

"Aye, lass. I want you too. More than I should. More than you know."

Her hand finds my cock through the outside of my dress pants. "Oh, I know."

With a growl, I kiss her again, reveling in the way her eager hands squeeze and touch and tease me. But when her thumb grazes the piercing, I jerk my hips back with a sudden intake of breath.

"Sorry," she says. "I didn't realize you were that sensitive."

Thank fuck she didn't notice the metal ball, but now what do I do? I've started the machine, but I forgot that she can't glimpse the machine's inner workings. If she sees my piercing, she'll know the truth.

"We should probably get to dinner," I say. "If Chef catches us fooling around, he'll lose his shit and turn us into the main course."

Quinn nibbles her bottom lip and raises the slit in her skirt a little higher. I see no panty line, and my mouth begins to water.

"Maybe you have time for an appetizer?" Her hand dips beneath the velvet and comes up glistening. "Here, have a taste."

I step forward and accept her fingers into my mouth. The moment her pleasure touches my tongue, my eyes close and I let out a low groan. Quinn tastes like every fantasy I've ever conjured. She tastes like my demise.

And I welcome it with an open mouth as I drop to my knees.

My arms slip below her legs, and my hands find the small of her back. I pull her toward my waiting lips and cover her glistening cunt with my mouth. Using the tip of my tongue, I tease her from her entrance to her clit. I refuse to leave a drop behind.

Her short nails rake against my scalp, and she tips her head back with a moan as my tongue eases through her slit again. I pull one of the plump lips into my mouth and suck, which earns another sweet sound from her. It's clear that I'm not cut out for protection work. If my boss were anyone other than Jim, this would get me fired. Something tells me Jim would just give me a promotion. This is what he wanted all along.

And now, it's what I want. More than anything.

I suck her clit into my mouth, and she rocks against me with a whimper. The lass is a green goddess as I look up at her and lave that warmth between her legs. My hands run up her thighs, reveling in that blessed thickness. I close my eyes and squeeze all that skin within my hands, and my low growl rolls against something sensitive. She jerks and rocks her hips again.

"Please fuck me, Aven," she begs on a whisper. "I need you."

The lower half of my body nearly rockets me to a standing position so that I can undo my pants and give the wee lass what she's asking for, but the upper half of my body—specifically, my caveman brain—screams that we can't. That damned piercing is seriously fucking everything at this point. Everything aside from what I want it to fuck!

I dive back into her pussy and hope that my oral skills are enough to derail her train of thought, but the girl is desperate for my dick. So desperate that she grabs my head and pushes it away from my dinner.

"I was enjoying that," I say as I try to get back in there, but she holds me at bay.

"Is there a reason you don't want to have sex with me?"

she asks. "It's okay if so. I won't keep pressuring you if it's not something you want."

I shake my head and stand. "No, it's nothing like that. It's not a matter of want. Just . . . Can you give me a little more time, lass?"

"Aye, I think I can manage that."

My cock throbs when she mocks my accent. God, the lass has no idea what effect she has on me.

"But I want both of us to go to dinner satisfied," she adds. "How about a little mutual masturbation?" Her eyebrow rises as her hand dips beneath her dress again.

I rub the front of my pants. Her offer is very tempting . . .

"Okay, but we have to have our backs together," I say. That way, there's no risk of her seeing the piercing. "And we have to be quick. If Chef Maurice catches us doing this, we'll never hear the end of it. We would be the 'it's a long story' at the next retreat."

Quinn is already spinning around on the table. "Say less. I can come in thirty seconds flat with the right motivation. Just don't be shy with the dirty talk."

Shit, dirty talk? I've never done that. Most women hear me speak fewer than ten words from the time we initiate sex to the moment I give them the brush off. Now she wants me to talk during? I don't think I can.

I place my back against hers and begin undoing my pants. Thank god I've been reading that smutty book. Maybe I can use some of that in my favor.

"I can't be the only one talking dirty," I say. My cock springs free, and panic ratchets my spine straighter as the overhead lights gleam on the metal ball. "Tell me what you're doing to that perfect little pussy."

"Mmm, fuck yes," she whispers. Her back moves

against mine, followed by the sweet sounds of a woman running her fingers through a very wet slit. "Tell me what you'd do to me."

I fist my cock and start stroking. Talking is already difficult, but talking while I'm flogging myself seems damn near impossible. Still, it's what the girl wants.

"I'd have spent longer between your bonnie thighs, for one," I say. "You taste like heaven, Quinn. I want to know if it's just as sweet when you come."

She writhes against my back. Little whimpers ease out of her, encouraging me to keep going.

Closing my eyes, I jerk myself harder and faster. Pre-cum provides a little lube as I envision what it would be like to have my mouth pressed against her when she comes. I'd swallow every drop and still want more.

"Once I've made you come, I'd be more selfish with you," I continue. "Would you let me use that pussy, lass? Would you let me fuck you until I was satisfied?"

"Fuck, I'm coming," she whimpers, and that's all the answer I need.

She shudders against me, and all the little sounds and motions push me over the edge. I look around, frantic to find a towel or rag or something to deposit my nut into, but four plates of chicken curry look up at me. Come spurts out of my cock at high pressure and lands on the plate in front. I grip the edge of the table as more pours out of me, right on top of the orange sauce.

"Shit," I mutter.

Quinn slides off the table in a rustle of fabric behind me, and I scramble to shove my softening dick into my pants.

"Well, that was certainly—" She freezes when she sees the glob of semen. Her eyes widen. "Jesus Christ, dude. I don't think you'll ever be able to come down my throat. I'll fucking drown."

"Ach, it's a normal amount." I pick up the plate and move toward the trash can.

Quinn grabs my arm, stopping me from dumping the meal into the bin. "First, that is not a normal amount. That is enough to choke a fucking mule. Second, why are you throwing it out?"

I hold the plate toward her. "Did you want to eat it?"

"Um, no. But maybe we should pay Desmond back for his little gift in my dinner the other night."

I lower the plate to the prep table. "Lass, I like the way you think."

We mix the giant glob of jizz into the sauce, then set a sprig of parsley on top so that we can tell the Cum Curry apart from the others. Wouldn't want the girl to end up with the wrong dish, after all. Right as we've finished concealing our treacherous act, Chef Maurice rushes in.

"Why are you two still in here? We're ready to begin service!" He hurries toward us with a flurry of waving hands. "Out, out, *out!*"

"Wait," Quinn says. "Another guest has dietary restrictions. Can you make sure he gets this plate?"

We give him the details, and he agrees before pushing us into the dining hall. Everyone is already seated at their assigned places, so Quinn and I take our seats near Jim and the rest of our inner crew, both of us sharing secret smiles across the table. I'm pleased to see Desmond not far down. We'll get to witness the debauchery up close and in person.

Now, we wait.

Chapter Twenty-Seven

Quinn

It's a shame I'm forced to skip the appetizer and salad, but my disappointment is all but forgotten when the servers begin wheeling out the entrees. My mouth waters when the chicken curry slides in front of me, but my gaze moves to Desmond further down. My dinner will taste even better once I've watched him gobble Aven's jizz.

My heart sinks as a plate of curry is placed in front of him. He tucks right in and starts eating without question, but there is no parsley on top of his dish.

Aven catches my eye, and we share a mental question: *Where is the Cum Curry?*

There's no time to consider anything as Eve's voice punches through my mental panic. "I didn't know curry was on the menu. How do I get a plate of that?"

"It's what Aven and I prepared so that I wouldn't get sick," I say. "I'm not sure there was any left."

"And you let *him* have some?" She pops her thumb toward Desmond.

The server stops and leans closer. "There were two more plates in the back. I could bring one out for you if you'd like."

Fuck.

"I'd love that, thanks." Eve passes the lamb back to the server.

I have to find a way to deter her from eating the curry. With the gusto of a malnourished dog, I start shoveling my food into my mouth. "God, it's so spicy that I'll have to eat it fast," I say as rice tumbles out of my mouth. "I'll be shitting fire for days after this. Are you sure you want to eat it?"

"As unappetizing as you're making it look, yeah," she says.

I stop shoveling. "It's not very good."

"Hey!" Aven says. "That's my ma's recipe, and I'll have you know it's the best fucking curry I've ever tasted. And I've been to India."

"That's all I needed to hear," Eve says.

I pin Aven with a glare, and he realizes what's going on.

"This isn't my best batch, though," he mutters.

But she won't be swayed. She even claps her hands and does a happy dance when the server places the dish in front of her. Meanwhile, I'm hyperventilating because I recognize that wilted sprig of parsley on top of the plate.

The world seems to move in slow motion as Eve grips the fork and dips it into the sauce. Before she can raise the utensil to her mouth, I knock it out of her hand and pull the plate in front of me. It isn't my proudest moment, but I start shoveling rice, curry, and Aven's essence into my fucking pie hole. With my hands, no less. I'm the picture of a maniac as I moan and groan and smack like a piece of shit.

"Sorry, I lied. It's the best curry I've ever had. I just wanted a little more to myself, and I was almost done with my plate." I keep shoveling, unable to look up for fear of all the eyes on me.

The server hurries off, and I don't stop eating until Eve has another plate in front of her.

She places a protective arm around her food. "I don't like to fight, but I will where my food is concerned. Don't pull that shit again," she says.

Fuck, she's pissed. And as I look around, I realize everyone is pretty annoyed by my presence right now. I'll have to explain this to the others so that they don't hate me. I guess it's impossible to avoid being the one they talk about at the next retreat.

I want to cry as I wipe my hands on the napkin. For someone who wants nothing more than to fit in, I have a bad habit of ending up on the outside looking in.

"It's my fault," Aven says, though he only speaks loud enough for the immediate group to hear.

My head pops up. Surely he isn't about to tell them what we just did. I planned to tell the girls, but I also planned to spin it in a way that isn't quite the truth. I was going to say Aven sneezed on that one, and that's why the parsley was there. They don't need to know that he sneezed with his dick.

"We put extra hot peppers in that one. It was meant for Desmond," Aven whispers. "Quinn just didn't want you to end up shitting lava for the next few days."

Eve's anger dissipates, and she laughs. The sound eases my worry almost completely. "Why didn't you just say so? I would have eaten it anyway, but at least I wouldn't have been cussing you out in my head."

"I panicked," I say, and it's the fucking truth.

The tension eases, and everyone has a good laugh about the misunderstanding. Everyone but me. As I try to enjoy the rest of my meal, I can't stop thinking about the copious amount of sperm currently swimming in my stomach. Rationally, I know they've long stopped moving, but that doesn't stop my mind from filling with images of my entire gut filled with semen.

It wasn't that much come, Quinn. Chill.

My stomach tenses, and I gag internally. Fuck this dinner. Can we cut to the circus, please?

Then I remember what's to come, and my stomach lurches for a different reason. Now that I'm getting closer to Aven, it might be best to say goodbye to Green Guy. Hopefully, our upcoming encounter helps me make up my mind. I can't keep spreading my heart between two men, no matter how much I enjoy spreading my legs for both of them. I love reading a good Why-Choose, but I don't want to be part of one in my real life.

No, tonight I'll need to have a difficult conversation, and I'm not looking forward to it.

The lights dim in the circus tent as the first act prepares to begin. A ringmaster steps into the center ring and tips his top hat toward us. As he straightens, I realize it's Jim. He raises his arm, and Kenny flies to him from offstage.

"Welcome, welcome," Jim says into a glittering silver microphone.

Kenny flies off his arm with a loud squawk and returns to the offstage area.

"That's probably best," Jim says with a laugh. "We're about helping the animals, not causing more trauma. But speaking of trauma, who wants to see someone get their bones broken?"

The crowd cheers, and even Aven claps his hands.

"Then look no further than the Slaughter Park circus, where the only way to earn a spot on our staff roster is to survive the show!"

Jim spreads his arms as two flame towers explode behind him in a show of sparks and heat. Loud organ music blares through the speakers as staff scurry around and set up a trapeze act behind him. He walks in front of them as they work, telling us all about what we'll see tonight: death-inducing acts versus death-defying acts. He also explains that anyone who survives will be offered a position at his animal sanctuary on Devil Horn Island, where they can remain for the rest of their days, paying penance for the abuses they've enacted.

I'm a bit disheartened to hear this, as I don't believe any of these people deserve a second chance, but then I see that the staff aren't wheeling a safety net into the ring. They're wheeling in a bed of spikes.

"Oh, this is going to get bloody," Aven whispers. "Maybe we should have sat in the splash zone."

"We can probably arrange a splash zone of a different variety this evening," I whisper back. "That's if you have anything left in the tank."

The low growl he offers goes right between my legs.

Speaking of the space between my legs, it's seeing more attention than it has in a long time. Well, from other people. Again, plural, and that's what's making me feel like a complete slut. I just rubbed one out with Aven, and now I'm planning to fuck Green Guy. I shouldn't also be planning to screw with Aven *again* on the same night.

But that's exactly what I'm thinking of doing.

If I can fuck them both, I can make a decision. After that, it's all smooth sailing. No more worrying that I'm cheating. No more difficult conversations. Just sex with a man who makes me feel something.

Man. Singular.

Jim's voice pulls me back to the event as he motions toward the trapeze and regales us with facts about dizzying heights and the survivability of landing on those spikes. I'm pleased to learn they'll suffer for quite a while, but that death is all but certain.

The spotlight clicks off, and a dark silence falls over the tent. The moment is broken when the cries of the terrified Cattle break through. Seconds later, the spotlight clicks on, and "Stars and Stripes Forever" drowns out the whimpering.

Jim is no longer in the ring, and two Cattle stand on either side of the towering platforms overheard—two women and two men. Glittery yellow leotards brand them all. One of the men steps forward and grips the trapeze with quivering hands as he inches to the edge of the platform.

I start clapping to the beat, and I'm thrilled when the girls join in. Before long, the excitement spreads, and everyone is clapping with glee.

The Cattle screams and steps off. I expect him to swing, and I think he expected that too, because he looks shocked as his grip slips. Down he goes. A metal spike drives straight through his abdomen, skewering him in place.

Up above, the remaining Cattle try to scramble down the ladders. The fire pyres blast off again, right beneath them, and all three scramble upward again. A brief argument ensues before a gunshot snaps them back to their senses.

"Remember the animals? Now you're in their shoes.

Your only chance to survive is to perform," Jim's voice booms through the speakers. "Any other option is certain death."

The remaining man on the platform grips the trapeze again. He says something to the woman behind him, and she nods. With that, he steps off the platform.

This man maintains his grip and swings fully to the other side. He yells something at the woman on the opposite platform as his feet level with her face, but she shakes her head and takes a step back. On the second swing, this repeats. On the third swing, he catches her platform with his feet and manages to remain steady enough to stay standing. Without releasing the trapeze, he plants his foot in her chest and sends her to the ground.

We stand and cheer as she screams the entire way down. She misses the spikes, but her head cracks open like a water balloon when it smacks against the sawdust-covered concrete.

"Clean up on aisle seven," Ice Pick yells, and we all laugh.

Everyone quiets again. The man on the platform is yelling something to the woman on the other side. She nods, unlike the other women, and I don't blame her. If I just watched a man kick someone to their death, I'd nod at whatever he said too. Then he steps off the platform and glides her way.

The woman reaches out and snags his feet. It almost looks like they're going to make it, that he'll be able to deposit her on the second platform, but whoever designed this trapeze didn't have very good depth perception. They realize the mistake too late, and the woman's back slams into the platform. The sudden, jarring stop snatches both down, and the Cattle land on the spikes with a crunch of bone.

King lets out a low whistle behind me. "The bastard took it right to the head."

I sit a little taller and look into the spikes. Sure enough, a single spike drove straight through one ear and out the other.

"At least we know the last thing that went through his mind," I say. "The spike."

Everyone has a good laugh at this, but my smile begins to fade as I realize the first act is coming to a close. It's almost time for me to make my exit.

"I need to use the bathroom," I whisper to Aven.

He nods and rises to stand with me, but I place my hand on his arm.

"I've got it," I say. "If anything tries to grab me, I'll scream."

He looks around, spots Desmond a few benches away, then nods. "All right, lass. Don't be long."

"I won't . . ."

. . . be back anytime soon, and don't come looking for me.

There is entirely too much shit to figure out, and I won't be able to do that if Aven interrupts my process. Namely, fucking another man to see how it makes me feel, but still. It's my process.

I get to my feet and hurry toward the exit as fast as my little kitten heels can carry me. At least Aven chose shoes that are easier to run in than stilettos. I can put plenty of space between me and this tent, and I'll be with Green Guy before he even knows I'm missing.

As I hurry into the evening air, I pull the phone from my clutch. There's already a text from Green Guy.

Exit the park and wait for me at the head of
the garden path.

The garden path? That isn't what we discussed, but I guess the change in timing forced him to adjust his plans. With a shrug of my shoulders, I head that way.

A blanket of unease falls over me as I walk, and I rub my arms to chase away the feeling. Some people enjoy liminal spaces, but I find them wholly discomforting. Places like this should be alive with people, not filled with dark, empty silence. The only sounds I hear are my heels clacking against the asphalt.

I peer around as I get the feeling that I'm being watched. Of course no one is watching me. Everyone is tucked inside that tent, and I'm already at the park gates.

Gary gives me a wave as I pass the final security checkpoint and exit the park. I wave back and take a little comfort from the bright lights and his gentle smile. It doesn't last after I walk a little further and thrust myself back into darkness.

When the path branches, I stop and wait. There's a bench nearby, but I'm too nervous to sit. Part of it is the excitement, but the other part is more akin to dread. It feels like I'm making a bigger deal out of this than I should, but it's turned into a big deal. I didn't make this happen. It just . . . happened.

Footsteps shuffle nearby, and I turn and find a man standing in the path. His frame blocks out the light from the tiki torch behind him, casting him in an ominous glow. I take a step toward him and expect him to do the same. When he doesn't, my blood runs cold.

"Green Guy?" I ask. I take a step back when he doesn't answer. "You're scaring me."

His head cocks to the side.

"Okay, now you're *really* scaring me."

The phone vibrates in my clutch, and I snatch it out and

read the text. It's a single word, but that's all it takes to stop my heart.

Run

In a blind panic, I turn away from the figure and take off. Green Guy couldn't have been the one to send that text if he was also that man, because that man was standing right in front of me. I couldn't see if he had anything in his hands, but they were clearly at his sides. That is *not* proper texting form.

That can only mean one thing. The man chasing me is Desmond, and Green Guy is trying to warn me.

Ferns and palm branches slap me in the face as I run. And that's fair. If anyone is going to punish me for being an absolute moron and following my pussy instead of my brain, why not Mother Nature? Granted, it's her fault I'm in this situation. Hormones will make a bitch do crazy things.

I dare to glance behind me, but I wish I hadn't. It's like a horror movie. He moves at a walking pace, yet he remains hot on my heels. Damn my short legs! Damn them to absolute hell!

I kick off the heels and pick up speed. When I glance back again, I no longer see him. That doesn't mean he isn't watching, though, so I keep running. Only once I get a stitch in my side do I stop and tuck myself in the foliage so that I can catch my breath.

Seconds later, a gloved hand clamps over my mouth and silences my scream.

Aven

The tiny purse buzzes at the girl's side, but she's too panicked to feel it. I clutch her squirming body against mine and try to think of a way to show her it's *me* without showing her it's *me*. I pull the phone from my pocket and shove it into her face.

Her green eyes widen, then focus. She relaxes against me.

I grip her tighter, asking if she's good now, and she nods. I let her go.

Without missing a beat, she starts pummeling my chest with her wee fists. She's so cute when she's mad.

"I thought you were my stalker! I thought you were trying to warn me that he was after me!"

I shake my head and type out another text.

> I'm going to chase you like one of those men in your books.

Seconds pass before the phone buzzes in her hand. Jim's rigged cell service is far from reliable, and the shitty signal takes ages longer than it should to reach her device.

Realization dawns as she reads it, and she smacks her forehead. "Oh my gosh. You were just trying to help me fulfill a fantasy."

I nod enthusiastically, and the black hockey mask nearly slides off my head.

"What happened to the signature green?"

I type another reply.

> I did the best I could with what I had on hand.

Quinn circles me, appraising me from every angle, and I'm melting under her scrutiny. Does she notice anything that reminds her of *Aven*? You know, the person I actually am? But she doesn't seem to make the connection as she stops in front of me.

"I mean, I'm not complaining. We just might have to change your name." She sighs. "Then again, after tonight, you may not see me again. Come have a seat on the bench. We need to talk."

She's about to break up with me so that she can be with me. How fucked is this? I should just stop everything right now and tell her the truth. Then she can be with me without any guilt.

Or she could decide you're a piece of shit, and then you'll never see her again.

Aye, there's that.

Fuck, this is why I don't do lies and secrets. It's too fucking complicated.

I join her on the bench, but I don't take her hands in

mine. The lass needs my strength, but that's an Aven thing to do, and I don't want to confuse her more than I have. Without anything to do, her hands begin fidgeting with her dress. It's killing me.

"I really like spending time with you," she begins. "Well, fucking you."

I almost laugh, but I bite my tongue.

"It's just not enough, though. I don't even know what you look like, and while I don't care, it's still hard to imagine things with you when I can't imagine you."

I respond via text.

It's complicated.

She reads the message and offers a humorless laugh. "This is what I mean. We can't even have a conversation." She shakes her head and lowers the phone. "Meanwhile, the man I can talk to and look at doesn't want to touch me. Or rather, he doesn't want *me* to touch *him*. Why can't the two of you compare notes?"

I wrap my arm around her before she can start to cry. What a godforsaken mess I've created.

"Worst of all, I still want to fuck you," she mutters. "Does that make me a bad person?"

I snatch up the phone and type as fast as my fingers can fly.

One last time for old time's sake?

I can't help it. I'm a monster, and she's the only thing that soothes the beast.

She laughs when she reads the message, and the sound

lightens my heart. "That's the whole problem. I don't want it to be the last time."

As she looks up at me, I know that I have to tell her the truth. There is no more room to run. After I fuck her senseless, I'll get a good night's sleep and break the news to her in the morning.

Run

She laughs again and shows me the phone. "Oh look, you sent it twice."

I stare at her and cock my head.

"Oh shit," she breathes. A grin slides onto her face. "You're serious?"

I nod.

As she jumps from the bench and takes off, she's more like a giddy lass than a woman running for her life. She's all smiles and squeals. No matter. I like my prey willing when it's her.

I give her a good head start before I rise and start the hunt. It's easy enough to follow her at first, but I soon lose the trail. When the path branches in three directions, I'm left scratching my head as I peer into the trees.

A flash of blonde hair disappears into the foliage. My quarry has gone off the trail, it seems, so I follow suit. Branches crack under my weight, and I push forward as glimpses of her spur me on. She's smiling still, but that smile will fade soon enough. I pull a blade from my hip and wave it at her the next time she turns around.

Just as I expected, her smile drops. "Oh, shit," she mutters before colliding with a tree. "We didn't discuss weapons!"

She knows the safeword. If she's smart, she'll use it. I won't stop unless she does.

Panic grips her in a chokehold as she rights herself and takes off again. I worry about her poor feet, but the ground is mostly leaf litter through here. She's choosing the easier way through. Unfortunately for her, it's even easier for those of us with shoes, and I'm on her in the next few seconds.

I band my arm around her waist, pinning her arms at her sides. In two flicks of my wrist, I've separated those elegant straps from the dress. The top falls away, exposing her breasts. I want nothing more than to lower my mouth and devour those perfectly pink nipples, but the damned mask prevents so much.

My hand moves to her mouth. She struggles and screams against the glove as I drag the dull end of the blade against her cheek. Her eyes close, and tears pop from the corners. I snatch my hand away from her mouth, terrified I've genuinely hurt her, but she's smiling behind my gloved grip. Confused, I hold her at arm's length and cock my masked head.

"What are you doing?" she belts. "Consensual non-consent . . . If I'm uncomfortable, I'll say the safeword. Now fucking use me!"

I step into her and grab her hair in a firm hold, snatching back her head.

"That's more like it," she says through gritted teeth.

I spin her around and pin her against a tree. She resumes the fight, but when I ram my knee between her thighs and force her to spread those pretty legs, she grips the trunk and steadies herself. The wee lass thinks I'm just going to have my way with her and be done.

Not even close.

I drop to my knees behind her and raise the dress. Moonlight catches on the curve of her full ass, and I'd give anything to drag my tongue up that glowing line.

I mean, she is facing away from me.

Fuck it. I raise the mask enough to expose my mouth, then drop my lips to her plump cheek. Smooth skin runs under my tongue, but it's not enough. My teeth sink down in a painful bite that I can't help.

Quinn clutches the bark tighter and sucks air through her teeth. I swirl my tongue over the bite to ease the sting, and she relaxes. When I bite again, she tenses. It's a glorious game of push and pull, and we'll both win in the end. I'll make sure of it.

Gripping her ass, I raise her hips just a bit to give me access to her dripping cunt. The son of a bitch is practically weeping with need, and I have just what it craves. I raise the blade and run the dull end through her slit.

Realizing the danger, Quinn sucks in another breath and holds it. Her pussy quivers as I flip the knife around and force the handle inside her. It's only three inches, but it's enough to have her standing on tiptoe and letting out a whimper.

Good lass. Let me have my way.

I watch as her pussy grips the handle with each pass I make. My tongue slides out to catch a bit of her excitement as it slips down the blade, and metallic essence coats my mouth. Ma always said it was a bad idea to lick knives, but frosting is easier to say no to than Quinn's pleasure. I'd thrust my tongue into a drawer full of knives if it meant getting a taste of her.

When I've had enough, I pull the handle from her and push my mouth to the source. She tries to step away, but I slide under her and wrap my arms around her thighs to prevent her from going anywhere. With my back against the tree trunk, she's locked in place.

I pull down, urging her to sit fully on my face. I want to drown in her. She refuses, as most women do, likely because she thinks she's too big. Here is a fun fact for all women. We dinnae care! Please suffocate us. The thicker the thighs, the sweeter the demise.

"Fuck, I'm going to come," she whimpers, and I immediately pull away. She grips my head and pulls it back toward her pussy. "What are you doing? I said I was about to come!"

I lower the mask, slide out from under her, and grip her hair again. The men in those books don't typically cater to the woman's needs. They're selfish and wanton with their passion, so that's what I'll give her tonight. She grunts as I force her to look forward again, but she understands what's happening when I start to raise her dress. She tries to help, but I take her hands and place them on the tree. When she pulls them away, I slap her ass and put them back where I want them.

"That's not a good way to get me to do what you want," she says with a cheeky smirk as she pulls her hands away again.

This brat.

I smack her ass again, then pull out the blade. When she spots it, she puts her hands back on the tree.

Good fucking lass. Stay just like that.

I position myself behind her and press my erection against her entrance. A long, low moan rolls from her mouth with every inch that slowly enters her. When I've fully soaked my length, I pull back and give her more force with the next thrust. Maybe too much, because her head bumps against the tree. I ease back to give her more room to adjust, and I nearly stumble over a fucking rock.

These things didn't happen in the book.

But I won't be deterred. I'm determined to give Quinn the fantasy fucking of her dreams if it's the last thing I do.

I move my grip to her hips and push forward. This time, she angles so that her shoulder braces against the tree, giving me the freedom to fuck her however I want. My pelvis slaps against her ass as I pick up speed—the only sound, apart from our heavy breathing and her occasional whimpers.

When I'm about to come, I pull out of her and spin her around. The dress is in tatters, yet she looks like a wild forest goddess. She looks like she badly needs to be kissed, too.

I raise a gloved hand and cover her eyes. Realizing what I want, she brushes my hand to the side and closes her eyes herself. I lift the mask enough to expose my mouth so that I can kiss her.

Our mouths meet with equal hunger. Her hands wind around my waist and pull me closer, and I grind myself against her. She reaches between us and grips my girth, moaning into my mouth, and I have to be inside her again. I don't care if I fill her immediately.

I lower the mask and step back enough to bend and get my arms beneath her thighs. I stand and brace her back against the tree as I lower her onto me. Her hands weave behind my neck, and she looks into my eyes as I bounce her on my cock. Each time she slams down, I grind upward to give her all of me and tease her swollen clit.

Loud music blares from somewhere nearby, and Iron Tiger roars across the tracks in the distance. The circus show must be over, meaning we're running out of time. In just a few minutes, anyone could wander down one of the nearby paths and spot us.

Quinn's head tips back as she lets out the most animalistic moan I've ever heard. Heartbeats squeeze my throbbing cock as she comes, and I release inside her. As my heat fills her, the cries rise until she's practically screaming. Our pleasure realized, we collapse in a breathless heap at the base of the tree.

"That . . . was incredible," Quinn pants as she lies back. "Oh my god, I never knew it could be like this."

I give her a thumbs-up, because same.

She grows quiet, and I turn my head to check on her. I expect to see her basking in the glow of one hell of an orgasm, but she just looks sad. I sit up and place a hand on her thigh, and she turns to look at me.

"Sorry, just in my head," she says with a wan smile. "Well, I guess this is goodbye."

Jesus, she looks like she's about to cry. I have to do something to make her feel better. Maybe if she thinks I'll pine after her, it will help. I grab the phone.

> Doesn't have to be goodbye. We could still sneak around.

> I really like you, Quinn.

I expect her to wave me off and say this is the way it has to be so that I can slink to my room and forget I ever pretended to be someone else. Is that what happens? No. Of course not. My last name is still Slade, after all.

"I really like you too, but I can't sneak around. That's not who I am." Quinn covers her face and groans. "This was supposed to be the fucking solution. Why is it just more complicated now?"

I place my hand on her arm, but voices in the distance snag her attention, and our heads turn toward them.

"Shit, I have to get back to my room before the others see me." She presses the top of her dress to her chest as she gathers her clutch with the other. "I'll text you," she shouts over her shoulder. "Either way, I'll see you again!"

"Aye, lass. You will," I whisper into the mask. But she might not want to. Tomorrow, I'm ending this, once and for all.

Chapter Twenty-Nine

Quinn

The next morning, I skip breakfast and the activities afterward. My nerves are shot, and I don't want to see anyone at the moment. Not even Aven or Green Guy. Maybe them least of all.

Neither of them seems to be struggling with this. Aven knows I've fooled around with Green Guy, and Green Guy knows I have feelings for Aven in spite of trying to deny them. Everyone is copacetic. Everyone but me.

What is wrong with me? Why are loyalty and monogamy so important? It's not like I'm trying to marry either of these men. Shit, in a few days, I'll still be crying over them while they're off on the next adventure. Is this really the life I want to live? It certainly wouldn't make my mother very proud.

Now *there* was a woman who never chased a man. She always said, *"Quinn, if you have to chase him, he probably doesn't have anything worth catching."* And then she'd go down the long list of STDs and their symptoms, which was meant to deter me from promiscuity. It didn't work, but I'd give anything to sit through another one of her lectures.

I've never missed her more than I do right now. What I would give to ask her advice.

The decision certainly isn't easy, and I can't keep straddling the fence. Last night with Green Guy was incredible. The sex was something I've never experienced, and it only made me question my decision more. Sex isn't everything in a relationship, but it matters to me. I couldn't attach myself to a man who wasn't good in bed, regardless of how much I enjoy everything else about him. Which is why I can't just strap a saddle on Aven and ride into the sunset.

Maybe that's the solution to all of my problems. If I can fuck Aven, I'll have all the input I need to make a decision.

I hurry to dress and get my face to a more presentable state. The messy hair can't be helped, but I run a brush through the loose waves anyway. When I've done what I can, I take a steeling breath and step into the hallway.

Aven's door is just across the way, but it feels like a journey as I step closer and raise my fist to knock. He's been trying to get me out of my room all morning, and I wouldn't even talk to him. Now I'm about to sexually assault him.

As soon as his door opens, I leap into his arms before I can change my mind again. He catches me and kisses me as he closes the door behind us with his back. He tries to say something, but I'm sick of talking. I need the other thing.

I lower my legs to the floor, then start unfastening his khaki shorts before he can argue. His massive hands block my fingers at every turn.

"Just let it happen," I squeal as I swat his hands away.

"Ach, what's going on? You won't talk to me all day, and now you're trying to jimmy your way into my giblets?" He turns and plasters his front half to the wall. "Unhand me, woman!"

I won't be deterred. I slam my chest against his back and worm my hands toward his waistband. But like a fucking snake, he slithers away, leaps over the bed, and holds his hands out as he stares at me with wild eyes.

"Stay back, witch!" He forms a ward against evil with his fingers. "You have no power here."

I grumble and step closer to the bed. "I don't want to *hurt* you. I just want to *fuck* you. Now give me your cock!"

I leap over the bed and grab his shorts, bringing them with me to the ground. You'd think he's hiding a fucking bomb in those things with the way he hops over me and dashes for the closet. By the time I've pulled myself from the floor, he's already dressed again.

"Did you buy an entire Target worth of khaki shorts? How many pairs do you have in there?"

"What's gotten into you, lass?" He runs his hands through his hair and tries to catch his breath.

I sit on the edge of the bed and pull a pillow into my lap. "Aven, I'm losing my mind."

"Aye, that much is clear." The bed sinks when he sits beside me. "Not sure how my dick will help you find it, but maybe we can seek another solution."

"Is it me?"

"Is what you?"

When I shift on the bed to face him, he gets to his feet. I roll my eyes and pat the bed.

"Sit down. I won't maul you anymore."

He doesn't take his dark eyes off me as he gingerly sits again. "Okay, let's try this again, but with words this time."

"Can you explain why you're so averse to fucking me?" I come right out with it. I'm sick of beating around the bush.

"It's just really confusing when you kiss me and touch me, yet you won't let me go any further."

He nods and runs his hands through his hair again. "Lass, there's something we need to talk about before we take that step."

"Oh my god, you're fucking married, aren't you?" I jump to my feet and start pacing. "It makes so much sense! A hot guy in his late thirties who's also single?" I stop pacing and look at the ceiling. "I've been the other woman!"

"What? No!" He grabs my hand and pulls me back to the bed. "Ach, it's nothing like that. Stop writing stories in your head." He eases me into his arms, and I can feel the truth in his words.

"So if it isn't another woman, what's the hold up?"

"I just . . . I can't be with you in that way until—"

"The other man in my life is gone?" I sigh. "I figured you wouldn't be interested in sharing me."

He opens his mouth to argue, but I place a kiss on his lips.

"No, I understand. You don't have to say anything. I'm being too pushy, and I have no right. I mean, you've been understanding enough, and I haven't even considered that you might not want to double dip."

"You aren't an inanimate object, lass," he whispers. "Don't think of yourself like a pot of food on a party table. You're a woman. A beautiful, witty, infuriating woman. While I don't like to share, I like degrading someone I respect even less, so no, I don't think of it as 'double dipping.' I won't say the other man isn't a problem, though, and that's what I want to talk about."

My heart shatters in my chest. "Aven, I can't make this decision without all of the information."

"Jesus fuck, would you stop talking and just listen to me for a moment? I'm trying to—"

"No, this isn't fair to you. You're right. If I can't make this decision without fucking you, then it just reduces *you* to an inanimate object." I shake my head and stand, disgusted with myself. "I'm sorry I even came over here now."

"Lass, that's not what I was saying. Just sit—"

I hurry to the door, embarrassed. I should have just stayed in my room. What a mess. As I rush into the hall, I bump right into Frankie and Maverick.

Aven's footsteps sound behind me, and his door clicks open, but I don't turn to look at him. I'm too ashamed. I fear that if I look at him, I'll burst into tears and everyone will know how stupid I am. Instead, I turn my attention to the couple and pray Frankie saves me somehow.

"Don't you two look cute," I say. "Where are you headed?"

Maverick tips his black ball cap at me. "I'm headed to the pool to have a soda with Ice Pick, and Frankie is headed to the room to do something for work."

I turn to Frankie. "Mind if I tag along?"

"Not at all," she says with a welcoming smile. "Though, I don't know how interesting it will be. I just have to make a note in a file."

Aven clears his throat behind me, and the other two give him their attention. I continue to give him my back, still too embarrassed about what just occurred.

"Didn't you want to finish our conversation first?" he asks behind me.

I shake my head. "Nah, we can talk later. But you've given me a lot to think about."

Frankie reads between the lines and grabs my hand. "She'll be safe with me, Aven." He tries to debate, but she gives him a wave, and we shuffle off. "We'll be fine, and I'll bring her back in one piece," she calls over her shoulder

"Thank you," I whisper.

Frankie smirks. "Don't thank me yet. You aren't off the hook until you tell me everything."

"Trouble in paradise has never been so orgasmic," Frankie says as she punches some inputs into the simulator's keyboard. "Now let's see if this baby can help you more than the idiotic men can."

Trying the simulator was Frankie's idea. After I told her all the sordid details, she figured the machine might have some input that we lacked. She even put in a call to King and had him and Jim scramble the security feeds so that Aven wouldn't see us sneaking down here. The last thing we need is an interruption when we're doing serious scientific work.

"All right, now go get in the chair so that we can see what it will be like when Aven fucks you," she says.

See? Serious scientific work.

I hurry to the egg chair. As soon as my ass hits the cushion, the chair starts its slow journey forward. Gripping the sides, I wait for the screen to come to life. Aven and I appear seconds later.

"I just have to remove the limiter," Frankie says through the speakers.

"Limiter?"

"Yeah. It seems not even Sim Aven is down to fuck. I'll just have to reprogram that part with a manual override, and then . . . that should do it."

"Will Sim Aven fuck anything else?"

"Let me check." A few minutes pass. "With the limiter active, he refuses to fuck anything. Without it, he fucks you, his hand, and even a pillow with a hole cut in it. He's not very picky." The keys click. "Wait . . . I take that back. You're the *only* woman he'll fuck without the limiter."

I smile and preen under this revelation. That is, until she comes back on the mic.

"I think we broke it when we removed the limiter."

"Fuck it. Run the sim!"

I don't care if it's broken. All I need to see is if he can make me come as hard as Green Guy can. If I have that answer, I can finally end my torture.

Sim Aven and Sim Quinn come to life on the screen. We plan to run the same scenario twice with both men. We're in a bedroom—Frankie chose the cruise cabins from their last retreat, as she assured me it was impossible not to fall in love there—and Sim Aven is currently kissing me. As Sim Quinn's hands unfasten his pants, I hold my breath and wait for the moment he tells her to stop.

But he doesn't. Sim Aven just groans into her mouth, encouraging her to keep going. Jim will need to clean the egg chair after this. Nothing is hotter than hearing a man hungry for a woman, and my panties are soaked.

"It's working," I say to Frankie, but then Sim Quinn pulls his cock from his pants, and the fantasy falls apart. "Why is it blurry? Who the fuck is censoring the sim?"

"The Chinese? I don't know!" Frankie taps on the keys, but the blurry box remains. "I can't get it to render his dick. The sim keeps saying I don't have clearance."

"When I was twelve, I watched scrambled porn on the Spice channel in hopes of seeing my first dick. Not even *that* was as infuriating as this!"

Frankie laughs into the mic. "Want me to try to start it over?"

"No. Just let it run. I'll use my imagination."

The speakers go silent, and the scene continues. By the end, Sim Quinn is thoroughly satisfied.

"I don't think a blurry censor box would leave my legs shaking like that, but okay," I mutter.

"Sorry it wasn't what you wanted," Frankie says. "It was still pretty hot, though, not gonna lie. When he picked you up and tossed you on the bed when he wanted to go from doggy to missionary . . . whew, girl."

"Yeah, that was pretty hot, wasn't it?"

"Ready for the next?"

I nod and settle into my seat as the simulation resets, this time showing Sim Quinn and Sim Green Guy.

"Does he really wear that atrocious unitard?" Frankie asks with a laugh. "And you can't decide which man you want?"

"He didn't have it on last night, but yes and yes," I say, though I'm laughing too. "You'd have to be there, girl."

"No thanks."

But our laughter tapers off abruptly as the sim starts again. From the kissing to the way he tosses me on the bed to change positions, the events play out identically. Granted, his dick isn't blurred, but that gives me no new information anyway.

"Yeah, I think we fucked it up when we removed the limiter," Frankie says. "Want to try a different setting?"

I nibble my lip and think. "Yeah, maybe one we're both familiar with. Put us in the rooms at the hotel. Run Sim Green Guy first."

Frankie gives the okay, and a few minutes later, a new chain of events unfolds. I pay closer attention this time.

They kiss, he chokes her, she rides him until she comes, and then she sucks him off.

This really has turned into a scientific experiment. I'm no longer even remotely horny.

"Ready for the next one?" Frankie asks.

"Run it."

Aven and Quinn kiss . . . He chokes her . . . She rides him . . .

Damn, damn, damn!

"Oh shit," Frankie says, but before I can ask her what's wrong, Aven bursts through the door.

I leap out of the egg chair. On the massive screen, Sim Aven and Sim Quinn fuck at a breakneck speed. My head turns toward the booth, where Frankie frantically mashes buttons. Now the sim characters fuck in reverse. It's almost worse now. Fabulous.

"Ach, you hens just use this machine for your sick whims! Perverts, the lot of you!" Aven reaches behind the machine and yanks the plug from the wall, casting the room in darkness. "If you wanted to see my bleeding dick that badly, you should have asked!"

Frankie raises a finger. "Is the bleeding the reason you don't want her to see it?"

"And I did ask!" I shout.

Aven turns and points at me. "You. My room. Right now. We're having this out once and for all."

I don't know whether to be scared or excited, but when he shouts for me to move my feet, I realize I will find out soon enough. Not even Frankie can save me now. She gives me a sheepish wave as I trot along behind Aven, prepared to learn my fate.

Chapter Thirty

Aven

Trying to do the right thing has never been more difficult, but my secrecy is driving the girl insane, and the insanity is catching. It's time to stop trying and start doing. It's time to rip off the bandage and let the wound do what it will. Whether it heals or festers, no matter. It needs light and air.

Aye, I could use some air myself.

I usher Quinn into my room and head for the floor-to-ceiling window. I can't open the damned thing, but maybe seeing the sky will help me feel less closed in. My back has never felt more against the wall, even when it's been against the wall in the most literal sense.

I turn to face the lass. She looks like the cat who ate the canary, and she *should* feel some shame. If she'd stopped yammering over me earlier, we could have handled this before my sexploits were plastered all over the sim screen for Frankie's eyes. We could have broken up three hours ago and ended this nightmare for us both.

251

Because that's the only way this can end. I finished reading the stupid romance book last night, and the moment the male lead told the woman the truth, she took off. He gets her back in the end, but this isn't a book and Quinn isn't a character. She's a woman with feelings and a heart I've likely broken with my lies.

"Sit on the bed," I say.

She nibbles her lip and does as she's told. "We weren't using it for porn," she whispers, and I almost laugh.

"All this fuss, just so that you can see my cock and learn if I know how to fuck."

"Sex is an important part of a relationship," she mumbles.

"Aye, but so is trust."

Her head jerks up. "I wasn't hiding anything from you. You know about Green Guy, and he knows—"

"Ach, that's not what I mean, lass."

"Why do I get the feeling you're about to break up with me?" She finally looks up at me, and the hurt in her eyes nearly breaks me.

"That's not it."

"Then what is it?" She looks at the carpet again.

I search for the words, but they won't come. Why is this so hard? "Quinn, there are parts of me you haven't seen, and—"

"So let me see them! Are you worried you're too small?" She eyes my crotch. "Too big?" Her gaze falls to the carpet again.

Fuck, I have to do something. She's spiraling.

"Lass, eyes on me."

Her eyes move to my face.

"The other part of me," I whisper as I grip my belt. "The part I haven't shown you."

Her parted lips close as her gaze drifts to my crotch. Her wee fingers grip the comforter tighter with each notch the belt slides past. As I unfasten the button and lower the fly, I realize I'm not even hard. Granted, the piercing is the important part, but I don't want to embarrass myself by flinging my flaccid penis at her.

I close my eyes and remember the way she looked last night. With all that moonlight on her skin. So delicate. So soft. I recall the way her breasts bounced so close to my hungry mouth. The mental visions do the job, and I stiffen in seconds.

"Holy shit," Quinn breathes. "Size is definitely not a concern."

"Lass . . ."

"I mean, maybe you were concerned I'd think it's too big, but you've seen what I do with those monster dildos."

"Lass . . ."

"Does it curve or something?"

"Quinn."

She looks up at me. "I really don't mind if it does," she whispers, and damn her for making me smile again.

I suppose one final happy memory doesn't hurt anything.

I reach forward and take her hands in mine. "What I'm about to show you might make you question everything you know about me. If you have questions, I want to answer them. Just please—"

"Aven, you're scaring me."

"I'm not trying to scare you. I'm just falling for you, Quinn, and I can't keep going until you know everything."

"Is it herpes? Oh god, it's herpes, isn't it?"

Before she spirals any further, and before I lose courage, I lower my boxers and expose my stiff cock, piercing and all.

Her gaze immediately falls to the shiny silver ball—the one part of myself I was unable to hide from her as Green Guy.

Quinn's eyes widen, and she covers her mouth as she scoots backward on the bed. Realization dawns in her eyes, and I brace myself, fully prepared for her to cuss me out.

"Oh my god. I can't fucking believe it."

I tuck my dick back in my boxers because now is not the time. "I'm sorry. I should have told you sooner or not done it at all."

"What? Are you kidding? Not get your dick pierced? I haven't slept with a single pierced man in all my life, yet in the span of a few days, I've bagged *two* of them? What are the fucking odds?"

"No, Quinn. It's me."

She looks me up and down. "Yeah, I know it's you. Why would you hide that from me? I'm not afraid of a dick piercing. I've learned that I'm the opposite of afraid of them."

"Lass. I'm Green Guy." I pull the phone from my pocket and wiggle it in front of her face. "It's been me the whole time. From the first night until now. It's always been me."

Quinn shakes her head. "No. No. No fucking way." She reaches into her pocket and pulls out her hidden phone. She taps out a message and hits send. "See? Your phone didn't do anything. You're not him."

"Lass, it's me. The service for these things is shit. That's why you got the message to run so long after I'd sent it last night." The phone buzzes in my hand. "See?"

Those details strike the mark, but it's still not enough. She snatches the phone from my hand and looks between the two. All of our messages are there.

"Holy shit," she breathes. Her skin has gone sickeningly pale. "What the actual fuck."

"Quinn, I'm sorry."

"Holy shit." She grabs a pillow from the bed, and I tense, certain she's about to leap on me and start denying me air. I'd let her. I fucking deserve it. But she doesn't do that. She just places the pillow over her face and lies back. "Holy fucking shit!"

Her voice is muffled, but I understand it all the same.

I take a step back as the lass lets out a scream and kicks her legs. Aye, I deserve that.

"You are a piece of shit!" she screams into the fabric.

Aye, I deserve that one too.

But when she pulls the pillow away and screams the next sentence, my heart actually breaks. "I fucking hate you, Aven Slade!"

So why is she smiling?

Chapter Thirty-One

Quinn

I toss the pillow away from me and leap into his arms. "Oh, you big, wonderful jackass!" I pepper his face with kisses as I feel lighter than I have in days. "I can't believe it. Is it really you?"

But instead of sharing my joy, Aven scrapes me off him and deposits me on the bed as he looks at me, bewildered. "Lass, are you even listening? I've lied to you. I pretended to be someone else, and I slept with you without your knowledge."

I raise my hand and count the points on my fingers. "You were deceptive for good reason. I can only imagine you were trying to protect me from Desmond. And I didn't care who was behind the green suit."

He shakes his head, still unable to process my reaction. He moves to the bedside table and pulls a familiar book from the drawer.

"Hey, I didn't know you were into smut. That's a really good one."

He looks from me to the book. "This is yours. I took it from your room the night I left the phone in there. That's how I got the idea to chase you."

His confusion clicks into place, and I realize what sort of reaction he expected.

"Aven . . . Clancy raped Charlotte's twin sister when she was in a coma. That's why it was so hard for her to forgive him for his lies. You haven't done anything wrong. If anything, I'm relieved the indecision is finally over." I stand and step into him, and my tension relaxes when he doesn't back away. "Making the choice between the two of you was killing me, and now I don't have to choose."

He licks his lips. "So . . . you aren't going to tell me you never want to see me again?"

"On the contrary," I say with a grin. "This was the best possible outcome. If anything, I'd like to see more of you."

He takes my hands in his and gives them a squeeze. "If you ever want to see me, just open your bonnie eyes, lass. I won't leave your side again."

His warm hands cup my face and draw me in for a kiss. The world tilts on its axis as two fantasies meld into one incredible moment. Things I valued in two men have combined within one incredible man that I don't want to say goodbye to at the end of this retreat.

"Whatever this is between us . . . it's real, isn't it?" I whisper against his lips. "I'm not just imagining it or writing stories in my head?"

"Aye, lass. It's real." He squeezes my hands and places a kiss on my forehead. "For better or worse, I've fallen for you completely. I fought it at every turn until I couldn't anymore."

I laugh when I remember that first meeting with Green

Guy and how nervous he was. "You really did try your best to be a good boy."

He lowers his mouth to my neck and gives it a nip.

"I like it when you're bad, though," I say. "Go a little lower."

His tongue cuts a path through goosebumps on my skin, and he squeezes the swell of my breast. "How low?"

With a smirk, I push the top of his head until he's on his knees. "About there should do it."

He reaches up and lowers my shorts, painting my thighs with more of those kisses as he works his way between my legs. His finger snakes beneath my panties and slides through my slit.

"I love what a mess you are, lass. So fucking wet." He puts his finger into his mouth and sucks it clean with a low growl. "Fuck, that's good."

I brace my back against the wall and step out of my shorts. My fingers run through his dark hair, pulling him closer to that needy part of me. I raise my leg and place it over his shoulder as he slides my panties to the side.

His tongue hits my clit, and I'm so hot down there that his mouth almost feels cold. The temperature difference makes every pass of his tongue more pronounced, and my toes curl as my eyes roll to the back of my head. This feels incredible. It's less about rushing my orgasm and more about making me feel good. And it's working. The slow tempo of each hungry lick of his tongue, each thirsty slurp of my sweetness—he's delaying my pleasure in the most delicious way.

With deliberate care, he eases two thick fingers inside me. They press against that hidden place each time he curls them forward. His lips wrap around my clit with gentle suction, and my legs nearly give out.

"Let's get you to the bed, lass." He stands and lifts me into his powerful arms, then deposits me on the mattress. My panties fall away as he drags them off and tosses them to the side of the bed. "Won't be needing these."

When his mouth drops to my pussy again, I tip my head back and sigh. Most men get down there and just start slobbering away, licking everything but what they're supposed to. Not Aven. His tongue finds my clit with every gentle pass, and his fingers keep massaging, coaxing me closer to pleasure.

The orgasm creeps so slowly that I don't realize it's happening. Warmth builds in my stomach. Instead of being slammed by hot, crashing waves, I'm bathed in them.

"Aven, I'm coming," I whisper.

My thighs quiver, and I grip the comforter as my teeth clamp together. I'm grateful for the steady pressure he keeps inside me while continuing to bathe the sensitive nub with gentle attention. The whisper of an orgasm grows to a shout, and I moan through each pulse of pleasure rushing through me.

Finally, I quiet, absolutely exhausted despite only lying here and getting eaten.

"I'll never tire of that sound," he says as he wipes his chin and smirks up at me. "Let's have another go, lass."

While I'd love nothing more than to lie here while he gives me orgasm after orgasm, I should really be thinking about work. I've all but abandoned my streaming services in favor of fulfilling my own fantasies, but when this retreat ends, I'll still have bills to pay.

I pat the bed beside me. "Let's have a chat instead."

"Ach, I never was much good at talking, but I guess I'll need to learn." He shuffles up the bed and lies beside me. "What would you like to chat about, lass?"

When he's reclined against the pillows, I pull a blanket over my bare lap and rest my head on his chest. Despite his cool demeanor, his heart hammers like a woodpecker against my ear.

"This . . . whatever this is—"

"Relationship," he says.

I settle against him with a smile. "This *relationship* . . . Is it something you'd want to explore outside of the retreat?"

"Outside the retreat, inside the retreat—so long as I'm exploring you, I can't be bothered with the location."

"Aven, I'm serious." I smack his chest, which earns a light chuckle from him. "I haven't been in a committed relationship since I tried college. Once I realized being a cam girl was my calling, I seemed to only attract men who wanted me to give it up."

"Ah, I see. You're worried I might want you to abandon your job so I can keep you barefoot and pregnant."

"Maybe not that."

"Or that I might be a little too possessive of you, which would make your job more difficult."

Yeah, that one.

His hand searches for mine, and I slide it into his. He gives it a squeeze. "I'll not do anything of the sort, lass. I'm possessive as they come, that much is true, but if being a cam girl is your dream, I'll support it."

"Well, I wouldn't say it was my dream."

"What would you say was your dream, then?"

I nibble my lip and sit up. "Promise you won't laugh?"

"No."

With a roll of my eyes, I reach across him and grab the book from the nightstand. "This. This is my dream."

His eyebrow rises. "You want me to rape your comatose

sister? No thanks, pal. I cannae be party to that fantasy. I'll murder whoever you please, but I draw the line at raping, even for you."

"No, you idiot. I want to be a writer." I lower the book. "Well . . . *wanted* to be a writer. It only took one professor in college to tell me to keep my day job. I shelved the dream and decided to go into teaching, which was out as soon as I realized flashing my snatch earns more money than educating young minds."

Aven sighs and pulls me against his chest again. "I know a little about shelved dreams myself." He grows quiet for a long time, but then he finally says, "I guess it's time you heard the tale of the Edinburgh Dragon."

Chapter Thirty-Two

Aven

I cuddle the girl against me, needing her support. She doesn't know it, but I've never spoken of this to anyone. Only my da knows, and it's why we've not spoken in the twenty years I've been in America. But if I want the lass to choose me, to really choose me, she has to know it all.

"As the tale goes, a massive dragon once terrorized the cities of Scotland. The great winged beast left destruction wherever he went. Farms were razed, herds of livestock slaughtered and devoured, and in his greed, the dragon only wanted more. Nothing could sate the creature."

"Shit, maybe you should be the writer," she says.

I smile and hold her closer. "When he finally landed to rest, so great was his exhaustion and so full was his belly that he never rose again. The earth grew around him and formed Arthur's Seat in Edinburgh."

"And you admire that?"

"Aye, I do. Because he stopped, lass. Because he knew when enough was enough, and he stopped."

"That's not how I see it."

"Tell me how it looks through those bonnie green eyes, then."

"It wasn't a choice. He stopped because his actions had consequences. If he hadn't been so bogged down with a belly full of sheep and cows, he might have had the energy to keep fucking shit up. It's a lesson in knowing when to stop, but you've gotten the ending all mixed up."

"Yeah? Well, here's another tale for you. Let's see what you make of this one." I run my hands through her golden hair and take a deep breath. "There was a dragon of another sort in Scotland. Just like the last, he was a mean one. Brandishing a fiery ax, he raised hell from one side of the land to the other. Aside from his ma and da, he cared for no one."

"Did this dragon kill the livestock and set the town on fire?"

I close my eyes. "Aye, in a way. He was hungry, and he fed himself until he was full. But it wasn't enough. He wanted more and more, and when he eventually looked behind him, nothing was left."

"I don't know how your mother died, Aven, but it wasn't your fault."

The lass is smarter than she realizes. Maybe she'd make a good writer after all. She certainly has this plot figured out.

"I'm not like the others, Quinn. I'm not content with killing hostages. I want to hunt, and I'm not particular about my prey." I close my eyes. "I almost wish I had your scruples. Then I wouldn't have been cast out of my homeland."

Quinn sighs and straddles my waist, which forces me to

open my eyes. I don't want to miss a second of her on top of me. "What makes you think I have scruples?" she asks.

"I just assumed, I guess. Then again, you didn't exactly waste any time when you killed the woman in the log flume." I smile when I recall the way she strangled her. "You knew she'd hurt animals, but you didn't have much more than the color of her jumpsuit. Most women struggle to make the kill without the inciting rage. Cat and Frankie did, anyway."

"Well, I'm not Cat and Frankie. And let's not forget who my father is."

I haven't forgotten, though I've tried not to think of it. The allergy discrepancy still eats away at me.

"So it doesn't bother you that I kill indiscriminately, and it doesn't bother me that you want to be a cam girl." I run my hands up her sides. "Sounds to me like we've gotten it all sorted."

"Not quite," she says, and a knowing look softens her face. "What happened to your mother, Aven?"

Memories flood my chest until I can't breathe. I look up at the ceiling, unable to hold Quinn's green gaze for a moment longer. Sensing my unease, the lass lies on my chest and strokes my hair. She doesn't push. She just waits for me to continue.

So I do.

"I started young, pretty much at puberty. My mother caught on quickly, and she did her best to steer me to greener fields, but as I said, I was hungry. The risks I took were increasingly ridiculous, but I thought I was untouchable. I can't even look fondly on the kills of my youth because I'm so ashamed. Not of the killing, but of the disregard for someone I cared for deeply."

"Your mother may not have been pleased to learn her

kid was a serial killer, but I'm sure she still loved you. And I know she knew how much you loved her." Quinn sits up on her elbows so that she can look me in the eye. "You don't doubt that, do you?"

I shake my head and manage a smile. "No, lass, I don't doubt my ma's love for a second. It was that love that cost her in the end, though. I didn't escape capture for all those years because I was careful. I escaped because, unbeknownst to me, my mother was shuffling behind me with a mop and bucket to clean up all the messes I'd made. Before long, most of our town knew the truth, that she was harboring a sicko, but no one could prove a damn thing."

"What did your father think?"

"I can't be sure. He was a man of few words before her death, but when he lost her, he refused to speak to me again. He blamed me, and he was right to. It still hurt when he called me a bastard, fatherless child, as if he could just erase me by denying his part in my creation."

"I still don't understand how it was your fault." Quinn drops down against my chest again. "You're leaving something out."

Aye, I am. The hardest part is usually the easiest to leave out.

Part of it is the fear of what she'll think of me. If my own flesh and blood couldn't stomach the sight of me after all was said and done, how can I expect the lass to stick around? But the only way out is through, and the decision is for Quinn to make.

As she relaxes against me again, I find the strength to tell the last of it. "One night, she asked me to stop. Point blank, just like that. 'Give it up, Aven,' she'd begged, but I wouldn't. I went out that very night, snatched up the first bloke I spotted on an evening walk, and brought him back to an abandoned mill near Grudie. Fields stretched out on all sides, and a herd of cattle often grazed in the distance. I could hear them lowing at night. It was one of my favorite places to kill."

"Because of the seclusion?"

"That, but the acoustics in the old mill were heavenly. The screams, lass." I hug her against my chest. "Ach, you had to be there."

"Maybe you could take me there one day," she says, and my heart shatters.

"I would if I could, but I cannae go back. You see, lass, I wasn't the only dragon in Scotland. There are many, all lurking in the shadows. And one night, I happened upon one on his evening walk, and I made a grave mistake."

"Oh shit," she breathes. "Was he a mafia boss or something? I've read about those."

I almost chuckle at her comparison, but the weight of the situation won't allow it. That heaviness presses down on my lungs, refusing to allow laughter to escape. You think I'd be used to it after living with it well into my late thirties, but no. That weight just presses down.

"Something similar," I say. "The head of an underground organization, so, close enough. I didn't care. Even when he told me what his people would do, that they'd avenge him in the most final way, I just laughed in his face and kept cutting off fingers to hear him scream. The bastard was ancient, but he put up a fight. Lasted for ten rounds with my ax before he finally shit his pants and died."

Quinn's arms tighten their hold around me. "And his people made good on his promise."

"They burned the pub to the ground while my mother was inside. She was identified via dental records. The fate

I'd bestowed on so many other grieving families had become my own."

"So why can't you go back?" She sits up again. "The pieces of shit got their pound of flesh. Isn't it settled?"

"Not even close. The man had a son, and he wasn't satisfied with simply killing my ma. He demanded I leave Scotland immediately and said I wasn't to return until I had the money to make good on what I'd taken from him. If I come back before I've paid him off, he'll kill my da and make it so that I can't so much as scratch my balls without the local government hearing about it."

"So why not take him out?"

Now I do laugh. "This isn't a romance novel, lass. I don't have a magic gun that grants a satisfying conclusion to any of this. For starters, I don't know anything about him. All communications were done via letters attached to burning rocks thrown through my bedroom window."

"Then how are you supposed to pay him?"

"He's moved to email now. I get one each year around Christmas."

"What a jolly fucking asshole," she mutters. "So how much do you need? I don't have much in savings, but once Jim pays me—"

"Absolutely fucking not!" I sit up on my elbows, but Quinn pushes my back to the mattress with one finger.

"Why not? You've been protecting me for weeks, and I've lost count of how many orgasms you've given me. You deserve a little compensation. And I want to help you."

I pull her face closer so that I can kiss her. The lass is an angel, but I won't accept her money.

"No, and that's final. Besides, Jim's paying me well after this, so I might have enough to make a dent in what I owe. Maybe I can take you to see Scotland eventually."

That earns a smile as I ease her off my lap.

"Now, I want you to get dressed," I say. "I've got a surprise waiting for you in the park."

I pat her ass as she hurries off to the closet. But instead of feeling relieved that I've told her everything, I can't help but feel the loss of my mother all over again. Maybe what I have planned for Quinn can brighten my mood.

Chapter Thirty-Three

Quinn

Aven leads me into a section of the park that's themed after the 1950s. Shops and restaurants line the strip of "street," making it look like a small town. A few classic cars even sit in front of a working diner. Further down the stretch of road, a couple of flat rides—a zipper and a carousel—have been set up like an old-school fair. As we draw closer, I even spot a fun house and . . .

"Please tell me we can eat funnel cake. And ride The Tunnel of Love!" I release Aven's hand and run to the massive pink heart that serves as the entrance. "I've always wanted to ride one of these, but I've never seen one in person. Look! They even have the swan boats!"

Aven grins and wraps his arms around my waist when he reaches me. "Lass, you can ride whatever your wee heart desires as soon as I've shown you your surprise. If you're good, I'll even chase you through the fun house after that."

I roll my eyes. "When am I not good?"

"Though . . . I suppose we could indulge in a little appetizer before the main course," he says. "You know, because you're such a good girl."

I shimmy my ass and move toward the small stand off to the side of the zipper ride. I go to the front to place an order, but Aven shakes his head and motions for me to go to the side entrance.

"We'll prepare it ourselves to make sure there's no funny business," he says, and we step inside.

Once he's kicked the staff out of the tiny kitchen, he sets to work. He tosses out the batter that's been sitting out for god knows how long and starts to prepare some from scratch.

"More of your mother's teaching?" I ask as I peer over his shoulder.

He nods and dumps the ingredients into the bowl. "Aye, she loved making funnel cakes. The little church in town held a bazaar each spring, and she'd set up a stand and sell sweets to the wee ones. I helped her a time or two."

I dip my finger into the bowl, and he studies me as I bring a glob of batter to my lips. My nose scrunches when the taste assaults my tongue. "Blech, what the fuck is that? That doesn't taste like funnel cake."

"It hasn't been cooked yet. The grease and heat will change the taste."

"No, I think it's missing something."

"Oh yeah? What's that, Betty Crocker? Sushi rice?"

I swat his arm as I get an idea. "No, but that special curry wasn't half bad. Maybe you should add a little of *that* to the mix."

"Okay. I'll just whip a little hairnet over my short and curlies and we'll be right as rain." He shakes his head with a laugh and goes back to stirring.

I step in behind him and wind my arms around his waist, going right for his junk. He growls as I grip him through his shorts.

"You're serious?"

"I am."

"Filthy little lass," he says with a smirk. "I think I'd rather try funnel cake of a different flavor, though. Drop those shorts."

My eyes widen. "I realize I have a tiny bladder, and I'm fine with it being the butt of some jokes, but I'm not pissing in my funnel cake, Aven."

"What? No! No piss. Ach, come here." He bands his arm around my waist and pulls me in front of him, wedging me between his firm body and the prep table. "Hand me the rubber spatula and drop your shorts."

I do as he asks and hand the utensil to him before disrobing below the waist. He picks me up and places my bare ass on the prep table, then places the bowl in my lap.

"Hand that piping bag to me." He motions with his fingers, and I slide it into his palm.

"What do you plan to do with that?"

He smirks and begins filling the bag with the spatula.

"Aven?"

He twists off the end of the bag, then secures it with a knot. "Spread those thick thighs for me."

"Um, no. You're not squirting fucking cake batter on my pussy, dude. Not happening."

"Wasn't a question, lass. Spread your legs and have a little more faith in me."

I can only hope I don't end up with a yeast infection after whatever he's planning. My legs spread, and his hands go to work between them. But instead of squirting the batter all over me, he maneuvers the thick plastic until it's inside me. Only the pointed tip sticks out.

"Okay, now what?" I ask. "I'm one sneeze away from making a fucking mess."

Instead of answering me, he starts positioning me how he wants me. I lie back, putting my ass dangerously close to the fryer. It's a wonder that I fit on this narrow counter, but I'm doing it. I feel more like a Sunday dinner than a sex symbol, though.

"Relax your thighs," he says, and when I do, he nods and lets out a deep growl. "Beautiful. Now let's get that batter into the oil."

Before I can say no, he grabs a pair of scissors and snips the tip of the bag. A spurt of batter squirts out and lands in the grease with a hiss. His fingers move toward my clit, and he rubs the sensitive nub with a slow, firm pressure.

My pussy clenches, and more batter jets into the grease.

"Oh, fucking lovely," he breathes. "Come for me, Quinn."

The smell of deep-fried dough drifts toward me, and damn me for getting more turned on. I can't help it. Funnel cake is my weakness.

The circles tighten, and the pressure increases. He drops his mouth to my chest, nipping my tightened nipple through my shirt. My back rocks on the cold metal, and the grease hisses again as I give it another offering. Within less than a minute, I've achieved lift off and damn near started a fucking grease fire with the high-pressure hose that is my vaginal canal.

When I'm fully spent, he eases the nearly empty bag out of me. He places it on the table and goes to remove the clumps of dough from the fryer.

"Doesn't look very pretty," I say as I eye what can only

be described as a disaster. Instead of the usual swirled pattern, it's literally just rods of crispy dough.

"No matter," he says as he sprinkles a little powdered sugar on top. "It'll taste amazing."

I go to take the plate from him, but he pulls it away.

"Wait just a tick. It's still hot for one, and it's missing the special ingredient." Much to my chagrin, he snags the baggy from the counter and places it beside the plate. "There. Now we have a dip."

"Fucking gross," I say with a wrinkle of my nose.

But he isn't joking. He plucks up a rod, then bounces it between his fingers before dragging it over the bag and popping it into his mouth. His eyes close, and he hums. "Damn, that's nice."

I forgo the special dip, but I give the rods a taste, and I'm shocked to find it's the best funnel cake I've ever had, even if it isn't the prettiest.

Our little side quest accomplished, we tidy up and return the food stand to the staff. Aven's hand finds the small of my back, and he guides me toward the diner I spotted. As we step inside, we're greeted by the smell of greasy food and the smile of a waitress in a pink uniform.

"Welcome to Jim's," the cooks yell from the kitchen.

The waitress steps forward and holds two menus toward us, but Aven waves her off.

"We aren't here to eat," he says, and the waitress nods.

"Follow me."

We're taken to a swinging door that looks like it leads into the kitchen, but when the waitress punches a few numbers into the keypad, then opens the door, I see a dark cement hallway lined with pipes.

"Y'all have fun," the waitress says with a smack of her

gum and a crinkle of her nose. "Your little friend sure as hell won't."

Her laughter cuts off completely as the door closes behind us. I peer up at Aven.

"Soundproofing," he says.

"And the *little friend* she spoke of? Does she mean Desmond?"

"Not yet, lass, but soon. That's what we're preparing you for."

"We?"

He huffs and urges me forward. "You know, if you stopped asking questions and started walking, you'd have all the answers you need."

Okay, fair. I hurry toward the metal door at the end of the hall. Excitement pings within me, and I'm a bundle of anticipation as I wait for him to use his key card to let us inside. His muscles tense as he grunts and swings the slab of metal open, revealing a square concrete room. A single bulb hangs from the ceiling, right above an empty wooden chair with leather straps on the arms and legs. Weaponry and tools of all kinds line the back wall.

King and Jim stand beside another door built into the right wall. As we enter, they give us a wave and come closer.

"Ready to practice your interrogation techniques?" King asks.

I smile up at Aven. "Really? You set this up for me?"

"*I* sure did," Jim says. "Had the team work through the night to build this room just for you."

"Well, it was my idea," Aven says.

"And my capital," Jim adds with a raised finger.

King looks between them. "Yes, you both did a bang-up job. You can yank your dicks over it later. For now, the young lady needs to meet her victim."

"Ah, yes," Jim says. "Gary, bring him in!"

The door behind them opens, and Gary leads a man by a metal collar fastened to his neck. When the man sees the chair, he balks, but Gary gives the chain a sharp yank and pulls him forward.

"I think you should start with his teeth, same as those lemurs he abused," Gary says as he shoves the man into the chair.

Jim laughs and rocks on his heels. "Gary, is someone getting a little taste for blood?"

Gary's eyes widen, and his jowls quiver as he shakes his head. "Not me, boss. I still don't have the stomach for it. This asshole needs to pay, though."

"This is Brickle," Aven says to me. "He's the jackoff we were talking about before. Think you can get him to tell us where those lemurs are?"

I look at the weapons against the far wall. "Yeah, I think I can."

"That's my cue to exit stage left," Gary says with a laugh. He hurries out of the room before I get started.

All eyes turn to me, including Brickle's. His lips haven't been glued or sewn shut, yet he remains silent and stoic. He tries to intimidate me with his glare, and I hate to admit it's kind of working.

"I like it better when they're scared," I mutter.

King steps behind me and places his hands on my shoulders. With a firm but gentle touch, he guides me a step closer. "Look at him. Not at what he wants you to see, but at what he's trying to hide. He wants to appear unbothered, but see how his hands grip the chair?"

Brickle's fingers relax, but not before I notice what King wanted me to see. He was clinging to that wood with everything he had.

"It's an act," King continues. "When you corner a spider, it may rear back and display its fangs, but that's not because it's brave. It knows the boot is coming, dear girl. It's sore afraid."

I look again, and he's right. The unbroken eye contact is this man's attempt to seem unbothered, but it's so intense that it can't be real. He doesn't scream or plead, but his eyes aren't the eyes of an unaffected man. There's fear there, even if it's buried beneath a whole lot of posturing.

I nod and step out of King's hold as I inch closer to Brickle. Gary strapped his ankles to the thick legs underneath the chair, so I have no fear of a kick as I kneel in front of him and look up.

"Where did you put them, Brickle?" I ask. "This doesn't have to be difficult."

He looks away from me. Using my femininity is out, then.

"Okay, difficult is fine with me." I stand and stroll to the wall of weapons. A chainsaw catches my eye, so I pull it off the wall. With a smirk, I turn toward the chair. "This would be so messy and fun, but too quick, right?"

Aven, Jim, and King nod in agreement.

"Entirely too quick, dear girl," King says. "And you want to be fair. Give the man a chance to walk away with at least some of his limbs still intact. That has to be the reward for giving us the information we want."

"Don't be silly," I say with a playful roll of my eyes. "Someone I admire once told me that death is the reward here."

The men chuckle at this. Well, not Brickle. He just starts breathing a little harder.

"As much as I'd love to stay and watch, I'm afraid King and I have other engagements," Jim says as he and King head for the door. "Enjoy your first taste of torture, and don't forget to lock up when you're done."

The duo leaves, and I return to the wall of goodies. Aven joins me, and together, we decide the hammer is the simplest place to start.

"Start slow," he says. "Ask a question and then give him a chance to make the right choice. If he doesn't, swing away."

I nod and step closer to Brickle. "Where did you hide the lemurs?"

He notices me eyeing his fingers, so he pulls them into fists.

"Last chance, asshole. Where are they?"

He remains silent, so I raise the hammer and drop it on his knee. His body jerks in the chair, and he lets out a guttural shout as his hands clasp and unclasp.

"Why do you give a shit?" he screams. "They're fucking monkeys!"

"They're prosimians, you moron!" I raise the hammer and bring it down on his other knee. Over his yelps, I shout, "And they matter more than your stupid ass!"

"Take out his eyes," Aven says, and the man's screams shut off as if he flipped a switch. "Aye, that's the ticket. Grab the melon baller and pop them right out. See if he can think a little more clearly with one fewer sense to distract him."

I grab the melon baller from the table and bring it closer to the man. He's begun to sweat, but his lips remain sealed. Pain isn't going to move him to tell us anything.

"I've got a better idea," I say to Aven as I drop the melon baller to the floor. Not all torture comes in the form of violence, after all. "Come here."

Aven joins me in front of the man, and I snuggle up to

my Scottish dream. I nuzzle his chest and let out a low whimper. He just looks down at me, confused.

"You want to fuck in front of him?" His eyebrow rises. "I don't think that's going to get him to tell us anything."

I give him the most performative pout I can muster. "Just cuddle me," I say in a baby voice. "I'm scared of the big woller coaster."

"Oh, fuck no," the man whispers as he finally starts straining against the straps. "Not this. Anything but this."

Aven catches on and joins the bit. "Is baby terrified? Does baby need daddy to snuggle his little pwincess?"

I nod up at him, my Scottish Cringe Lord, and he pulls me against him. For the next few minutes, we pretend to be an annoying couple standing in line for a ride. It's the most torturous thing I've ever had to witness, so I can only hope it will push Brickle to the brink of madness. We baby talk and comfort each other as loudly as possible until Brickle finally lets out another scream.

"Nine-two-nine Wester Drive," he says. "They're in Texas. Just make it fucking stop!"

I stand on tiptoe and place a kiss on Aven's nose. "Thanks, *daddy*," I whisper with a giggle before I skip straight over to Brickle and raise the hammer again. "Any last words, asshole?"

"They said you should be fair!" he screams.

"When it's their turn to torture someone, they can extend grace if they'd like, but I'm fresh out."

I bring the hammer down on his skull. The first blow sends his eyes looking in two different directions, but he doesn't die. He just starts sort of jerking like the chair has been electrified. After two more blows, he finally stills.

As I drop the hammer at my side with a satisfied sigh,

Aven steps into me. Pulling me close, he looks down and smiles. "You're so feral, lass. I fucking love it."

With a growl, he drops his mouth to my neck and cleans away the blood spray with his tongue. I tip my head to the side to give him more access. My eyes close, and I wrap my arms around his neck.

"I wish it had lasted longer. I should have saved that move for the finish," I say.

"You're already an ace at torture. Just look how you torture *me*." He takes my hand and lowers it to his crotch. His stiff cock fills my hand through his pants. "Now how about that fun house?"

"It'll have to wait," a voice says through an overhead speaker, and Aven and I jump apart and look skyward. "Sorry, forgot to mention that we installed cameras and mics. Hope that's okay."

"Jim?" Aven says.

"And King," a British voice says. "We've got a problem. We need both of you to meet us in Jim's room. ASAP."

Chapter Thirty-Four

Aven

As Quinn and I board the swan boat, the mood is decidedly different from this afternoon. Gone are the easy smiles and laughter. Instead of getting flirty and crawling all over me, her hands sit still in her lap. Her green eyes look at the ride attendant as he checks the seatbelt over our laps, but she doesn't really see him. She's miles away.

I wrap my arm around her shoulder and pull her closer. "Hey, it'll be okay, lass. Let's worry about Desmond when we need to, yeah?"

She nods and tries to smile, but I stop the attendant from sending the swan boat into the tunnel.

"Give us a sec," I say, and he nods and steps away.

Water drifts under the boat and gently splashes against the sides of the tunnel as it continues into the darkness. I firm my hold on her and bring her closer. She doesn't protest. She just slides over until she's pressed against my side. Her head drops against my shoulder, and her hands find mine. I give them a squeeze.

"They'll find him. Jim has cameras everywhere." I kiss the top of her head. "Just stick with me until they do."

"Will you stay in my room tonight?" she asks.

I smile against her hair. "Aye, I've already had it taken care of. When we get back to the room, my things will have been moved over. Jim saw to it."

That relaxes her a bit, and she squeezes back. "It wasn't as scary when I felt like we had the control, but now that he's gone missing, I'm terrified. He could be anywhere."

When we met with Jim and King, they didn't pull any punches. Desmond isn't in his room, and the last footage they have is of him boarding the gondola that takes park-goers from one side of the property to the other. The footage showed his ride vehicle arriving at the second station, but it was empty. Jim didn't have any cameras stationed along the track, so there's no way to know when or how he exited.

Worst of all, Jim reiterated that we aren't to take him out if we find him. He still hasn't broken the cardinal rule in a way we can prove, and until he does, we can't kill him. Not without becoming complete outcasts.

But what Jim doesn't know is that I overheard King speaking candidly to him before they realized I'd arrived at their door. It was only two sentences, but they left me with too many questions.

"He isn't to kill him, and neither is the girl. The right is mine, and I'll be damned if I'll be robbed of it again."

I shake my head and sigh. "There's more to this than they're telling us, lass. If they've been hunting Desmond all these years, why haven't they taken him out? Why did they need to keep using you as bait?"

"They need something else from him, I guess. Something we're unaware of. And until they have it, they don't want to kill him. I just hope it doesn't end up costing my life."

My heart shatters when I consider a world without Quinn in it. I've never been happier to be annoyed by a wee lass in my life, and I cannae let that go now. "That'll never happen. I won't allow it. As long as Desmond draws breath, I won't leave your side. He can't hurt you if he can't reach you."

She offers a weak smile and squeezes my hands. "Let's just try to enjoy ourselves and forget about him for a bit."

I call for the attendant, and he sets the ride in motion. This one is much gentler than the log flumes, and there's no murder activity to take my focus away from Quinn. I'm just able to enjoy her amusement as we float into an enchanted scene and soft, romantic music plays overhead.

"Oh, Aven," she breathes. "It's so beautiful."

Aye, even I have to admit it's pretty incredible. Purple lighting casts a faux weeping willow in a romantic glow as we pass beneath its drooping branches, which have been shaped into a sort of tunnel entrance. As we pass into the next scene, however, a record scratches, and the music changes from gentle and romantic to playful and fast.

"Fucking Jim," Quinn mutters. "Can we not even have a romantic boat ride? It sounds like he produced this shit on his iPhone."

"Aye, he fucks around with that Garage Band app all the fucking time. That bird of his loves it."

The tunnel opens up, and we float through a picnic scene. Two animatronic figures—a young man and woman —sit on a blanket by a large basket filled with food. They're dressed in fifties attire, which well suits the theming for the area, though the music is more like something out of the eighties. Their heads rock from side to side with the playful beat as a large bipedal rabbit hops into the scene and begins to sing.

Two animatronic birds descend from the ceiling, each of them holding a butcher knife in their scaly feet. They sway to the beat, then swoop down and slice open the animatronic throats. The robotic heads tip back, and blood jets over us as we jerk back in shock.

"What the fuck kind of love tunnel is this shit?" Quinn says with a laugh. "I fucking love it."

The boat jerks forward again, and the song continues its refrain behind us, with the happy animals occasionally belting, "At the picnic!" as we depart.

The merry tune gets a bit softer. This time we're stopped in front of a drive-in theater. We can only see the shadows of two figures in the car, but it's easy enough to figure out what they're doing. The car rocks with their efforts as two animatronics—a smiling hot dog and a dancing popcorn bucket—bounce into the fray. The music picks up again, and they begin to sing.

"What the fuck is even happening?" Quinn says with a laugh.

Both the popcorn and the hot dog brandish knives and start stabbing into the windows as they croon the next part with unrestrained glee. More blood sprays out and splatters over our skin, but when I look down, I realize it's just warm water. The lighting makes it look red.

"I'm going to have this idiotic tune stuck in my brain for eons after this," I groan.

Quinn gives me jazz hands as the boat lurches forward again. "At the drive-in."

"Ach, don't you start."

The next scene is more of the same, this time featuring a

couple getting engaged by the very stream we sail down. Just as the animatronic man gets down on one knee, a pair of sentient garden gnomes appear from the bushes and start singing about how great love is down by the river. Then they pull out machetes and lop off the heads of the man and woman. It shouldn't be romantic, but somehow, it is.

Just knowing that Quinn and I share this secret sickness the forest creatures sing about is enough to make my heart swell.

The ride floats beneath another purple willow, and we're back at the station. I exit the swan boat first, then help Quinn onto the platform. We exit the ride and squint into the fading afternoon sun.

"Well, that was an experience," she says. "It certainly wasn't what I expected."

"No, but it was good fun."

"At the picnic," she sings, then skips ahead a few steps. As she spins to look at me, I can't help but pinch myself. She's a fucking dream.

I don't know what I've done in my sorry life to deserve a gift such as her, but I sure hope I've done enough to keep her forever. I want her to get on my last nerve for the rest of my natural life. Maybe the next as well. What a life we'll have in Scotland if I can only get us there.

"Wait up," I say as she skips toward the fun house.

She looks over her shoulder with a flirty smile, the trouble with our missing stalker all but forgotten. "Catch me if you can, Scotland Yard."

And with that, she darts into the building.

I don't run to catch up with her. The wee thing needs a head start, and I'm going to allow her that. When I catch her, however, I won't allow much of anything other than whimpers as I make her come. I'll pin her down and—

"Looking for someone?"

The hairs on my neck rise as Desmond's voice reaches my ears. I turn toward him. He's standing a few feet away beside a drink stand, clutching a lemonade in his hand. With a smirk, he draws the straw into his mouth and sucks some of the tart liquid down his throat. He smacks his lips and smiles at me.

Footsteps pound nearby, and Jim and King round the corner at a sprint. When they spot me standing a few feet from Desmond, they come to a halt. The men look between us, then come closer.

"Desmond, there you are," King says with a forced smile. "We've been wondering where you'd got off to."

The man runs his hand through his dark hair, and sunshine glints off the gray running through his sideburns. "You caught me. I spotted something on the gondola ride and wanted a closer look. Didn't mean to raise the alarm."

"No alarm raised," Jim says. "I just prefer to keep a constant head count. We lost one of our own at the Sinners Retreat one summer, and I don't want to go through that headache again."

Desmond clucks his tongue. "Such a shame. Did you ever catch the bloke who did it?"

Bloke? Since when do American men use the term *bloke?*

King seems to catch the slip as well, and we share a look as Jim brushes right past it.

"No, we never did catch the man who killed Eighties, and we likely never will. Water under the bridge, but not a river I'd like to float down again." Jim rocks on his heels with his hands behind his back. "Will you be joining us this evening for the fireworks show? I've had it specially arranged to mimic the same array the park used in its heyday."

"You don't say . . . I wouldn't want to miss it, then." A sparkle glints in Desmond's eye as he turns to me. "You and Quinn will be there as well?"

I nod once.

"Sounds like a party," Desmond says. He tips his lemonade toward King and Jim. "Sorry to worry you men. I saw what I needed to see, though, so you won't have to worry about me disappearing again. See you tonight."

He strolls off, sipping his lemonade and looking around at the park as if he has a right to. Fucking idiot.

Quinn pops out of the fun house. She looks irritated until she spots King and Jim. Worry replaces the agitated furrow of her brow, and she hurries over to us.

"What's going on? Did you find him?" she asks.

"No, he found me," I say. "The asshole popped up when I was about to join you."

"We know where he is now, though," Jim says, "so there's no need to worry. Go and have your fun, and we'll all have a big surprise tonight at the fireworks show."

I turn to Jim. "What are you planning, old man? And why don't I have a good feeling about it?"

King shakes his head and walks off, and that only reinforces the rising feeling that Jim has something dastardly up his sleeve.

"All things in good time, my boy." He laughs, then hurries to join King.

"I don't like the sound of this," Quinn mutters, and I'm inclined to agree.

But I have better things in mind at the moment.

I give her ass a firm pat. "You'd best get back in that fun house. I was trying to give you a chance to get away. You don't want to know what I'll do to you if I catch you in there."

"Or maybe I do?" She nibbles her lip and takes off again.

This time, not even Desmond will deter me from having a bit of fun.

Chapter Thirty-Five

Aven

A large tunnel rotates in front of me, and I'm dizzy before I ever step into the damned thing. At least the lass isn't here to see me fall on my ass. The walls drag me upward, and I scramble out before the spinning walls dump me onto my face. On the other side of the suspension bridge in front of me, I spot my quarry climbing a wobbling rope ladder to the floor above.

"Gotcha," I whisper as I grip the bridge and begin to cross.

But all of my confidence goes out the window when the damned boards start to sway. My fingers clench the bridge's flimsy handholds a bit tighter as I creep to the other side. The lass really does have a head start now.

Despite seeing the ladder from the bridge, it's unreachable. A plexiglass partition separates me from access, so I take the side path down a dark hallway. As I open the door at the end, a large jack-in-the-box pops out for a cheeky jump scare. I swat the damn thing away and push on. Around the corner, I find the ladder.

I start the climb, which is more difficult for me than it was for the lass. By the time I reach the top, I'm beginning to wonder if this is even fun for her. But then I hear her giggle and catch a glimpse of her golden ponytail disappearing down a red slide.

"Oh shit!" she squeals as she descends.

In my haste to get to the slide, I don't realize the floor is composed of skinny rollers. The first step sends me onto my back with a groan. The structure shakes with the force of the impact.

"Are you okay?" the lass says somewhere below me.

I open my mouth to say yes, but no sound comes out. Only a squeak.

"Need me to slow down?"

I force my lungs to push air over my vocal cords. "Not a bit. You'd best run!"

She giggles again, and her footsteps patter off somewhere below me. Meanwhile, I'm on my hands and knees, trying to navigate these shit-ass rollers. Whoever called this disaster a *fun* house should be flogged. I'll have Jim burn it to the ground after this.

When I finally reach the slide, I'm too exhausted to haul myself the right way round, so I take the son of a bitch headfirst. The slippery tube curves to the left as I'm hurled toward a ball pit at the speed of sound. Bright colors explode against my face as I land.

"Fuck," I groan.

These authors need to write more realistic chases. I'll be missing teeth and covered in bruises by the time I catch up with Quinn, but hopefully my dick will still work. That will make up for everything. I just have to get to her before she can escape.

I drag myself out of the ball pit and through a maze of hanging punching bags. Strobe lights flash overhead, and loud rushes of air randomly accost my face. I struggle through and reach the end after being smacked in the skull by no fewer than four bags.

As I navigate another dark hallway, more jump scares pop out. I dodge a swooping ghost, then punch a hanging skeleton in the face for actually fucking scaring me, but it's all forgotten when I step into the next room.

Mirrors surround me on all sides, and I see no sign of Quinn. I can't even hear her footsteps nearby. But then the wall shudders, and the girl lets out a groan.

"Shit," she whispers.

I cover my mouth and laugh silently as she collides with another mirror somewhere further in. My laughter is short-lived when I realize I have to navigate this monstrosity myself. With my hand outstretched, I take a few steps and immediately collide with a wall. The mix of clear and mirrored panels is really doing my fucking head in.

"When I catch you, I'm going to punish you," I shout toward the ceiling.

Quinn lets out a squeal and collides with another wall, then another. She's close. I can feel the vibrations each time she makes a misstep. Plus, all the grunting helps.

I turn a corner, and there she is. She sees me in a reflection and turns to run away, but she collides with my chest. I band my arms around her as she giggles and fights to get free.

Lowering my mouth to her ear, I whisper a simple question that quiets her immediately. "Do you want me to take you so that I can use you until I'm satisfied? Or would you prefer to have your own needs met? Choose wisely, lass."

She sucks in a breath and looks up at me. "Take me."

I spin her in my arms and pin her against the nearest clear wall. Unfortunately, there is no wall, and we end up stumbling forward when only air meets us. But that's just fine, because as we stumble into another winding section, we're surrounded by more mirrors than clear panels. No matter where we look, there we are.

I can't wait to see her from every angle.

When I push her forward again, I'm finally greeted by a wall. With a smirk, I pull her hair to the side and nip her neck. "Hands on the wall, lass, and don't pull them away until I say."

She does as she's told and braces herself against the clear plexiglass as I drop to my knees and snatch her shorts to her feet. I lean forward and sink my teeth into her ass, and the lass yelps and pulls her hands from the wall. I smack her other ass cheek and bite harder.

"I didn't tell you to move," I growl.

She slams her hands on the wall again and pants through the pain, so I reward her by kissing the bite mark.

"There's a good lass. Don't be disobedient, now. I hate having to punish you."

"Liar," she says.

I smirk. "Aye, that was a lie. I live to bring you pain because it makes your pleasure that much sweeter."

I crack my palm on her ass again before ripping away her lacy purple panties. She won't be needing them anymore. Once I've discarded the flimsy piece of torn fabric, I spread her cheeks and drag my tongue across her back entrance.

"Pineapple!" she squeals.

I arch a brow. "All the shit we've done, and eating ass is your hard line?"

"If you ever want to kiss me again, yeah. That's my hard line." She nibbles her lip in the mirror, clearly uncomfortable with setting this boundary. Her hands drop to her sides, and she fidgets with the hem of her shirt.

Meanwhile, I'm delighted to learn more about her likes and dislikes. I move my mouth higher and kiss her lower back instead. "If you don't like ass play, you don't like ass play. I'll always listen to your boundaries, lass. I'll honor them and cherish them. But if you don't put your hands back on that wall, I'll do something far worse than worshipping your asshole."

This lightens the mood, and she places her hands on the wall again. She'll need to brace herself more than that for what I have planned, though.

I slide my hands up her thighs and drag my fingers through her swollen pussy. She's already dripping. Not wanting to waste a drop, I pull my fingers into my mouth and suck. God, she's delicious.

My dick throbs in my pants, straining against the denim and aching with a ferocity I can't take for another second. When she lets out a whimper as I stand behind her, it takes every ounce of willpower to stop myself from pulling out my cock and splitting her in half. Still, there's an embarrassing amount of desperation in my movements as I begin unfastening my belt.

After snatching the strip of leather free, I bring it down on her ass, right over the bite mark. Quinn's back straightens, and her hands go for the red welt. I step into her and grab her ponytail, forcing her breasts against the wall. With a clenched fist, I snatch her golden locks so that she's forced to look at me.

"I warned you, lass. Now you're in trouble." I lean down and kiss her hard on the mouth, and despite the way I tug her scalp, she releases a needy moan.

I lean back and wrap the belt around her wrists, tying her hands behind her back. With one hand gripping the strap, I use the other to push my cock against her glistening pink slit. My head tips back, and I groan as her neediness pulls me in.

I move my free hand to her hip while snatching back on the belt, keeping her back perfectly arched. She turns her head to the side and breathes through it as I ease in and out of her. I move slowly at first, letting her feel every inch of me as I glide through that glorious, squeezing heat.

"Spread those legs wider, lass." I snatch back on the belt a bit, and she complies. This drops her hips down a few inches, and when I thrust forward again, she lets out a whimper. "Oh, did that feel good?"

She nods her head and whimpers again when I bottom out.

"You like it deep, don't you? You like the way that piercing feels when it punches all those delicate places." I tug the belt, holding her at a nearly impossible angle.

She looks up at the ceiling with tears in her eyes as she chokes out a strangled, "Yes!"

I fuck her harder, faster. My hand revels in all that softness around her hips as I squeeze until her skin turns purple. And she's everywhere. When I look to the left and right, I see her from new angles. There's no hiding the pleasure on her face or the way her thighs begin to shake. I see it all.

"Oh, fuck," she whispers.

I pull out of her before she can come all over my cock. The poor thing nearly collapses as I release the belt.

"What the fuck are you doing?" she cries. "I was about to come!"

I unfasten the belt from her wrists, spin her around, and point to the floor. "On your knees."

Her disappointment dissipates as she remembers she chose this, and she hurries to get to her knees. And I'll be damned if she doesn't open her mouth and look up at me.

I gently smack her cheek and smile down at her. "Finish me off, and don't you dare waste a drop of what I give you. Do you understand?"

She nods up at me, then takes me into her mouth. Stars explode behind my eyelids as they clench shut, and I suck air through my teeth. Her warm, wet tongue slides around my head before she guides me to the back of her throat. I'd planned to grab her head and skull-fuck the shit out of her, but now I'm inclined to let her work her magic. She clearly knows what she's doing.

As her head begins to bob, my toes begin to curl. Her green eyes look up at me, filled with tears as the metal ball repeatedly assaults her throat. She gags and keeps going like a fucking pro.

My fingers wind through her hair and massage her scalp with my nails as she sucks my soul from my body. Fuck, I cannae feel my legs anymore.

Seconds later, my balls tighten. The lass can sense what's coming, so she keeps the same steady pace as she coaxes more pre-cum from the tip. Unable to hold off a second longer, I grip her head in both hands and hold her still as I fill her throat. Quinn gags repeatedly, but she doesn't try to pull away.

When I'm finally spent, I pull back and drop to my knees in front of her. "Fuck, lass. That was fan-fucking-tastic."

She swallows and wipes her mouth, then looks down, almost as if she's ashamed.

Confused, I dip a little lower so that I can look her in the eye. "Hey, what's wrong? Was I too rough? Ach, I'm sorry. I won't do it again."

She shakes her head and finally meets my gaze. "No . . . it's not that."

"Then what it is?"

Nibbling her lip, she hesitates, then scoots back a bit, revealing a small puddle underneath her. "I kind of pissed myself when I was gagging, and it's fucking embarrassing. I have a weak bladder. That's why I have to pee all the time."

I pull off my boxers and use them to wipe away the minuscule puddle. "No need to be embarrassed about a little piddle. Happens to the best of us."

"It doesn't happen to you," she mutters.

I shrug. "I'm not the best of us."

That earns a smile. "How can you be the biggest asshole while simultaneously saying sweet shit like that?"

"It's a gift, really. Now, let's get you dressed so that we can head back to the hotel. Maybe we can finish you off in the hot tub, pissy britches."

"All right, now. No need for jokes." She plucks up her panties and holds the shredded fabric up to the light. "Did you have to rip them?"

"Aye, I did. They were separating me from—"

My throat closes up when I catch movement behind Quinn. Looking through the clear plexiglass panel, I spot Desmond standing there and watching us. Quinn follows my hardened gaze and sucks in a breath when she spots him.

"How long has he been there?" Quinn whispers as she

hurries to get her shorts over her bare ass. "Was he watching us?"

"I don't know, but he'll never watch anything again when I'm through with him." I go to take a step forward, but Quinn wraps her hand around my arm.

"Hey, remember what King and Jim said. We can't take the kill."

I shake off her hold. "Fuck what they said. We don't play by their rules, remember?"

"Aven, I don't think—"

"It's fine, lass. You head back to the hotel and keep your nose clean." I bend and kiss her lips for what I hope won't be the final time. Then I hurry to find my way out of this damned maze as Desmond smirks and makes his exit.

This ends today.

Quinn

The elevator spits me out on the ground floor, and I check my reflection in the mirror across the way. A smile eases onto my face. I'll never look at a mirror again without thinking about the way Aven used me. The bruise on my hip is a delicious reminder. I close my eyes and brush my fingers over the ache, reveling in the way it hurts just right. It's tucked under my pool wrap—a hidden reminder of my man.

It's been over an hour since he took off after Desmond. On my way back to the hotel, the girls spotted me and asked me to join them for an impromptu pool party, complete with activities. I figured it would be a good way to keep my anxiety at bay while Aven is chasing down my stalker and potentially breaking Jim's rules. If he pops up and says we need to run away to Scotland, my bag is already packed.

It might not make any sense to the average woman, but when you know, you know. Aven is it for me. Maybe I'm delusional. Maybe I've read one too many dark romance books. But I no longer care. As long as I have Aven, I'm going to be happy. I feel it in my soul. He won't abandon me.

Your mother didn't abandon you, Quinn . . .

Didn't she, though?

The smile drops from my face. She was there one moment, holding my hand and remarking on the fireworks. The next, she was gone. Per my therapist, my mother likely felt she was doing what was best for me by leaving me at the theme park. She made a difficult choice, and by all accounts, it paid off. I was well cared for, and the Parkers loved me as one of their own.

I press the bruise on my hip. At least some painful memories are pleasant.

"There you are!" a voice says to my left, and I turn to find Eve coming toward me. "We were about to send out the search party. You ready to slaughter some Cattle?" She pulls me closer and spins me so that she can get a better look at the bruise on my hip. "Tell me it was consensual, and I'll give you applause. Tell me it wasn't, and he can join the fucking Cattle."

I nibble my lip to hold back a wide smile. "Completely consensual and welcome."

I'm practically bursting at the seams to tell the girls how everything worked out, so I go ahead and fill in Eve.

"My kinky little friend," she says with a beaming smile. "Welcome to the club."

"You like it rough too?"

"I want my lady to toss me around like a rag doll and sit on my fucking face. I feel bad for all of you women who will never know what it's like to be suffocated by pussy."

I laugh at that and hook my arm through hers as we start

toward the pool. "I'll just live vicariously through you. Are you currently in a relationship?"

Her smile softens. "Not anymore. I want commitment and marriage, but I seem to only attract women who like to cheat. I'm taking a break from the dating scene while I lick my wounds."

"I'm sorry, Eve."

She pats my hand and offers that musical laugh that has a way of setting everyone at ease. "Don't you worry about me. I go home and cry into my Louis Vuitton pillowcases, so I think I'll be okay. I just need to make better choices."

Gentle aloha vibes trickle from the speakers as we open the lobby doors and head toward the pool. Neon purple lights give the water a pleasant glow as we approach. The girls sit on the pool's edge, chatting among themselves. Frankie and Kindra sport waist-snatching one-piece suits, while Eve, Cat, and I rock bikinis. I don't think I've ever seen a more attractive friend group.

We join the others, and Gary brings out a tray of piña coladas as I regale the crew with the tale of two cocks. As a reward, I'm treated to the story of Bennett's pineapple love-fest as we wait for Gary to bring out something more exciting than drinks. We're all here for one reason, after all —the murder.

I just hope it can take my mind off my worry for Aven. I can't talk about his current absence. Aven didn't have time to give me any rules or words of warning before he took off, but he didn't need to. I know that Jim can't know what he's off doing right now. He didn't need to reiterate the need to keep this silent.

Gary returns to the pool with a few other staffers, and the Cattle trail behind them. Each victim is dressed in a color-coded swimsuit. Their hands are secured behind their backs, and they're connected by a chain around the waist rather than by their feet, which have been left free for once. Judging by their silence, they've had their lips secured shut in some way.

"I don't quite have Jim's panache when it comes to games, but I'll do my best," Gary says with a nervous chuckle. "What does he usually say?"

The girls laugh, then say in unison, "The game is simple!"

"The game is simple," Gary says. "You just need to swim the length of the pool one time, then try to kill the sorry shitbag of your choosing. The weapons are in the cabana at the other end."

"What are our options?" I ask.

Gary glances back toward the cabana. "I scrounged up a couple of power tools, the gun that bird used to kill a guy, some—"

"No, not the weapons," Kindra says. "The Cattle. What did they do?"

"Oh, right!" Gary raises a finger and nods. "I forgot you guys like to know their crimes. We've brought a serial rapist, two dog-fighting assholes, a child molester, and a lady who got her kicks from abusing the elderly."

I feel a little foolish, as I was asking about the weapons. I don't really care what these assholes have done.

"Dibs on the child molester!" Kindra yells, and the man in the pink speedo wets himself.

Eve turns to me with a shimmy of her shoulders. "What's your poison, honey?"

I shrug. "Doesn't matter to me. I'm a bit different from you guys. I definitely enjoy righting wrongs and killing bad guys, but I'm fine with killing for the sake of killing."

"A woman after my own heart," Eve says. "Those three need a reason, but I just need the motivation."

"You say that like it's a bad thing," Frankie says.

Eve goes to her bag by a lounger and pulls out a covering for her hair, which she fastens in place without a mirror. Not a single micro braid pokes out, and she still looks stunning, so I'm becoming more convinced that she knows magic. "Not a bad thing. Just different. Different doesn't have to be bad."

"You got another one of those?" Cat asks. "I really don't want to have to wash my hair before the event this evening."

Eve tosses a second cap to Cat, and the girl begins tucking away her blonde hair.

"I kind of feel like it's the other way around," I offer. "The differences, I mean. Like, maybe we're looked down on because we aren't choosy."

"I don't look down on you. My mother always said that folks who look down on others must feel silly up on their self-made pedestals, so I've always tried not to stand on one." Cat tucks the last of her hair into the cap, though she doesn't look half as cute as Eve. She looks more like a Kewpie doll, but I'll never tell her that.

Frankie nods in agreement. "Besides, have you seen the penis-to-vagina ratio at these shindigs? I refuse to alienate another woman who could become a sister."

My heart squeezes when she says this. She has no idea she has a sister in the most literal sense. We secretly share the same DNA.

A few of the men stroll by the pool, and Bennett is among them. He sees Cat and immediately begins laughing.

"Who made my girlfriend look like a fucking Kewpie doll?" he yells toward us.

Cat reaches up to snatch off the cap, but Eve covers her hand and stops her.

"The cap makes her look like an adorable doll. Meanwhile, you look like a fucking moron all the time by nature's design," I yell back.

Eve nods, then looks at him. "At least she can take off the cap, honey! You're stuck with that melon head."

That earns a laugh from all of us, and Cat lowers her hand. *Thanks*, she mouths to me.

"Don't mention it," I say as the men shuffle off toward the hotel.

"You guys gonna line up to begin?" Gary asks, and we all remember that we're supposed to be playing a game, not bonding.

We hurry to the shallow end of the pool. The entire thing is massive, and I'm pretty sure I'll be winded after swimming the length of it. I'm also nervous about how I'll kill any of these people when they have legs to kick with, but then I see that Gary is busy buckling their ankles together as we prepare to start the swim.

He looks up from the first set of legs, and I nearly laugh at his excitement as his buggy eyes bulge. "Try not to make it too bloody, as I'm a bit squeamish. I'm trying to get over it."

"We've got you, Gare Bear," Eve calls. "Let's get this train rolling!"

He moves to the next Cattle and starts fastening the woman's legs, but she kicks out and lands a blow to the dented side of his head. Gary crumples to the concrete with a groan.

Eve is on her way over before Gary has a chance to get to his feet again. "This motherfucker," she mutters before snatching the woman by her hair and looking straight into her eyes. "Didn't your mama teach you to keep your hands and legs to yourself? If she didn't, you're gonna learn today, bitch. If I spot a chainsaw in that cabana, you're gonna pay for what you did to him in the most excruciating way."

"I might need to go to the infirmary," Gary says with a nervous laugh.

"Yeah, you might," Eve says as she releases the woman. "It's definitely getting bloody now."

Gary hurries off as we consider the best way to run the game without our officiant. What we come up with is a different game altogether. We'll each take turns removing a body part until the bitch is dead. The one who makes the final cut is the loser.

We send back four of the five Cattle, leaving only the bitchy woman who kicked Gary. Working together, we strap her midsection to one of the loungers via some of the rope from the cabana. When we're certain she isn't going anywhere, we hurry to pick our tools for the game.

The gleaming gun catches my eye first, but that will end the game of body-part Jenga too quickly. Instead, I go for the reciprocating saw.

"This should help us drag this out," Kindra says as she holds up a small soldering iron. "We can cauterize any major vessels."

"Stop it, you're turning me on," Frankie says as she raises a katana and swipes the blade through the air.

Eve plucks up the chainsaw, Cat opts for the tray of surgical tools, and Kindra chooses the biggest set of pruning shears I've ever seen. With our murder weapons tucked under our arms like prizes, we scurry back to the woman on the chair.

"Let's let Quinn make the first cut," Cat says.

The girls agree, and I step forward with the tool and

turn it on. The blade whirs to life, and the woman's eyes widen. I grip her wrist and cut through the zip ties so that I can pull her arm around front and focus on a single finger, but she wallops me with her free hand and immediately tries to undo the rope around her waist.

Like hyenas, the women descend on her and pin her flailing limbs to the lounger. Knowing what I want, Eve ratchets the woman's wrist and presents her quivering fingers toward me. So many choices.

Sensing my indecision, Cat offers some help. "The thumb and index finger contain the most nerve endings. Break through the center bone rather than the joint to inflict the most pain."

"That nursing-school education is paying off in spades," Eve says as she grunts and readjusts her grip. "Chop, chop, Quinn! She'll have less fight once she loses some blood."

The woman screams through her nose as I press the vibrating blade against her thumb. It melts through the skin, but when the teeth hit that thick bone, the blade stutters to a stop. I pull back and come at it from a different angle, and I'm rewarded with a loud *pop* as the bone splinters beneath the vibration. The thumb remnant drops to the concrete.

"Fucking sick," Kindra says with a grin.

Eve passes the arm to me, and we trade places. "My turn! And I'm going to take a risk. Get that soldering iron ready."

Cat grabs it from the lounger and turns it on. "It's heating up. I'll cauterize any vessels that won't clot."

Eve nods and yanks the chainsaw's starter. In the silver bikini and black bathing cap, she looks like a deranged synchronized swimmer as she slings the whirling blade toward her prey. She leans forward and, wearing the most maniacal grin imaginable, proceeds to lop off the woman's right foot. The appendage skitters across the pavement and spins into the pool.

Blood gushes from the open wound, and now that she's down a foot, her legs are free to kick. We didn't exactly think this through.

"Hold her still!" Cat screams.

We do, figuring she's preparing to seal off the bleeding stump at the end of the woman's leg, but she's wielding the scalpel. She attacks the kneecaps with surgical precision, and the lower parts of the legs become more like spaghetti noodles.

Cat swipes some sweat from her forehead and sits back, pleased as punch. "There. It'll be hard for her to kick without any ligaments."

Tears stream from the woman's eyes as she hurls curses at us from behind her sealed lips. Her nostrils flare, and she's looking a bit pale. How wonderful.

Cat sees the change in pallor and hurries to close off the red jets.

"My turn," Kindra says. She gets on her knees in front of the woman and slides the large pruning-shear blades over the big toe on her remaining foot.

The woman jerks her leg free, and Eve and I move to hold it down.

"As bad as it hurts to stub this little shit, I can only imagine how much pain you'll feel when I chop it off," Kindra says as she lines up the cut again. Before slicing down, she situates the blade's edge so that it covers all five toes. "Then again, shouldn't all the little piggies go to the market together?"

Kindra closes the blades, and toes pop off like jumping beans. When she pulls away, only the tiny digit on the end remains, wiggling in the wind. We collapse in a fit of giggles, unable to continue without cracking at least five jokes about the Brave Little Toester. Then Frankie uses the katana to lop it off as well, and we're sent into gut-aching laughter again. I guess those piña coladas are kicking in.

But the laughter is cut short when Jim's and King's voices reach us. They're yelling about something—or at someone—and my heart ceases beating. Did Aven finally catch Desmond, and now *they've* caught *him*? I stand and look, but I can't see them.

"What's going on?" Frankie asks.

The men step out from the garden path and finally come into view. I don't know if I'm more shocked or relieved to see that Aven isn't with them. They're just yelling at each other. But why?

Then their voices reach me.

"He got onto the gondola with Desmond, but they didn't show up at the second station. It was just like before," Jim says. "I love him like a son, King. We have to find him."

Their voices fade as they hurry into the hotel, but Jim's words echo inside my brain. The girls are ready to get back to the game, but not even torture can pull me out of this mental tailspin. If Jim and King are worried about Aven, then I am too.

I make my excuses—much to the girls' displeasure—and hurry up to my room. If I want to go on a rescue mission, I'll need to dress for it. I choose jeans and a snug t-shirt in case I'm forced to climb. Something about that gondola is the key to all of this.

My suspicions are confirmed as I'm buttoning my jeans. The secret cell phone buzzes in the nightstand, and I nearly trip over my feet as I rush to read the message.

> I've trailed him and found his hiding place.
> Meet me at the gondolas.

There's no time for questions, so I shove the phone into my pocket and bolt out the door. I hurry back to the pool area. The girls are gone, and some crew members busy themselves with cleaning the blood from the concrete. I can only hope no one has removed the table of weapons yet.

Inside the cabana, I'm relieved to see everything exactly how we left it. Well . . . mostly. The gun is no longer on the table, and that's exactly what I planned to take with me. Everything else is too bulky to wield with any efficiency.

With empty hands and a lot of hope, I exit the cabana and hurry to the park entrance. Security gives me a nod as I rush through the turnstile and jog toward the gondolas at the other end of the property. I don't know which one is considered station one, so I'll just ride it both ways until I see something.

Hot breath saws in and out of me by the time I reach the station, but before I can board one of the swinging cars, I find the missing gun. It's in Desmond's hand as he pushes the barrel against my back and leans down to whisper, "Gotcha."

Chapter Thirty-Seven

Aven

Cat, Kindra, Ezra, and Ice Pick sit in the lounge area off the side of the lobby as I hurry toward the elevators. I search the surrounding area, but I see no sign of Quinn. Doubling back, I ask if they've seen her since we parted ways at the fun house.

"She heard Jim yelling about his damned bird, so I think she went to help look for him," Cat says. "She took off toward the park about an hour ago."

"And you let her?" My eyes bulge, and my hands clench into fists at my sides. I never found Desmond, so the lass is at risk every second we're apart. I never should have left her.

Cat's eyebrows pull together, and she takes a step away from me.

Ezra rises and places a hand on my shoulder. "Steady, old man. Just have Jim check the cameras. I'm sure he can find her in no time."

I shake my head to clear the rage, then look at Cat. "Sorry, pal. I'm just worried."

"It's fine, but I usually only let Bennett talk to me that way, so watch it."

"Be careful, Aven," Kindra jokes. "Your give-a-fuck is starting to show."

She's right. Quinn's made a visible change in me, and I don't even care. Let them see my vulnerability. If it will help me save the girl, let them see it all.

"Jim's up in his room now," Ezra adds. "Might as well go before he heads to the park for the fireworks shit. Though, he may cancel the entire evening if he doesn't find that bird."

He'll definitely cancel the entire evening if we don't find Quinn. I'll cancel it myself. I'll raze this entire island to the ocean floor to find her.

I leave the group and take the elevator to the top floor. King answers almost as soon as I knock, and the two men look as frazzled as I feel.

"I want all the files," I say. "Right now. I want Quinn's, and I want Desmond's first of all. After that, I want the files on her mother and father. Not the redacted shit you gave me, either."

"Redacted files?" King looks at Jim. "We didn't redact anything from Grantham Carter's file. And what's going on? This isn't about Kenny, I take it."

"I went after Desmond, but he escaped. Now Quinn is missing."

"We told you—"

"Fuck what you told me!" I shout, cutting Jim off. "Fuck the mission, fuck your stupid rules, and fuck you, too! Give me the files so that I have the information I need to save the woman I love or I will take up my ax again and chop off every appendage until you do what I require."

King strolls to the side table and pours whiskey into a

short glass, then passes it to me. "I know you don't drink on the job, but cooler heads often prevail."

I accept the drink and knock it back in one swallow. It won't cool my head, but it will dampen my anxious mind. "There. I've had your drink. Now give me the files."

Jim and King share another look before Jim says, "We can't do that. We don't have much information on her mother, and the file I gave you on Carter was complete. Nothing was redacted, I assure you."

"What do you mean you don't have any info on her mother?" I ask. "You have a file a mile thick on Bennett's, Ezra's, and Frankie's mothers. You know more about that Daddy Carter asshole than any swinging dick in the bureau."

"Watch it," King says.

"Aye, I *am* watching it, and this is what I see. You either don't have information on Quinn's mother because Quinn isn't who you say she is, *or* you do have information and you are once again holding out on the big idiot. Is that about right?"

Jim sighs and rubs his eyes. "No one thinks you're an idiot, Aven. Please, sit down and let us explain."

"No, I'm not giving you time to think up more lies. I want the truth. Why don't you have a file for Quinn's ma?"

"Because she was Desmond's first victim." King's voice cuts through the air with finality. He leaves no room for doubt or question.

I shake my head and look at the ground. "So, she's dead, then. She didn't abandon the lass at all."

"It's true," King says, his voice somber. "Quinn's mother lived a nomadic life. There was no stability for the young girl, but there was no lack of love, either. It was that love that pushed her to make a terrible decision. She abandoned the girl, in a sense, but not in the sense she's been made to believe."

"Her mother answered an ad in the local paper," Jim says. "It simply mentioned an odd request and a little once-in-a-lifetime wish fulfillment. She had a wish and hope, so she called him." Jim looks at his shoes, and not even King makes a sound as he continues. "We can't be sure of the agreement, but Quinn found her way into the Parker's hands not by way of the state, but via private adoption."

King sighs. "Her mother was never found officially because she was never missing officially. She ran in darker circles, mind you. Not the sort to run to the police. The only one who ever missed her aloud was her little girl, but even that was silenced. The girl's therapist was instructed to tell the girl her mother abandoned her. Eventually . . . she believed it."

The whiskey glass shatters against the wall the moment it leaves my hand. I glare at them. "I won't keep it from her. It's her business, and she's going to know it by morning."

"Let's not be hasty," King says, hands raised in a placating gesture. "At least wait until after the fireworks. We think this will push Desmond to act."

"Do you even hear yourself, man? Why do you insist on carrying on with these insipid rules? Quinn is likely in danger because you've kept my hands tied." I shake my head to fight back tears of rage. "No, not anymore. As soon as I find him, he's dead. Quinn isn't your bait anymore."

King flops onto the couch with a sigh and covers his eyes with his hand. "The girl is probably fine. Jim, go check the footage. I need to speak with Aven."

Jim nods and hurries off, and King motions for me to sit. When I fold my arms over my chest and continue standing, he pushes on anyway.

"Is Quinn your first love, Aven?"

I hadn't considered it, but yes, she might be. The lass I fancied in my teens certainly doesn't count, considering I ended up slitting her throat. Even if Quinn cheated on me like that cunt did, I can't imagine killing her. I'd rather live in a world of hurt than live in a world where she doesn't exist.

"Aye, she is."

King nods. "Desmond took my first love from me. Twenty years ago at this very theme park, in fact."

The blurry picture comes into focus. "You were in love with Quinn's mother," I say.

"She was meant to be a victim. I picked her up on a street corner with plans to practice my knife skills. My black heart had other plans. From the moment she spoke to me, I knew there would be no death for her that day."

"Then why didn't you help her? You parade around in designer suits and drive fancy cars the same as Jim. Why didn't you get them off the fucking street?"

King turns his icy-blue gaze toward me. "Do you think I didn't try? She refused to take a handout, and her various addictions prevented her from straightening out her life. And I'll give you one guess as to why she couldn't attend a proper rehabilitation program."

"Her daughter."

"She'd written me, asking if I'd help her fight to get Quinn back once she was well again. By the time I'd received the letter, it was too late. She'd already enacted her plan and become Desmond's first victim. And there's more to it than—"

"Oh no!" Jim shouts from the next room, and the hairs on my neck stand on end before he even rushes in and says the next dreadful sentence. "You were right to worry,

Aven. Desmond has her, and he's taken her to the gondolas."

"What?" King and I shout in unison.

"He had her at gunpoint. It looked like Kenny's gun." Jim runs his hands through his hair, and the mess it leaves behind is so unlike him that it makes me feel sick. He's terrified enough to forgo his usual act of keeping up appearances, so I'm more than right to be terrified myself.

I turn to leave the room, and King shouts after me.

"Where are you going?" he asks.

I open the door and pause. Unlike them, I won't keep anyone in the dark. "I'm going to the gondolas. To save Quinn."

"Wait!" Jim shouts. "We haven't run this situation through the simulator. We don't know what could happen."

"I don't need a simulator to tell me that," I say. "I'm going to save the girl, pay off my debt, and then she and I are taking a one-way flight to Scotland. If her brothers and sister wish to visit, I'll send the fucking address."

"About that," King says. "There's one more bit of information we've been withholding, and I think it's time you knew. Desmond isn't just tied to Quinn and me. He's linked to you as well. You killed his father."

Chapter Thirty-Eight

Quinn

Desmond pushes me forward, and I stumble onto the narrow metal platform running between the trees. The rust and general disrepair of this service area tell me Jim doesn't know of its existence. Leaves and gnarled branches obscure it from view when you're on the gondola. It wasn't until Desmond opened the door and told me to get ready to step out that I saw it myself. I damn near missed the step when I hopped off, too.

Something tells me this service entrance wasn't known by many. There's no way someone would have okayed this death trap. The only way onto this walkway is to hop from the gondola, which is definitely an OSHA violation. This is one of those theme park "secrets," like the tunnels under Disney.

"Keep moving," Desmond says as he rams the gun's barrel between my shoulder blades.

I point at the gaping hole in the metal grate under our

feet. "I'd fucking love to, but I forgot my winged shoes this morning."

"It's a damn shame I want to fuck you so badly. Otherwise, I'd send your stupid ass to the forest floor. Jump."

My jaw drops, not because he told me to jump the gap but because he thinks he's getting anywhere near my pussy. And I'm the idiot? I may not have a weapon, but I'll be damned if I'll go down without a fight. If my stubby little nails can claw out his icy eyes, it will be enough.

"Do you even know who you're fucking with?" I say before making the leap. I turn to face him after I land safely. "Do you know who my father is?"

Instead of looking concerned, he merely smirks and jumps over, putting his chest level with my nose when I refuse to back up. "Oh, I know exactly who your father is. The question is, do you?"

He grips my shoulders and spins me around, and I roll my eyes. Up until a week ago, the answer would have been no. Thank fuck Aven came through with my very own Maury Povich moment. It's just a shame Daddy Dearest wasn't there to run off screen, screaming about how it's not true.

How will my brothers and sister react when they learn of their new sibling? I want to smile when I think of it, but there is a very real chance they won't even know until after I'm dead.

"How'd you do it?" I ask. The curiosity is too much to bear. If he killed Aven and took the tiny cell phone, I want to know so that I can just jump off this platform right now. "The text message, I mean."

"Jim had to set up something special for the two of you to communicate on the island. I merely tapped into it via one of the lobby computers." He pulls a small phone from his pocket. It's similar to the ones Aven and I use, but it's not the same. "This certainly helped. Jim really should invest in some better locks for his supply rooms. Now quit stalling and start walking."

The walkway pushes through the trees a bit more before our destination is revealed. Built into the canopy and completely hidden from view is a small wooden shack that looks like Satan's Treehouse. The red paint may be faded, but I can still make out the dancing demons plastered over the aged boards. Their black eyes seem to stare at me as I draw closer.

As we step onto the porch, I hear a familiar screeching from inside.

"You plan to kill Kenny?" I turn to glare at Desmond. "You bastard."

Desmond flicks the barrel toward the front door. "Stop stalling. I stole the bird to keep Jim occupied so that I could go after what I really wanted. Now get inside and give me the show I've been waiting for. I've even got a fun little setup for you in there so that your new friends can watch me rape you until you beg for death."

"You're fucking gross, you know that?"

"You have no idea, princess. Now move those feet while you still can."

As I grip the handle and open the metal door, the metallic stink of blood rushes toward me. I cover my nose and take an instinctive step backward, but Desmond blocks my exit. Then my eyes adjust to the darkness, and I see the reason for the smell.

In the corner, Desmond's lanky friend lies in a crumpled pile. A discolored tongue lolls from his swollen, purple face. The skin on his neck nearly obscures the rope cinched around it. Blood pools beneath a few shallow defensive wounds in his arms.

"What the fuck did you do to him?" I ask as I move toward the opposite corner.

Desmond closes the door behind him and locks it. "He started asking too many questions, and when he followed me here, I had to take care of him."

"And why me?"

Desmond steps toward me. When he reaches out to run his fingers through my hair, I pull away. He lowers his hand with a scowl, then slaps me. My head rocks to the side, but I don't give him the pleasure of a yelp. I straighten my spine and brush my hair out of my face, staring at him and daring him to do it again.

"Why you?" he says as he appraises me. "You'd love for it to be because you're so beautiful, wouldn't you? It should be some enigmatic quality that I see within, but it's not. It has nothing to do with you and everything to do with my very specific needs."

He places the gun on a side table near Kenny, who perches on a branch jutting through a broken board. A tiny chain around his scaly ankle keeps him fastened there. He keeps picking at the clip connecting the chain's tail to itself, and I can only hope he figures it out and pulls a Lassie for me.

What is it, Kenny? Quinn's stuck in the old treehouse?

A plastic zipper bag is shoved into my hands, pulling me out of the rescue fantasy. "Put this on," Desmond says. "I'll even give you a bit of privacy." He motions toward a wooden door in the back wall.

"No thanks," I say with a smirk, and I begin stripping off my shirt. I refuse to give him an ounce of power over me.

I pull the clothing from the bag. The shorts drop to the

floor as I hold up the shirt and try to make out the design in the dim light. It looks like a vintage band tee from the eighties, but I don't recognize the name of the band. Still, the shirt is somehow . . . familiar.

"Put it on," Desmond says with a widening smile. "I can't wait to see you in it."

I roll my eyes and swallow the unease when I spy a dark stain near a slash in the shirt's side. I've watched enough episodes of *Criminal Minds* to know what's going on. He's dressing me like one of his past victims so that he can relive some fantasy. Gross.

My gaze darts around the room, trying to focus on anything other than the asshole in front of me. A monitor and webcam sit on the floor on one side. An ax hangs above the side table beside Kenny. Aside from all that and the single dangling light bulb, the room is empty.

Seeing no way out, I ease the shirt over my body and pull the shorts from the floor with a cock of my head. "Have you seen the size of my ass, Lord Fuckwad? I can't fit my right thigh in these things, let alone my waist."

He nods and appraises me again. "Yes, you look just like her in the face. Same golden hair and bright green eyes. It's a shame you didn't learn how to push yourself away from the table."

"Excuse me?"

"Don't get indignant. Your mother might have been a fatty had she not loved meth more than she loved *you*."

Rage coils low in my gut, and I breathe through the urge to hurl myself at him and claw out his stupid eyes. "You didn't know my mother."

"Oh, have I struck a nerve?" He chuckles and steps closer. "I did know your mother, Quinn. I knew her before you did. My da sent me to America at a young age to learn all about his business, and your mother was one of our best clients. A beautiful, strung-out junkie who was willing to get dicked down for her next fix."

"Shut up!"

"I wasn't a killer when I met her. At the time, I didn't even know what I was capable of. That didn't come until your little boyfriend chose to murder my father."

My chin begins to quiver, and I take a step back, then another. Before I know it, my back is against the door in the most literal sense, and I have nowhere left to run. I look down at the shirt, and a memory flashes in my mind. I see my mother, smiling as she points at the starry sky. Colors explode, and her hand slips from mine.

"This is the shirt my mother wore the night she disappeared."

"That's right, Quinn, but she didn't disappear. She's been here the entire time." He tosses his head back and laughs as I try not to puke on my feet. "It was entirely too simple. I made an offer she couldn't refuse, and she fell right into my lap. While you were bleating like a little lost lamb, your mother was bleeding out. I've been chasing that moment since that night, and I've never experienced it again, but when I heard that Jim planned to buy Laughter Park—"

"You thought you could recreate the moment with her daughter."

"I've kept tabs on you all these years. When your little friends thought they were orchestrating my capture, I was the one plucking the strings. Who do you think tipped off King to my sudden reappearance? Who do you think sold this theme park to Jim?"

"But why my mother?"

Before he has a chance to answer, Kenny lets out an

ear-piercing screech and begins flapping his wings. Underneath all that squawking, I hear a familiar voice yell my name. I can't be certain if it's my hopeful imagination or a miracle, but I don't respond. Kenny is louder than I ever could be, and I have to hope Desmond didn't hear anything.

"Shut that damned animal up!" he yells as he flails his hands toward Kenny. That only makes the poor creature screech more loudly.

While he's focused on the bird, I lean backward and unfasten the door lock. Now I just have to hope Aven gets here before Desmond realizes he's on his way. Fighting him myself isn't an option, and playing hopscotch on that crumbling walkway as I run for my life is not a possibility.

I glance back at the bird. The latch around his leg has come open, but it's still hooked in place. With a little finesse, I could probably free him.

"Let me handle him," I say. "He doesn't like loud sounds, and you're a fucking bullhorn."

After grabbing the gun from the table, Desmond steps back with a scowl, and I use my back to block his line of sight as I stretch my arm toward the bird. Kenny eyes my arm, then quiets and steps up.

"Good boy," I whisper.

"What are you telling him?" Desmond barks.

I roll my eyes and flick the latch away while gripping it so that the chain doesn't fall to the floor. "The secrets of the fucking universe. He's a bird, you moron. I'm just being nice to him so that he'll calm down."

I place Kenny on the branch, careful to keep the chain draped over it so that Desmond doesn't realize the bird is free. Whether Aven shows up or not, a plan is forming in my mind.

I turn back to Desmond. "Now answer my question. Why did you choose my mother?"

"You seem to have forgotten who has the control here." He wiggles the gun in the air, then motions for me to move to the other side of the room. "Get on your knees in front of the camera."

I step toward the monitor and camera on the floor, then get to my knees. If being compliant can buy a little more time, so be it.

Desmond steps closer and turns on the devices. I fill the screen, though not with my usual glamor. The single dangling bulb above my head provides such shitty light. This is not at all flattering, and my stomach sinks to my ass when I see an active chat pop onto the screen.

EVE: We're looking for you, honey.

CAT: Don't give up hope!

I close my eyes. It's not just me anymore. It's not just Aven, either. We have friends, and I finally have family, and right now, they're all hunkered down somewhere, giving me their support. As soon as they save me, I'm telling them everything.

"How touching," Desmond coos. He kneels behind me, and I want to vomit when he leans closer and smells my hair. "Knowing that your friends will watch me destroy you is icing on the cake."

Using the gun's barrel, he pulls my hair to the side. I try to move away, but he brings the butt of the gun down on my shoulder and snatches me back in place by my hair.

"Is there anything you want to tell them before I kill you, you little *brat*?"

Aven should have gotten here by now. I must have wanted to hear his voice so badly that I imagined it. No one is going to find me out here. In case this is the last thing I get to say, I'd better make it good.

"I want everyone to know something about me. I've been keeping a secret, and no, I don't mean my feelings for Aven." I swallow around the lump in my throat. "Killing isn't just a hobby I discovered here. It's in my blood. I'm . . . a Carter sibling."

The chat explodes, the words zipping by too quickly for me to read. Desmond starts laughing behind me, and an icy feeling grips my spine. The cold barrel presses against my nape and rakes up my skull.

"Killing is in your blood, that much is true," Desmond says, "but Grantham Carter is not your father. I am."

I lunge forward and disconnect the webcam, then rise to my feet and kick the monitor until it hisses. It can't be true. It can't, and I don't want anyone else to hear his spurious bullshit.

"You're a liar!" I grip the broken monitor and spin around to face him. "You're only trying to piss me off!"

"Your response is certainly more than I hoped for." He chuckles again, and my blood begins to boil. "Your mother answered my ad because she already knew me. She'd been dealing with me for years, just as I said. One of my best customers, and the whore to bear my demon seed."

I shake my head and toss the monitor at him, but he ducks out of the way. "It's not true."

"How does it feel knowing your little boyfriend was the match that lit my fire? Had he not killed my father, I never would have discovered this glorious hobby."

Aven's story flashes through my mind. "Aven killed your dad in Scotland."

"That's right, princess. Now you're putting it together." He motions toward the ax on the wall. "With that very ax, he ended my father's life. And now I'm going to use it to end yours."

I blink up at him. "If I'm really your daughter, how have you been watching my fucking sex streams? And you want to rape me? I don't buy it."

"What can I say? I'm a disgusting man with a disgusting taste for revenge." He raises the gun and points it at my chest. "I'm finished talking, princess. You don't have to believe me if you don't want to, but you're going to get what's coming either way."

"Wait!" I hold out my hands. "I have one more thing to say."

Desmond rolls his eyes and drops the gun to his side, which is exactly what I hoped for. "Go on."

"Kenny . . . bang, bang."

Chapter Thirty-Nine

Aven

A gunshot rings out as I leap onto the metal platform from the gondola, and Kenny's screeching spurs me forward. God bless that loud-ass bird. If it hadn't been for him, I never would have spotted the walkway. Unfortunately, it was a moment too late, and I had to take the ride around again to get back here.

Quinn's scream reaches my ears. I take off into a sprint, and when the walkway ends ahead, I use the momentum to leap to the other side. The metal groans when I land, and the platform cants to the right. I lose my footing. Rust scrapes away as I slide, and I claw for any sort of handhold. My hand wraps around the railing at the last second, and my boots dangle toward death. With all the strength in my upper body, I haul my feet back to the slanted platform and drag myself onto the next.

Darkness clouds my vision as I push forward, and another gunshot pierces the silence. I'm close enough to hear the sounds of a scuffle—boots scraping on wood; grunts and wing flaps. The gun fires again, and Quinn screams. If he shoots her, I'll kill Desmond before ending my own life. Not even Scotland is enough to live for if she isn't there.

Desmond has been the barrier to all of my happiness. King and Jim were keeping quite the secret, but now it's out in the open. Now I know that the only thing stopping me from returning to Scotland is also the only thing preventing Quinn from living her best life. It's time to destroy the wall and bridge the fucking divide he's created.

I shoulder the door and take it down in one hit. I stumble forward and spot Desmond and Quinn on the ground, fighting over the gun. Kenny flies past and zips out the door, and it's for the best. He doesn't like loud noises, and it's about to get very loud in here.

There's no time to see if Quinn is shot. She and Desmond both have their hands on the weapon, and it's a dangerous game they're playing. The barrel shifts position, moving from her head to his, but she's getting weak.

I lunge forward and bring my heel down on Desmond's ribs. He grunts and recoils, but he doesn't loosen his grip on the gun. Quinn leans forward and sinks her teeth into his clenched fist, and the gun fires again.

The pain is immediate. Heat explodes in my right side, and I grunt and clench my teeth to stop from screaming. Glancing down, I spy a small hole in my shirt. There's very little blood when I press my fingers to the wound, though the sharp, searing, ripping ache damn near causes me to faint.

No matter. Jim always said the simulator predicted I would die to save the girl, and I'm inclined to prove it right. So long as she lives, I can die happy.

I bring my leg down on Desmond's ribs again, and something cracks. His hands finally release the gun, and

Quinn grabs it and scrambles backward on her ass while keeping the barrel leveled on his head.

"Don't you fucking move, asshole!" she screams.

I rush to her side and drop to my knees. "Lass . . . are you hurt?"

The gun quivers in her hands, but her resolve is steady as she shakes her head. "He says he's my father. Is it true?"

I place my hand over the gun and try to lower it, but she shakes me off.

"Is it fucking true?" she screams. She keeps the gun and her fiery green gaze locked on her target.

"Lass . . ."

Quinn pulls the trigger, but the gun just clicks. It's either jammed or empty. She screams and tosses it aside, and Desmond continues writhing and gripping his cracked ribs as he fights for air.

I pull her into my arms as she begins to cry.

"Tell me it isn't true. He isn't my father. I was supposed to have found my family, Aven. I was supposed to be where I belong." She cries harder, and I wish I could tell her it's all a lie. But it's not.

"You have found family, lass. You've found me." I wince and grit my teeth as she brushes against the bullet hole in my side. "The others don't even know that Jim lied about you being a Carter sibling, and they still welcomed you with open arms. Your lineage doesn't change a damn thing. You're one of us, and we aren't letting you go."

"You knew?" she asks, and the betrayal in her voice almost breaks me.

I stroke her hair and kiss the top of her head. "Only just, lass. Only just. King and Jim told me everything before I ran down here to play hero. I never would have kept this from you. Quinn . . . I love you."

"I love you too."

"And I love you three and four," I say before I kiss her forehead. "Don't ever forget that. I cannae live without you, lass."

Desmond groans and rolls to a sitting position. "This is all very touching, but if you're going to try to kill me, could we get on with it? I have a flight back to Scotland in just a few hours, and I'd hate to miss it."

I rise to my feet and move toward the far wall, only now realizing what hangs there. I pull the ax from its holder and close my eyes as the familiar weight rests in my hand. "You ever watch *Star Wars*, Desi boy? Yoda has one of my favorite quotes. 'Do or do not, there is no try.' I don't plan to leave you breathing, you bastard."

My arm rises, prepared to make the first swing, but the floor spins under my feet. A deep numbness washes over me, and I stumble into the wall. I slide into a slump on the floor, my stupid arm still wielding the ax above my head.

"Aven!" Quinn shouts. She scrambles on her hands and knees until she reaches me, then pulls my upper body into her lap. "What's wrong? Are you hurt?"

The lass feels me all over, and I'm too weak to stop her from discovering the hole in my shirt. Her fingers dart forward and raise the fabric, revealing the weeping wound in my side.

Desmond whistles and lets out a hoarse chuckle. "Damn, that sucks. Have fun bleeding out, though."

He gets to his feet with a groan, and Quinn is powerless to stop him as he starts out the door. He pauses to deliver a parting blow before he exits.

"Oh, and one more thing." He raises a finger with a smile. "Once your little boyfriend is dead, I'll be back for you, Quinn. I won't stop until you've joined him in hell, and now that he won't be there to protect you, it will be easier than ever. This isn't over yet."

"You're right," King says as he steps into the tree house. "It isn't over."

My consciousness is fading fast, but I cling to the shreds as King, Jim, and Ezra step into the room. If they're about to end Desmond, I don't want to miss a second of it.

Quinn clutches me a little tighter. "He's been shot," she says toward the men.

Ezra passes a gun to Jim before hurrying to my side. Jim raises the weapon toward Desmond, who lifts his hands and backs toward the wall. Ezra looks at the hole in my side and shakes his head.

"Damn, this is a sorry business," he whispers. He looks back at the men. "He could be bleeding out internally. We need to get him to hospital."

"Ach, I'll be fine. I just feel a little weak. Get what you need out of the asshole, and then kill him so I can die knowing Quinn is safe." I wave him off, and he backs away. "The girl knows it all now, so let King get what he needs."

Desmond cocks his head and breathes a little harder. I can only assume he's working with a punctured lung at the moment. Good. I hope it hurts like hell.

"King?" Desmond says. "King doesn't factor into any of this."

"That's where you're bloody wrong, Desmond." King steps closer and pulls some cuffs from his pocket. "Until I know what you've done with Marcia's body, you'll enjoy some downtime in the Cattle barn."

A light sparkles in Desmond's eye. "Oh, so I wasn't the only one who enjoyed slumming?"

King pulls back his fist and sends it into Desmond's face. Something cracks, and his nose begins to bleed.

"It wasn't slumming. I loved her. I offered her all that I had, but she refused. I thought loving her from a distance would keep her and her young daughter safe from my sickness, but it wasn't enough." King fastens the cuffs around Desmond's wrists. "You made sure of that."

"She wouldn't take your money? She was more than happy to accept mine," Desmond says. He grins, showcasing his blood-stained teeth. "I took it back, of course. Right after I fucked her and slashed her up."

A white fog begins to descend over my vision. I'm fading fast, but they're so close to finding Quinn's mother. I can't derail the momentum by whinging about a little gunshot wound.

"She has to be here," Quinn says. "There's no way he got her body out of this death trap." Her gaze darts to the door in the back wall. "He wanted me to go in there to change."

I can't feel Quinn's warmth anymore. Everything is so cold. Footsteps clomp over the boards, but I can't see anything. Voices filter through the haze and reach me from miles away.

"I see a skull . . ."

"Aven? Aven!"

"I'm sorry, son. I've tried to protect you. I've tried to protect all of you. Please . . . just wake up."

The English accent filters through the fog. It's somehow familiar and entirely foreign at the same time, but I follow it out of the darkness. My eyes open, and I discover a man in a white coat standing at my bedside.

When he notices my open eyes, he lowers the tablet in his hand, pulls off his glasses, and tucks them into his coat pocket. He holds his hand toward me, then pulls back when I don't accept the handshake.

"I'm Doctor Mott, and I've been overseeing your care. How are you feeling?"

"Like I've been eaten and shit out by a bear," I say. I make a mental note to find the owner of that voice, because it definitely isn't this guy. He's too high-pitched. And American. "Where's Quinn?"

Doctor Mott checks his watch. "She stepped out to shower for the first time in three days. She'll probably—"

"Three days?" I fling the blanket off my lap, then hurry to cover myself when I realize I'm naked. "Where the fuck are my clothes?"

"Settle down, now. We had to drain a few of your friends to make up for all that blood you leaked into your abdomen. It'll take some time to recover. The bullet ripped through several vessels and a couple of organs."

"And did the bullet also take off my clothes? Ach, I'm naked as the day I was born."

I take a deep breath and flop back on the pillows. This asshole can't answer any of the questions I have, so I guess I'll just have to wait for Quinn to show up. It's not like anyone else would be waiting for me to recover. I didn't exactly make friends like she did.

The door bursts open, and Quinn nearly breaks her ankles to get to my side once she realizes I'm conscious. She throws herself onto the bed, and I don't even care that she's yanked out my IV and sent blood squirting all over the pristine sheets. The doctor rushes over to slap a tourniquet on it while I use my other arm to hold the girl.

"Oh my god," she wails. "I thought you'd never wake up!"

"And miss hearing about how you all killed Desmond? Lass, tell me he's dead." I brush her hair out of her face as she sits back. "Tell me you found your mother and that it was you who ended him."

Quinn offers a sad smile, then kisses my forehead. "We found her. She was in that little closet, reduced to bones and dust, but it was her. Our DNA matches, and so do mine and Desmond's. He's really my father."

"He *is*? I was hoping for more of a he *was*."

"And let you miss out on the kill? Not a chance." Her smile shifts to something happier, and she eases off the bed and starts for the door.

"Hey, where are you going?"

She pauses and looks back at me, her eyebrows pulling together. "To tell the others."

"Others?"

"Yes, silly. Jim, King, the entire group—everyone is out there waiting for good news. Ice Pick and Grim even showed up yesterday. Everyone has been coming in shifts."

"For me?"

"I'm not the only one who loves you, Aven." She pulls the door closed again. "You're just going to have to accept that."

Aye, I will. And with open arms, at that. My days of keeping to myself are over, and I think I'm okay with that. The isolation was always a reaction to my father's treatment. He never understood me. Never even tried. Then the people who wanted to understand me were never given the chance because I'd already closed myself off.

"There's one more thing you need to know," Quinn says as she steps closer, and my heart begins to hammer.

I shake my head. "I won't hear it. Not yet. Not until we're married."

"Married?" Her eyes bulge, and she takes a timid step toward me. "What sort of drugs do they have you on?"

The doctor looks up from his tablet. "Morphine, mostly."

"Thanks," I say. "Think you could give us a little privacy?"

The doctor nods and leaves the room, and I pat the side of the bed. Like the obedient little lass she is, Quinn shuffles over and sits down.

"I mean it, lass. I want to marry you. As soon as I'm out of this bed, we'll hop a boat to Scotland and begin our lives, and the first time we step foot on that soil, I want it to be as man and wife. I don't care if it's sudden. What I feel for you was sudden, too, and it's the best thing that's ever happened to me."

"Aven . . ." Her lashes flutter, and she fidgets with the blanket. "I don't know what to say."

"Ach, say yes. Jim's already become an officiant so that he can marry Kindra and Ezra. We could get him in here and have it done right away."

She bites her bottom lip and considers this. "Quinn Slade . . ." She wrinkles her nose. "I kind of hate it. I'd gotten used to thinking of myself as Quinn Carter."

I shake my head and pull her closer, breathing in her toasted-vanilla scent. "We won't be taking my da's last name. He was never a father to me. Not any more than Desmond was to you. He abandoned me at my lowest point. Meanwhile, your mother never abandoned you."

"I finally know the truth," Quinn whispers. "That she thought she was giving me a better life. Did you know she planned to get me back after she went through rehab?"

"Aye, lass. King told me everything. Your mother loved you something fierce. Could we take her last name?"

"There is a reason I was okay with taking the Parkers' last name," she says with another wrinkle of her nose. "Quinn Butts never really sat well with me."

"We could be the bonnie Butts of Scotland, lass. I can picture it now. We'll have two wee ones named Harry and Rosie."

"And a little dog named Itchy," she says with a laugh. I close my eyes and revel in that sweet sound. "No, I think we'll have to come up with something better."

The door bursts open, and Jim practically falls into the room. Quinn spins in my arms to face him as he offers the most sheepish smile I've ever seen.

"Sorry, couldn't help overhearing your little discussion," he says with a wiggle of his fingers.

I roll my eyes. "Come off it, pal. You were eavesdropping again."

"It's a nasty habit, and I'm working on it," he says. "But that's beside the point. You see, I may have a simple solution to your little surname issue. That's if the two of you plan to be wed?" He rocks on his heels and looks at us with an expectant gleam in his eye.

"We don't want to be the Madigans, but thanks for the offer," Quinn says.

"No, no. Not my last name. One of your very own." He grins and shakes his head. "But I'm getting ahead of myself. Why not make a game out of it, hmm? If you let me marry you right now, I'll tell you your new last name."

Quinn and I share a look.

"Think of it," Jim continues. "I'll marry you here in the hospital room. After that, you can go off on your honeymoon to slaughter Desmond on the island. You'll have the entire park to yourselves."

"That does sound incredibly romantic," Quinn says with a nibble of her lip.

"Then it's settled!" Jim claps his hands and turns to leave the room. "I'll just grab our witnesses, and—"

"Wait!" Quinn holds up her hands. "I don't even have a ring! I can't get engaged without a ring." She turns to face me. "And you didn't even ask me. You *told* me."

The door opens again, and King falls in this time. He straightens and brushes his tie before clearing his throat. "Apologies. Jim's little habit is catching, it seems, but I may have a solution to that jewelry problem."

He steps forward and places a tiny black box in my hand. The corners have been rubbed white from years of sitting in someone's pocket. I open the box, and Quinn gasps. A massive diamond sits in a cluster of smaller stones.

"I asked your mother to marry me no fewer than three times. You were there for all of them, though you were too small to remember." He smiles at the lass as he nods toward the ring. "Don't make the same mistake. If you love him, say yes, child."

I pull the ring from the box and hold it toward her with a shaking hand. "Quinn, I cannae promise our life together will be perfect, but I promise it will always be a life *together*. Will you marry me?"

She nods her head and holds out her hand, and I slip the ring over her finger.

"Oh, happy day!" Jim says with a flail of his hands.

King pulls a handkerchief from his front pocket and passes it to his weeping friend.

"One change of plans, though," I say. "If I could wear

more than a hospital bed sheet as I say my nuptials, I'd appreciate it."

"And could we at least throw together a dress?" Quinn asks.

"Oh, hell, let's just make it a wedding!" Jim says. "Eve, Cat, and I can plan something for tonight. Just meet us at the hotel."

With that, Jim and King leave the room, and Quinn's eyes bulge when she looks at the ring again.

"Holy shit," she breathes. "We're getting married."

Chapter Forty

Quinn

Eve pins a rhinestone belt over the see-through corset top. She had the dress flown in from a designer friend in California. The designer friend came along as well, but once he'd stitched the last stay in place, he tootled off for a drink with Jim.

My mind is a whirlwind of excitement and trepidation. What I'm doing is a terrible idea. I'm about to marry a serial killer who was excommunicated from his homeland for killing a fucking mob boss. Not to mention the fact that I've known him for less than three months. Not to mention the fact that we've only spent a night together.

This would make for one hell of a book plot.

I shake my head and look at myself in the mirror as Eve steps away. For better or worse, for richer or poorer, I'm doing it. I'm marrying the man I love.

"Ready?" Eve says.

I nod up at her. "I think so."

"Not yet, you aren't!" Cat yells as she barges into the

lobby bathroom. She shoves a pair of earrings into my hand. "You need something old. My brother gave me these for my seventh birthday. Well, technically my parents, but still, they're important to me. And I want you to have them."

"And you need something new," Kindra says. "Since you're getting married before me, I want you to have these with my blessing."

I look down as she passes two ring boxes to me, inside of which rest two gold bands. I shake my head. "Girls, I can't accept these. This is too much. Kindra, these were meant for you and Ezra."

She shrugs. "We're planning a destination wedding in California before the summer retreat. We're taking our sweet time, and I think we've decided to have our rings tattooed in place anyway. Please take them."

I clutch them to my chest as tears fill my eyes. "Thank you."

"I've got you covered on something borrowed," Eve says with a raised finger. She goes to her clutch and fishes out a long box. "I snagged this from one of the assholes I killed. He bought it for his mistress, and it can definitely be traced back, so I kind of need it back after the wedding."

I open the box and reveal a stunning diamond chest piece. Eve fastens it around my neck, and it hangs perfectly, stopping at the swell of my breasts.

"It's beautiful," I breathe.

"Something blue . . ." Frankie mutters. She looks around the bathroom, then realizes there's nothing in here for a bride to carry into battle. Then her eyebrows rise, and she smiles. "I realize this isn't conventional, but it is blue. I used the gun blue on it myself just last week."

She slips something cold and metallic into my hands,

and I slide the small weapon into my dress pocket. "Thanks, Frankie."

"It's just a little twenty-two, but she'll get the job done if you're ever in a bind."

There's a knock on the door, and Grim appears when we tell him to enter. He shuffles into the large bathroom, looks around once, then clears his throat. "Everyone is ready to begin, and I grow impatient. Some of us had other plans today. Could you please hurry up?"

He turns and leaves before I can respond, but my heart swells a little. He said please. My grumpy neighbor never says please.

"Okay, I'm ready now," I say. "Let's go get married."

We're a gaggle of giggles and excitement as we exit the bathroom. They hook their arms together and snag me in the middle, and as a group, we march toward the ballroom. As we reach the doorway, Gary pulls it wide with a smile. I'm happy to see he's looking much better after his accident.

"You look beautiful, Quinn," he whispers as we line up. "Jim has a little surprise for you in there." He winks at me, and a trill of excitement zips through me. I hope it's a murdery surprise.

The bridal party begins its slow march inside. The men are already lined up on Aven's side. My groom is blocked from view, but Ezra, Bennett, Maverick, and Ice Pick stretch out to the left of the room. They each smile at their women as they make their entrance. Ice Pick just smiles at everyone.

And then it's my turn.

As I step through the doorway, everything around me seems to fade until I can only see Aven. A black-on-black suit hugs every muscle perfectly. His broad shoulders quiver a bit when he sees me, and he covers his mouth as he fights back tears. I've never felt more beautiful or desired in my life. And as I look at all the people here to support us, I've never felt more like I belong somewhere.

Rosie plays the piano in the corner. She tickles the keys with a professionalism I didn't expect. Grim sits on the bride's side, and King sits on the groom's side, each of them acting as witness and support for us orphaned killers. Jim stands at the head of the party. His smile nearly rivals Aven's.

Even Kenny is in attendance, perched right beside Jim. He flew straight to the hotel after escaping the tree house, and he hasn't left Jim's side since. It's only fitting that he's part of the wedding, considering how he provided the perfect distraction for me to attack Desmond. If it hadn't been for Kenny, I might not be moments away from the happiest moment of my life right now.

Then I spot the surprise nearly halfway down the aisle, and my feet stop moving. Kneeling in front of Jim, dressed in a white suit, is my father. His hands have been fastened behind his back, and a white ball-gag keeps him from speaking. He looks like shit, so I can only assume he hasn't been very well cared for during his stay in the Cattle barn. How wonderful.

My focus returns to Aven, and I find the strength to move forward again. I feel like I'm carried on wings as I close the distance between us. When I'm nearly there, Aven reaches out for me, and I take his hands in mine.

He gives them a squeeze. "Ach, damn you for being so beautiful. You've made me cry."

I squeeze back. "Damn you for being so sweet, because you're going to get me started too."

A gentle laugh eases out of our bridal party, and Grim rolls his eyes.

Jim gets started by telling the group a little about each of us. Aven is so closed off and I'm so new to the group that everyone ends up learning something they didn't know. That includes me. As it turns out, I'm marrying into a very extensive vintage toy collection. I'm not mad about it.

Aven learns that I have a very extensive collection of my own, though it's books rather than toys. Granted, if you count sex toys . . .

"I hope that the two of you continue to explore and learn new things about each other for the rest of your lives," Jim says with a beaming smile, and now he's crying. He pulls a handkerchief from his pocket and blows his nose. "Do we have the rings?"

Desmond has been sitting quietly through all of this, but knowing that I'm about to get my happily ever after must be too much for him to bear. He forgoes his stoicism and starts thrashing his shoulders as he tries to wiggle out of the ropes on his wrists.

Ignoring his theatrics, I pull the rings from my pocket and pass mine to Aven. "Right here."

"Wonderful," Jim says with a sniffle. "Quinn, do you take Aven to be your lawfully wedded husband? Do you vow to clean up his kills without complaint and keep his secrets faithfully?"

"Ach, I don't need her cleaning up after me."

"I do," I say with a smile.

Jim turns to Aven. "And Aven, do you take Quinn to be your lawfully wedded wife? Do you vow to protect her from the evils of this world and be silent when she's reading?"

"Aye, I do," he says.

"Normally, the happy couple would exchange rings and vows at this time, but I thought we'd do things a bit differently, hmm?" Jim looks toward the back of the room and motions for someone. "Gary, bring them in!"

Gary is all smiles as he strolls toward the head of the room with two axes in his hands. I recognize the aged one from the shack in the trees, but the one in his left hand looks brand new. Its handle is white instead of wooden.

"The life of a serial killer is often a lonely one," Jim says. "The two of you are blessed to have found someone who shares your most secret desires. I am a firm believer that the family who slays together stays together, so it's only fitting that you begin your new life with a kill."

Desmond drops to his chest and starts worm crawling across the floor. No one stops him. Gary merely steps over him and pushes the axes into mine and Aven's hands.

"Congrats to the happy couple," he says before hurrying out of the room. He already knows this is about to get messy.

Aven smiles down at the ax, then spins it through the air one time. "Feels good to have her back in my hand."

"Anything special I need to know?" I ask as I test the heft.

"Just don't get too carried away with the swings and lop off your own limbs," he says with a laugh. "I'll love you either way, but I prefer both legs wrapped around my waist."

"Noted," I say as I step toward our prey.

Kenny flaps his wings and lets out an excited screech.

Desmond hears our footsteps and rolls onto his back. The entire wedding party files in behind us and closes in to watch. Even Grim shows a moderate amount of interest as Aven nudges the prone man's head with his boot.

"Looks like you missed your plane back to Scotland,"

Aven says. "Such a shame. But no matter. We'll make good use of your refunded flight."

Desmond shouts something behind the ball gag. Instead of looking terrified, he just looks pissed.

I raise my foot and bring it down on his groin. His eyes pinch shut, and he rolls to his side. With a guttural scream, I raise the weapon and bring it down on his hip. The ax head breaks through fabric and skin, then gets lodged in bone. Desmond keeps screaming as I place my foot on his thigh and wrench the weapon free.

"I didn't write any vows," I say. "I feel like this is where we should be saying our vows." I raise the weapon and aim for the bloody spot, but I swing a bit wide and make a fresh gouge in his upper thigh.

Aven shakes his head and widens his stance. "Lass, watching you hack your father with an ax is the best vow you could have written. Actions sometimes speak louder than words."

My mouth nearly waters as I watch him raise the ax. My very own Paul Bunyan. He swings for all he's worth, and the ax takes off one of Desmond's arms at the shoulder. Blood jets out, but Desmond only sees an opportunity. With the removal of his left arm, his right is now free. He unfastens the leg ropes, then reaches up to wrestle the ball gag from his mouth before rising to his full height and stumbling forward. All the while, his dismembered arm dangles from the rope tied to his other wrist.

Unfortunately for him, that hack job I did on his leg prevents him from getting very far, and he collapses before he even reaches the doorway.

He spins onto his back with a whimper as the mob approaches. Aven and I stand at the head, both of us wielding our bloody axes as if we've been possessed by

Lizzie Borden. Forty whacks wouldn't be nearly enough for this asshole.

"Any last words?" I say as I stand over him. "You were kind enough to offer me that, so I figure I should do the same."

"Fuck you." He spits at my feet.

Aven raises his boot and brings it down on Desmond's teeth, reducing them to picket fences after a fight with a car. "You want to finish him off?"

I shake my head. "I don't need that for closure. I've gotten everything I wanted, and that's the best sort of revenge."

"Aye, you're right." Aven pulls me in for a kiss. "Let's give the honor to someone else."

"Could I try?" a small voice says.

Everyone's heads whip toward the entrance. We're all shocked to see Gary standing there.

"Gary?" Frankie says. "You want to kill Desmond? What about your blood phobia?"

The tiny man licks his lips and takes a timid step forward. "I'm trying to get over it, but I think I just need to toss myself into the deep end. Can I . . . kill him?"

I offer my ax to him. "You have my blessing."

"And mine," Aven says.

Gary eyes the ax and shakes his head. "I don't think I can use an ax."

I remember the gun in my pocket and push it into his hand with a grin. "Try this, Gary."

"No," Desmond says. He repeats the word, starting at a whisper and rising to a scream. "You can't let some nobody kill me!"

"Honey, that isn't a nobody," Eve shouts from the back.

"That's Gare Bear, and you'd better say his name with a little respect next time."

"There won't be a next time," Gary says with an evil smile. Well, as evil as he can muster for a tiny little balding man with bug eyes and a dented skull. God bless him.

He raises the weapon and fires. Unfortunately, the bullet misses Desmond's skull and lodges somewhere in the floor.

"It's okay," Maverick says, encouraging him. "Take your time, Gare Bear."

He nods and fires again. This time, the bullet punches through Desmond's gut.

Grim takes Rosie's hand and leads her out of the room, ever the impatient one.

"I'll get it this time," Gary says, determined.

And he does. When he fires the weapon again, Desmond's head rocks to the side as a vacancy sign slams over his eyes. The lights are still on, but no one is home. His chest heaves a few more times, weaker and weaker, and then he's gone.

The group breaks into applause, and everyone claps Gary on the back for a job well done. The wedding is all but forgotten until Jim brings us back to the reason we're all here.

"I won't make everyone line up, but I still want to introduce the new couple for the first time. Exchange your rings."

This is the moment we've been waiting for. The moment we learn what our new last names will be. It was risky, letting Jim secretly fill out the forms so it would be a surprise, but he promised it wouldn't be Madigan or Butts or Slade. Our hands are shaking as we slide the rings onto each other's fingers, both of us eager to learn our fate.

"Aven, you may kiss your bride." Jim looks like he's about to explode with anticipation for whatever he has in store. "Go on! Pucker up! I can't announce you until you do!"

Aven pulls me into him, and everyone erupts in another round of cheers as we seal the deal over my father's corpse. It's poetic, really.

"Everyone, I'm pleased to announce . . . the Carters!" Jim claps his hands, but he's the only one. Everyone else just stops and stares.

The happiness drains from Aven's face. "Jim, you cannae just give us the name we want. That's their heritage, and I won't steal it." He motions to Ezra, Bennett, and Frankie.

"Fuck it," Bennett says. "You're as much a brother to us as anyone else. I don't care if you take the last name. I want you to."

"I second that," Ezra offers. "Family is about more than DNA, Aven. You're both family to us now."

Frankie raises her finger. "I've only just recently learned that I'm related to these idiots, but I welcome one more. Please accept, Aven."

Jim finally butts in with a fit of laughter. He shakes his head and holds out his hands, and we patiently wait for him to quiet enough to explain the punchline. "No, no, no. You don't understand. Aven, your last name is Carter and always has been. The man you believed to be your father was impotent. That's why he knew you weren't his."

"It's true," King says. "Your mother had a momentary night of weakness that resulted in your conception. I'm sorry we kept it from you, but the simulation predicted that this was the best way to get you to stick around. If we'd told you everything from the moment we knew the truth, you'd have run off."

I smile up at Aven and brush my thumb over his cheek. "And here I thought our relationship was fate."

"Well, now that everything's out in the open, we'd best clear out so that these two can enjoy the park alone," Jim says. "There'll be time for a family reunion later."

Understanding Aven's need for solitude, they start heading for the door.

"No," Aven says, and everyone stops to look at him. "We don't need to be alone. I've spent too much time in isolation. If I'm part of this fucked-up family, then I want to start acting like it. I want everyone to enjoy the park tonight. With us."

My cheeks ache from how wide I'm smiling when he looks down at me. My heart is full to bursting.

"Well, then I suggest everyone get outside," Jim says. "I have one more surprise in store."

We hurry out of the building and into the cool evening air. Starlight twinkles above, and only a few hazy clouds mar the night sky. Jim says something into his radio, and the park lights shut off. We're doused in darkness. The moment is eerily familiar, and that creepy déjà vu feeling isn't helping set me at ease.

Seconds later, the sky explodes with color and light. Fireworks pop and hiss overhead as everyone oohs and ahhs. Everyone but me. My heart rate is currently climbing toward tachycardia as I feel my mother's ghostly hand slipping away from me again.

But then a real hand slips into mine. One that is warm and alive. A hand that won't let go. It squeezes mine with a pressure that says, *You are safe, lass.*

I finally smile up at the fireworks. Aye, I am.

Epilogue

Aven

I lick my lips and stare at the line snaking around the corner outside of the bookshop. Quinn doesn't seem a bit nervous, and she's the one they came to see. Meanwhile, I'm a fucking wreck.

We pooled our money and bought a small cabin in Vermont—close enough to the others that we can hang out regularly, but far enough away that we can still have our privacy. We've been living off the remainder while Quinn worked to get her dream off the ground, and judging by that line, she's well on her way to the sky.

She wrote the first book in just two weeks. The lass has plenty more where that came from, too. She's had them knocking around in that bonnie brain of hers for years. For the past six weeks, she's been busy okaying covers and formatting and working her ass off to follow her editor's corrections. The release was a week ago, and it was an overnight success.

Granted, Eve might have helped a little, what with her

visibility on social media. She and the other girls have become a veritable street team, recommending the book everywhere they can. But the book is good, and now word of mouth does all the advertising for her. No one can take that away from Quinn Carter.

"I think I'm ready," Quinn says. "You can let in the VIP winner first."

I nod and stroll to the front of the bookstore. The owner unlocks the door and lets the first visitor inside.

"No funny business," I tell the woman. "Keep your hands to yourself and you'll make it out of here with both of them attached to your body."

"Oh my god," she squeals. "You're the husband from her bio, aren't you? You really are Scottish!"

"Aye, and I really am serious about keeping your hands to yourself."

She nods up at me, her blue eyes bulging with excitement. "I promise. No touching."

"Aven, stop being a bull and let Andrea through," Quinn says behind me, and I step out of the way.

The woman nearly knocks me over as she rushes forward and holds her book toward Quinn. "I want to buy a special edition too, but can you please sign this tattered copy? I've read it three times since it released, and it's helped me through a breakup."

"You aren't buying anything. I'll sign that copy and your free special edition. Thanks for your support, love." Quinn takes the book from the girl's hands, then scrawls her signature in the front with a metallic silver pen. "And I don't care what my husband says. You're giving me a hug."

I roll my eyes as she stands and pulls the flabbergasted woman closer. "Lass, I cannae do my job as bodyguard if you keep breaking all the rules."

"Breaking rules is what got us here," she says over the woman's shoulder. She pulls back and looks Andrea in the face. "Now, tell me all about your book collection. We have about fifteen minutes before Aven lets the horde through."

I stand to the side as the girls gush about their favorite authors. My head remains on a swivel. She may no longer be a cam girl, but ravenous fans are still ravenous fans. I'm happy to retain my post as faithful watchdog for the rest of my life.

And it will be the rest of my life. This marriage thing has turned out to be the best decision I ever made. I wake up to the woman I love. I come home to her. Every day is spent anticipating seeing her again and knowing she'll be there. Granted, it's taken some getting used to. Remembering to lower the toilet seat has been the hardest bit, though.

We've experienced our first fight. We've had our first makeup sex. It was pretty epic. I'm okay with losing fights to her if it ends with my dick in her mouth. Yeah, I'd say this is pretty much the best.

My musings are interrupted by a commotion around the front door as a man fights his way through the crowd of agitated women. He flails a small leather satchel as he pushes through. I'd better save his ass before they rip a second hole in it.

"Grab the door," I say to the worker near the front. "I know the guy."

The woman opens the door, and Jim falls into the bookstore, landing on his ass with a grunt.

"Well, I never," he says as he rises and dusts off his tailored suit. "They're like hyenas."

"And there's their queen," I say with a nod toward Quinn.

"Is everything okay?" She peers around the woman in front of her. "We weren't expecting you until after the signing."

He raises the leather bag and gives it a wiggle. "I got some news today, and I was too excited to wait. Could we have just a moment?"

Quinn nods and jots something on one of her business cards, then passes it to Andrea. "I hate to cut this short, so let me take you to dinner. That's my number. Text me later, and we'll set something up."

Andrea pulls the card against her chest and jumps up and down. "Oh my god, I have Quinn Carter's *phone number!*"

I grab the girl by her shoulders and start moving her toward the door.

"Thank you, Quinn! Best day ever!" Andrea yells over her shoulder as I shove her outside.

Once the door is secured once more, I hurry back to Jim and Quinn. He's already pulled a few papers from the satchel, and he places them on the table as I approach.

"This is an email chain that was intercepted by Frankie last week. Look at the country of origin."

I raise the printouts and read through them. The conversation is heavily coded, but it's not hard to figure out they're discussing a hit. The country of origin is listed as America for one and Canada for the other.

"I'm failing to see what you want me to see," I say.

"Same," Quinn says.

Jim taps the page in my left hand. "That's Grantham Carter. And he's currently in the States."

Quinn's eyebrows pull together. "What does that mean? Is that a big deal?"

"It's the biggest deal," Jim says.

"No one's seen him for years." I read the emails again. "Are these dates accurate? The emails were exchanged last week?"

Jim nods. "He's in the wind again, but if what he says holds true, he's about to embark on a cross-country spree before retiring for good."

"Well what are we waiting for?" Quinn says, and she's already packing away the books on the table. "Let's go get him!"

"It's not that simple, lass." I place her books back on the table. "Besides, you've got a book signing to handle. You can't let them down." I motion toward the rabid women pressed against the glass shopfront. "They might kill you. Or me."

"I'm already working on the next steps," Jim says," but Frankie thought I should clue you in as soon as possible so that you can plan around your book tour. I've purchased a slew of RVs, so get ready for a road trip. We'll chase him down, then land in California for Ezra and Kindra's wedding."

Quinn bounces on her toes. "Oh my god, how exciting! This will give me so much inspiration for an upcoming series. I can't wait." Her excitement fades when she realizes I don't share it. "Aven, what's wrong?"

"What do we do when we find him?" I ask Jim. "What's the point?"

"Perhaps he could be convinced to make amends with his children, for starters," Quinn says. "I mean, if that's something you guys want."

I shrug and shake my head. "I don't really know what I want. I haven't thought about it. I guess we'll find out when we catch the guy."

"Right." Jim shoves the papers back into his bag. "Well, I'm off to meet with the others. Don't forget about dinner!"

He hurries off, leaving Quinn and me in the silent shop. She strolls around the table and resumes her seat. I take up my post beside her and try to swallow the building anticipation.

"I almost wish he hadn't told us," I say.

Quinn reaches over and gives my hand a squeeze. "Hey, we'll get through it together. If we survive the road trip, that is."

"Aye, there's that. I only hope he doesn't make us share an RV with Ice Pick. He could clear an event space with his nighttime gas."

"Yuck. I'll talk to Eve to make sure we're with her."

That brings a smile out of me. A few months ago, I would have been looking for a way out of this. Now I'm planning ways to make it work.

"You ready to meet your fans?" I ask, and she takes a deep breath.

"With you by my side, I'm ready for anything," she says.

I couldn't agree more.

Get ready for the final installment of the Slaycation series! *Sinners Reunion* coming summer 2026: Books2read.com/ SinnersReunion

If you want to take a darker road trip, check out all of the dark, hitchhiker romance standalones in my Ride or Die series. These can be read in any order.

Hitched: Books2read.com/Hitched
Along for the Ride: Books2read.com/MFMHitchhiker
Driving my Obsession: Books2read.com/
DrivingmyObsession
Across State Lines: Books2read.com/AcrossStateLines
Don't Stop: Books2read.com/Dont-Stop

If you aren't ready for the darker books just yet, here are
more dark-lite books you can check out.

Stranger Session: Books2read.com/StrangerSession
Her Fantasy: Books2read.com/HerFantasy
Last Mistake: Books2read.com/LastMistake
Protect Me: Books2read.com/ProtectMeNovella
Dark Decisions: Books2read.com/DarkDecisions
Morally Grey: Books2read.com/MorallyGrey
Edge of Sin: Books2read.com/EdgeofSin

Ready to go pitch-black?
Captured (banned as an ebook and audiobook):
Books2read.com/Capturedbook
Never Let Go: Books2read.com/NLG

Connect with Lauren

Don't miss a thing from Lauren Biel! Check out all of her books, social media connections, and other important information at Campsite.bio/LaurenBielAuthor and Lauren Biel.com

Acknowledgments

To my VIP gals (Jessie, Nikita, Lexi, Grace, and Kim), I'm so glad this author journey brought me to you all.

Thank you to my husband, who is my own grumpy guard dog.

Whitney @whit_bookish (Bayside Books) and Kelsey @between.pages.with.kelsey, forever "mayo" bonded.

To Andrea @andrea_reads_alot, my special VIP reader in the book, I love you and our friendship. Your support means the absolute world to me.

Brooke, my editor, thank you for making these books everything they are and continue to be. I couldn't do any of it without you.

Hey, Mom, thanks for taking us to the one amusement park every year until we became too old. This is the "adult" version. And Dad, I hope you love this cockatoo too. We miss you!

Thank you to my valued Patrons. Your contribution helped make this book happen: Stalker Chelle, Kassandra R, Lisapooh98, Jenna J, LucyInDaSky, Ranae G, Veronica M, Alyssa S, Jessika W, Ashley S, Elvira, Amber C, Morgan,

Melissa D, Elle (Queen of Smut), AdorablyFeral_Reads, Tabby R, Samantha H, Raquel O, SimplyDevine, Hollie C, SamAndBigDaddyD, Tanja, KitKatLaughAttack, Ashley M, Laura F, Megan L, Leslie Mae, Ashley S, Rebecca C, Kaat, Lauren.loves2read, Kimberly G, A.Reads, Danielle M, Danielle N, Sunshine_the_Bookie, Sara M, Harley B, Heather M, Bonnie F, Marguerite, Courtney R, Vikki S, Amanda T, Lisa W, Court's Bookshelf, Nicholetta88, Emily S, SerenaLorraine, Heather S, Jennifer S, Just Jen Here, Briyanna M, Jesi D, Charmaine B, Michelle, Christy P, Callie K, Arnica S, Maxine T, Leslie W, Smitty, Brooke, Anna S, Shelby F, Tiannah J, Sharee S, Courtney P, Kristiana B, Vero A, Sara S, Samantha R, Jessica G, Kimberly S, Tabitha F, JesStenger, Eugenia M, Nineette W, BoneDaddyAshe

Also by Lauren Biel

To view Lauren Biel's complete list of books, visit: https://laurenbiel.com/laurenbielbooks/

About the Author

Lauren Biel is the author of many dark romance books, with several more titles in the works. When she's not working, she's writing. When she's not writing, she's spending time with her husband, her friends, or her pets. You might also find her on a horseback trail ride or sitting beside a waterfall in Upstate New York. When reading her work, expect the unexpected. To be the first to know about her upcoming titles, please visit www.LaurenBiel.com.

www.ingramcontent.com/pod-product-compliance
Lightning Source LLC
Chambersburg PA
CBHW030111310726
48970CB00004B/1237